The Black Feathers

By the same author

The Whistling

The Black Feathers

REBECCA NETLEY

MICHAEL JOSEPH

PENGUIN MICHAEL JOSEPH

UK | USA | Canada | Ireland | Australia
India | New Zealand | South Africa

Penguin Michael Joseph is part of the Penguin Random House group of companies
whose addresses can be found at global.penguinrandomhouse.com

First published 2023
001

Copyright © Rebecca Netley, 2023

The moral right of the author has been asserted

Set in 13.5/16pt Garamond MT Std
Typeset by Jouve (UK), Milton Keynes
Printed and bound in Great Britain by Clays Ltd, Elcograf S.p.A.

The authorized representative in the EEA is Penguin Random House Ireland,
Morrison Chambers, 32 Nassau Street, Dublin D02 YH68

A CIP catalogue record for this book is available from the British Library

HARDBACK ISBN: 978–0–241–53401–4
TRADE PAPERBACK ISBN: 978–0–241–53402–1

www.greenpenguin.co.uk

To my indomitable grandmothers: Patricia
Whish and Mabel Kelly, with love

Even before I arrive, I dream of Guardbridge. I dream of leaning chimneys, bowed ironwork and meandering passageways. It is not always myself in the dreams, but another, one who walks with quick steps and direct purpose.

This woman paces the corridors, but now and then she stands outside and gazes up at the windows, her heart as narrowed as the pupil of a snake.

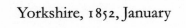

Yorkshire, 1852, January

I

From the carriage window, the scenes blur with snow and blend with my strange transitionary state of being: churches and hills, beaches with their solitary walkers, then wintry copses – all seen at a distance, all awaiting some signal to move on.

Beside me, Edward has his head turned to the opposite pane. We do not speak, but I have learned already, in the year we have been together, that he is a man of few words, a man of restrained action. This suits me well, because there are many things of which I can never talk and secrets that must be kept.

The term 'husband' still feels remarkable on my tongue, as if it were a foreign word of which I had only a vague sense of meaning. But we have managed well so far, even if love is not part of it. I recall what my mother said: 'Do you think marriage is about love? He may not be handsome but he's rich and you won't need love if you have money. But mind him well – men are fickle.'

I have not seen signs yet that Edward is fickle and I have come to think a marriage without love must be safer than one that relies only on the heart's mercurial nature.

Agnes sits opposite, our son asleep and red-cheeked on her lap. I swallow and turn away because John makes me think of you, and I squeeze my palms tight until my hands ache and the feeling passes.

Of all the things Edward must never learn, he must never learn of that.

'What is the time?' I ask.

Edward reaches for his watch chain, his clever fingers elegant inside the gloves. His movements are unhurried, almost languorous, but he cannot hide the burr of excitement that is lodged within him and his eagerness to return to Guardbridge.

'We still have a long way to go.'

I have imagined Guardbridge often, as described through Edward's eyes: the main square of the house rendered in dark stone, with two wings spread out on either side like a bird stretched for flight or a cormorant drying its feathers perhaps. It has many windows and staircases but much of the house lies sleeping, collecting dust and mouse holes, and the north wing, which suffered a fire in one of the rooms, has now been abandoned. I imagine the fast river that runs behind, and beyond that oak woods that chatter and creak in the wind.

As if sensing my thoughts, he says, 'Are you looking forward to seeing Guardbridge?'

I take a moment to examine my expectations. Arrival will mark an escape from the condemning gaze of my parents, and more than that — at Guardbridge I will begin again.

It is many months since we began our bridal tour in Bath, where the days passed too quickly and the late-winter sun left no shadows and then the early bleed that had us confined to town. I think back to the long confinement in Mordoch Street and the hours I had lain watching shadows play on the ceiling and wondering whether the child inside me would live or die. The sound of the doctor's rap on the door, his cane rattling into the umbrella stand and the click of heels as he mounted the stairs. One thing I am sure of is that I am sick of rest.

As we travel further into Yorkshire, we reach wilder country, with rocky tors and birds that circle high in the white cloud, and all the time the snow slips down, softening sound until the journey falls into the slow drifting territory of dreams.

When we finally hit the moors, the sky is full of shadow and I am wide awake. The wheels tick against the newly iced surface like a faulty clock. It is dusk — the sun is low and the moor catches the glint of afternoon light, fires of red sunset on the frozen surfaces. I cannot stop shivering.

'See that copse?' Edward says. 'Beyond there is where

I used to go for plovers' eggs. And that mire is where Ned's horse went down.'

It is as we turn a corner banked with trees that Guardbridge comes into view. Trees ring a crumbling wall and in the garden are the shapes of bushes and statues, but it is Guardbridge itself that draws the eye – a fortress of stone with panes of glass that glitter from discoloured frames. It is half buried in snow, like an animal crouched in its lair, but there is something else. I have the curious notion that it is not the first time I have been here. Nothing I see is surprising or unexpected. There is the north wing, with its smoke-blackened stone, just as described, and the arch below that reveals a glimpse of the river.

A memory comes to me – of Mrs Breach, a friend of the family, a woman my father spoke disparagingly of and who was instantly recognizable in her elaborate hat, a bird stitched to its rim. She never lost an opportunity to tell me of the great friendship she had shared with my aunt, and I would stand bored and distracted as I listened to some recounted anecdote, waiting for a pause in the conversation to make my excuses and leave.

On this day, however, she had begun, 'I'd heard you're to be married, Miss Edge?'

Marriage was nearly all I could think of then and I had been enthusiastic to reply that indeed I was. By that time I had become accustomed to the responses of pleasure, the beams of goodwill, but Mrs Breach remained strangely unmoved.

'You have all my good wishes,' was all she said.

I had paused, wanting to stress again how favourable a union it was to be: to a man not only of money but a portraitist too, when Mrs Breach had put a hand suddenly on my arm and her brow had creased.

'Is it to Guardbridge you go?'

'Yes, it is.'

Mrs Breach had stepped back a little, her eyes growing grave.

'You've been to Guardbridge?' I asked.

She had shaken her head and pulled her coat closer. 'No, but I've heard of it. It's not what you want to hear, I'm sure, my dear, but I owe it to my treasured friendship with your aunt to suggest that you don't go ahead with this proposal.'

Familiarity with Mrs Breach's eccentricity made this response to the declaration of my marriage less alarming than it might have been had it come from someone else. Even so, I had said a little sharply, 'What possible reason would I have to break my engagement?'

'It's Guardbridge itself that concerns me, you know, and the women who are born there.'

'What of them?' I had pressed.

Mrs Breach had looked a little awkward then. 'Forgive me. I can see I've upset you. Guardbridge has a reputation. Not a good one. I'm surprised that you haven't heard this already.'

'A reputation for what?'

'It's said that the house is a bad place, a place where bad things happen.'

And in spite of the sun, and my scepticism, I had thought of the tragic, untimely deaths of Edward's previous wife and son, and shuddered.

The carriage comes to a stop, jolting me from my thoughts, and as I am helped down, my foot sinks into a drift and Edward sweeps me up into his arms, dislodging my hat.

'Well, wife,' he says, 'welcome to your new home.' But his eyes are already looking upwards to the windows, his thoughts far away. Momentarily his grasp loosens and there is an instant when I nearly fall. Then he wraps me tighter, and I think of the home I left all those months ago.

All will be well now. All will be well. I am finally free.

The front door opens and frames a woman, hands clasped nervously to each other. She does not come forward, but hovers a little back, keeping to the hall.

'Is that Iris?' I ask.

'That's Iris, yes.'

We take the steps and enter the house and now I see her clearly: tall and gaunt, sparse hair pulled back over a high forehead and eyes that are large and grey.

She cannot be but a few years older than me, yet her skin is remarkable in its smoothness, almost without flaw.

'Edward.' She takes him in an enthusiastic embrace, kissing him on both cheeks, then stands back to inspect him. 'You look very well, I'm pleased to say.'

'And you're as pale as ever and far too thin.'

'Nonsense,' she says. 'My dresses fit me as wholly as they ever did.' Now she studies me.

'Annie, I've been longing for you to arrive. It's been too many months we've had to wait. Do you mind terribly if I call you Annie? We are, after all, sisters now?' Her look is tentative and a knot of apprehension is dispelled with the recognition that it is Iris who is the most keen to please.

I tell her I am happy to be called such and as we enter the hall I think with pleasure of what it will be like to have a female companion; Edward has already warned me that he will often be away. I glance at my surroundings: the panelled walls and stone flags, a great marble fireplace framed by bronze stags.

It is Edward's portraits that I am most keen to see and I would like to stand before each one and examine it at leisure, but Agnes is coming up the steps with John, and Iris's expression grows brighter.

After cooing extravagantly she says, 'He's perfect.' But when she looks up there is sadness and I am reminded that not long ago Edward's first son might have run into her arms or taken her hand and begged her to play. 'I've been excited to show you your rooms and the nurseries. We spent an age choosing fabrics and furniture. I hope you'll approve.'

'Annie is tired and must rest. Perhaps you'd show Agnes the nurseries,' Edward says.

'I'm not tired. I would like to see them,' I protest.

They all turn to me but Edward puts a firm hand on my arm. 'It's been a long day and you're still not recovered. You'll come and get warm and eat something. You ate too little at lunch.'

Taking my elbow, he guides me with easy familiarity along bewildering passageways and finally to a large room with a blazing fire.

I think fleetingly of home – the frosted inside panes of the parlour, my father slamming through the house with demands to find a lost item that one of us women must have misplaced. I see him now scowling down at me, although we were nearly the same height.

Edward sprawls on the chair opposite with a comfortable sigh and takes out a cigar. It is as if he has never left, that all the time we were away he has really been at Guardbridge in this very seat.

My eyes find the portrait that hangs above the mantelpiece. Without being told, I know that this must be Evie, Edward's first wife. With her image before me, she moves from some fictitious location in my mind and is made real. It is jarring – it has been too easy to forget that Edward has been married before, and the very image of her sparks a moment of pointless jealousy. I study it further. Her hair is held away from her face and at her neck is a string of pearls, polished to the whiteness of tiny bones.

'Do you mind?' he says, gesturing to it. And I wonder what he is thinking – is he considering the difference in his affections, because I have come to believe that when he married Evie, unlike with me, it was for love.

The scene of our initial meeting floats to the surface of my thoughts. He had come to Helmsworth for a commission, and when I had crossed the market square towards home he caught a glimpse of my face that pricked his interest. An introduction had been sought, and I recall how we sat that first time in the parlour and I learned of Edward's recent loss. But I did not need to be told; it was there in the pain of his expression, in the way he seemed cowed by sadness. A widower, and father, both wife and child lost to scarlet fever.

But I did not care because as he talked of his estate, I marvelled at his wealth and talent and could only think of leaving Helmsworth. There was never talk of love. We both knew what it was we sought – he company and an heir and myself an escape from my shame.

But here is Evie: beautiful, or nearly so, and I will

have to compare myself to her every day, as surely he will.

'I mind a little,' I admit. I want to ask more – what was she like? Was she a good mother? Did she run Guardbridge well? But it has been made clear from the very first that Evie and Jacob are never to be discussed.

'But you will paint me soon.' And a thrill runs through me when I imagine how I will feel to see my own image upon the wall.

Edward rings the bell and instructs the maid to prepare our baths. A little later she returns to tell me that the water is ready, and I follow her along the icy passageways. As we move further from the drawing room, there is a change of atmosphere. The hallways narrow and the lamps barely touch the dimness but appear suddenly out of the gloom. The maid's candle flame slips back and forth uncertainly on its wick and any noise our feet might make is smothered by carpet until occasionally there is a gap of timber and then the halls rattle with the sound of our heels. Sandalwood and lamp oil permeate the air everywhere.

My eyes take in everything and nothing, and by the time we have ascended the stairs and followed another corridor, I could not have described one painting or one item of furniture I had passed.

Once, I turn, sensing that someone is behind us, but am presented only with the cloistering darkness.

'How much further from my chamber are the nurseries?' I ask, filling the silence.

'They are no great distance. Would you like to see them?'

'Not just now. Perhaps when I'm bathed and dressed.'

The maid pauses and turns to me, the candlelight paling the end of her lashes. 'This is your room, ma'am.' She smiles and opens the door, standing back for me to enter.

It is more lavish than even my imagination had conjured. Grand furniture and hangings, two vast windows looking out to the moor, rugs and carpets and a walnut dressing table set with lamps.

A tub has been placed behind a screen in front of the fire. But no sooner have I appreciated its splendour than I wonder whether this was where Evie once slept.

As if sensing my thoughts, the maid says, 'The furniture in here is new. The previous Mrs Stonehouse's is on the other side of Mr Stonehouse's bedchamber.'

'Oh.' I regard the room with a keener eye. 'What's your name?'

'Flora, ma'am.'

My trunks have been unpacked and after I have bathed and dressed I sit at the mirror as Flora puts up my hair. I open my jewellery case and gaze down on the emerald necklace and earrings that Edward had presented to me after our wedding.

'I'll wear these tonight,' I say with pride.

Flora peers down. 'They're beautiful.'

'They belonged to his mother.'

Behind me, the bed awaits, and I am not as afraid as I had been in those first weeks. My body has grown accustomed to Edward's touch and even though I keep it at a distance, it is not as distasteful as it had been. And one night, when we were in Bath, it had filled me with a strange longing that I did not understand. But as I view the bed now, I think of Evie and how Edward might turn to me and in a half-dreamlike state expect her, not me.

'I would like to see John and the nursery now,' I say.

Back in the corridor the chill is frigid. We meet another passageway and finally a lobby where a faint moon shows through a dusty skylight. Flora turns the handle carefully and we step inside where the room is lit by one milk-glass oil lamp that diffuses rose-coloured light. Agnes stands from her comfy chair, putting down a mug of ale and wiping crumbs from her apron. She puts a finger to her lips and nods to the cot.

The scene is already complete. I am the interloper. I can only tiptoe to the crib and look down at my son, so peaceful in sleep.

'I'm hoping we can keep to the routines of Mordoch Street,' Agnes whispers. 'You still need to recover your strength.' Her tone is gentle, but it is almost a physical pain to see John there and to admit to myself that I feel so little. It is as if my heart has retreated to some place where it can no longer be touched.

And so instead, I study the bright pictures and oak chests lined with toys and objects, the pile of folded linens and the nappy bucket. At least John can be happy and safe here.

'I hope you'll be comfortable,' I say.

'It's very well equipped; your sister-in-law and the housekeeper have done wonderfully well. Everything has been arranged and carried out with the greatest consideration. Now you see to it you have a good supper and if John needs you, I'll find you.' She gives me a kind smile.

Outside, I pause and feel the sting of my inadequacy. Agnes is good with John. It is best this way. But even so, as I walk away, my feelings turn uncomfortably.

The housekeeper, Mrs Ford, oversees dinner: five courses. Quenelles of chicken, then game and fish, sauces sitting in elegant jugs, glasses and silverware that catch the candlelight.

Timbers creak and wind knocks the panes. As we eat, part of me is still waiting for my mother's impatient demands or for one of the children to tug on my skirts for attention.

'Doesn't Iris eat with us?'

'No, she keeps largely to her own quarters.'

'Why is that?'

Placing a napkin to his lips, he says, 'It's been like this for as long as I remember. She's not alone. She has Mrs North for company.'

'The devoted Mrs North. Iris is lucky to have her,' I tease.

He looks at me wryly. 'I shouldn't jest, Mrs North has been the rock that's weathered all storms.'

'You haven't often talked of Iris – even at my prompting, I'd even begun to wonder if there was something about her you were trying to hide from me. But my first impression is that she will make a perfect sister.'

He gives me a playful look. 'Iris is a little eccentric, but you'll not find her unkind or unpleasant.'

'What makes her eccentric?'

He raises his brows in a light-hearted gesture. 'You'll find out soon enough.' The candle wicks gut, sending tongues of shadow across his face. He lifts the carafe and pours more wine.

Later, Flora accompanies me again to the bedroom. Lamps are already lit, the covers turned down. Despite the fire, the air is sharp with cold. As Flora helps me out of my clothes, we speak only of practicalities: how I want my hair, what needs taking for laundry. A tentative dance of learning each other's ways.

A nightgown has already been chosen, one we bought in Bath with lace and broderie anglaise, roses along the hem, but I can only think of that first moment of panicked resistance when he climbs in beside me and wonder if it will ever change.

We both turn to a noise from Edward's dressing room.

'Will that be all?' Flora asks.

'That will be enough, thank you.' I sit up against the headboard and watch the door, but when he finally comes through I start.

As my husband stands beside the bed, I do not feel as if he can be real, and now he is here I do not want him to be. He is dressed in a nightshirt, open at the neck where a web of hair escapes. I recall the cramped mattress of home where I and my sisters had lain like matches in a box. I remember the smell of their sour breath and in summer the sticky sweat of their bodies and know, in this instant, that I would rather be there. I hold myself tight and watchful inside my skin.

He takes the side of the bed, causing the boards to creak and dip beside me. When it is over, I fall asleep – and when I stir later there is an empty space where he had been and I know, as is his custom, that we will spend the remainder of the night alone.

I cannot sleep again, and eventually curiosity has me get up and see where Evie slept.

Taking a candle, I step out into the corridor, which seems narrower for the darkness. Wind whispers in distant places and my feet soon chill on the rugs.

I tiptoe past the dressing room to where Edward has his own bed. Laying the flat of my palm to his door, I press an ear to the wood as if I might hear him, but there is only silence.

I take the few paces to the next room, which must have been Evie's, and pause. For an instant I believe there is movement inside, but leaning closer there is nothing. I push down on the handle but it will not give.

As I am about to leave, the candle catches the glass of a painting, another of Evie. I search the face avidly for flaws, but as I look I am drawn deeper into her gaze and see there, embedded in the iris, not a smile but something else altogether.

Still curious, I turn back and place my eye to the keyhole of her room, expecting blackness, but there is a faint light. I spring back. Someone must be in there, and I can think only that it must be Edward. Did he hear me at the door? Hear me try the handle? Guiltily I hurry back to my own chamber.

Inside, the cold has intensified, and the air feels as if it has been disturbed by something even in my short absence. My palms prick. I scan the corners and opaque spaces but there is only the sound, far off, of wind whining as it chases across the landscape.

Back in bed, shapes created by the candles weave across the ceiling and as hard as I try, the memories that I have been trying to keep back all day begin to emerge. Memories of *you*. I want to resist them, but the silence and perhaps even the great moor that lies outside forces the door open a little wider than usual, and you are there. You, who I held only for a short time, until my mother took you away.

I wonder, as I always do, where you are now. Are you sleeping? I imagine your fine strong limbs upon the sheets and the happy dreams that might pass through your mind. I hope they are happy. I think of the brother you will never meet, who will never know you exist. And shame and failure cut me through and I weep silently – face pressed to the pillow to muffle the sound of my grief.

2

'I hope you slept well, Mrs Stonehouse. The snow's still coming down,' Flora says, drawing back the curtains.

'How is John? Have you seen Agnes?'

'I believe he had a good night,' she says.

Through the window the moor dazzles and the hills beyond glitter in the brightness.

'Is Mr Stonehouse up yet?'

'He was up and breakfasted early,' Flora says, as she readies the washstand. 'I hope you were comfortable?'

I tell her I was, and after dressing I sit as Flora brushes my hair.

'How long have you worked here, Flora?'

She regards me shyly. 'Eleven months.'

'Do you like it?'

'Yes, I was fortunate to gain the post. Mr Stonehouse has a reputation for being a fair master.' Her words should bring comfort but her gaze, in the mirror, does not quite meet mine and I wonder why.

Afterwards, as I go downstairs, I notice more fine things: vases and tables, paintings and Queen Anne chairs. I try to imagine my mother complimenting me on my new home, but such warmth seems impossible and a little of my pleasure is reduced.

Breakfast is held in a room that catches the morning light. A table is set with a newly pressed cloth and laid with napkins, fruit and meats. I view the variety of food stuffs with bewilderment. Just over a year ago I would have been cutting bread and separating my sisters in a quarrel, running a hand over my youngest brother Albert's sweet curls and urging him to eat up. At the head my father would have put his cup down without a word and waited for me to refill it. I pause and think of Albert with a longing that nearly takes my breath away.

After breakfast, I have my first consultation with the housekeeper. We discuss menus and the household routines, and as I leave I gaze down at the list I have made and think about all that I am expected to remember. Flora finds me and tells me that Miss Stonehouse is expecting to receive me in her quarters.

Iris. I recall the unsatisfying conversation with Edward and how it has piqued my curiosity about my sister-in-law further.

I follow Flora to another wing, where the walls hold paintings of earlier times: a flat-faced Madonna and child, profiles of Elizabethan ladies. Iciness steals through the sashes where snow continues to fall silently beyond. Halfway along the passageway is an oriel window with a wide bay that leans out towards the back of the house and overlooks the river and woods.

'It's a pretty scene, isn't it?' I say.

'Very pretty,' Flora agrees.

We continue on and reach a door where Flora places her tray on a well-situated table and knocks.

The room we enter is large, with fading wallpaper and curtains. Several windows look out to the moor and one to the striking view at the rear of the property – but my eyes are soon absorbed with the figures who inhabit the chairs by the side of the fire.

Iris is dressed in a striking tunic of green with embroidered details of silver thread. Opposite is a neat woman with greying hair tightly held beneath a widow's cap. They stand and Iris comes and kisses my cheek.

'This is Mrs North, but we call her Southy.' She gives her old nurse and companion a nod. 'Edward and I considered it witty at the time.' She gestures to a chair. 'We hardly had time to say hello yesterday, and I don't think I even asked you if your journey here was smooth? And, of course, I hope that you had a comfortable first night?'

'The journey was good and I'm very comfortable, thank you.'

'And Guardbridge?'

'I very much like what I've seen.'

'The countryside must feel strange after being so long in town.'

'It does. For over six months my whole world comprised four walls and a bed, but I'm sure I'll quickly adjust.'

'And Edward was away with several commissions too. Weren't you lonely?'

I think back to those days, which seemed without end while I waited to see if I would lose our child. Edward did not like to sit with me in the bedroom; I think it made the possibility of that loss too real and he was absent more often than not, but Agnes had been there and for that I was grateful: sensible Agnes with her deep, quiet voice and careful way of moving as if considering the impact of every action.

'It was lonely,' I admit.

'But your family – you have parents still alive – did they come to visit?'

'They didn't.' I put a palm to my cheek that has grown suddenly warm.

'Not even your mother?'

'She's needed at home. We had only one maid and a daily and so there was always so much to do.' But I know that was not the reason; she could have come with my sisters and brothers, even if it was for only a day. I recall the final goodbye from which she had turned as soon as she could, and a band of pain creases my midriff.

'Well, I'm sure she would if she'd been able.' But a gleam of pity suggests that she guesses. 'Have you a large family? It'll be hard to be away from them, I think. Edward tells me you have many siblings?'

'Not so very big. There are five of us,' I say. 'I have two sisters and two brothers.'

'Will they come here to visit?'

'I hope so. Albert, the youngest, is keen to see where I'm living. It was the very last thing he said to me. He's five now, and Lizzie is just nine; they will most likely travel to Guardbridge as soon as it can be arranged. I plan to write to my mother this week.'

'I hope Edward's told you how delighted I am to gain a new sister,' Iris says a little shyly.

'And I too. My siblings are all younger than me by some years; there was no one I could call both friend and sister.'

'There, my dear —' Mrs North places a palm on Iris's arm — 'I told you that Mrs Stonehouse would feel nothing but happiness to have you here. Miss Stonehouse was a little afraid that you may have no time for the likes of a sister.'

'Quite the opposite,' I assure them. 'And I must thank you for your decoration of the nurseries and of my own room.'

'You're pleased?'

'Very,' I say, and Iris colours with pleasure.

'John is a darling boy. Southy and I both went this

morning when he woke. I wanted to see the shade of his eyes again. You know, he's more like my brother than you, I think.'

Mrs North says, 'Children change quickly, quickly indeed. Next week he'll look like his mother and a week after that everyone will remark that he has his grandfather's chin.'

Iris pours tea and hands me a cup. When we have finished, Iris's expression becomes a little grave and she pauses before saying, 'Did Edward tell you about me? About my hobbies?'

'No,' I say. 'He didn't.'

'Well, I believe he's not forthcoming about it outside Guardbridge.' She gives an uneasy laugh. 'So many people would consider me eccentric or worse; there are many ignorant views of such things.'

'Of what things?' I ask.

She sits a little higher in the chair, but rather than pride I sense she is on the defensive already. 'I'm a psychic and medium.'

Of all the eccentricities that I might have imagined, this would never have occurred to me in a hundred years of pondering it.

'I've shocked you,' she says.

'No. I mean, you have in as much that it's such a surprising ability to have.'

'And one which many people object strongly to,

especially those of religious faith.' They both watch me closely now to gauge my response.

'I expect my father's profession as a preacher has led you to expect I wouldn't look favourably on what you do?' I say. And I wonder if this was also the reason Edward did not reveal it.

'It's occupied my thoughts a lot,' Iris says.

Mrs North nods vigorously.

'You needn't have worried. What you claim doesn't cause me any moral qualms.' And it is true. I do not hold beliefs that the dead can be communicated with, and my father is not here to dictate what or what not I should think or feel. 'But, tell me, what does it mean to be a psychic? I've heard of people with such gifts but I'm not sure I fully understand what it entails.'

'To be psychic is to have the ability to see what is hidden from other eyes – truths and certainties are revealed to me – it's a mysterious gift, one that goes hand in hand with my ability to communicate with those who have passed on to the other world.'

For all my scepticism I have a moment of alarm at the notion that she might be able to see what I keep hidden.

'It's a gift that's passed down to all Stonehouse women; my aunts and great-aunts were all born with it.' She smiles. 'You look concerned, Annie. Don't worry, John is safe. But if you have a girl, you can expect her to have the capability too.'

This gives me pause; the idea that a daughter would inherit such talents as Iris claims is not a happy one.

'Once a month, on the full moon,' she continues, 'I conduct a small séance here in this parlour. It's only myself and Southy who are part of the circle, but I have dared to hope that you too would join us?'

I think again of my father and how he would react if he received this piece of information. An image of him comes to me, red-cheeked and angry, his grey eyebrows frowning into the creases of his forehead, and I flinch. For an instant he could be standing before me, his rage poised to come raining down with a slap or worse. But the idea that I can do as I wish without his judgement is liberating.

'Yes,' I say with force. 'I'd be most interested.' I'm aware that my enthusiasm is perhaps stimulated more by the idea that I am no longer restrained by my father's will rather than for the event itself.

Iris lets out her breath. 'I'm not so afraid now to admit that I have another unusual hobby – although it's more popular these days.' She indicates a diorama of small stuffed animals. I look round and see more, and one above me that hangs from the ceiling on a hoop of polished wood. Birds are tastefully arranged on its branches and it turns gently in the air, giving the impression of flight.

'You made all these?' I say, and getting up I go to the table and study another tableau. Each creature is perfectly preserved, and rather than disgust I feel a pulse of unexpected admiration. Iris's artistry has kept the animals so lifelike that even in death it is as if, at any moment, they could fly.

'I don't know why Edward chose to hide this skill from me.'

'Some consider it morbid.'

'I don't think so,' I say. 'Our own parlour sports a bearskin rug and a display of parrots that belonged to my great-aunt. You must tell me what you use to keep mites away – I'm afraid our parrots suffer dreadfully from them. You must have been doing this a long time to become so adept.'

Mrs North says, 'It takes many years to accomplish the craft. Would you like to learn?'

'I'd be happy to teach you,' Iris adds.

I know a little of taxidermy's methods, but the idea of handling flesh and the visceral nature of preparation makes me recoil. 'I'm not sure I could do much credit to it. I was never very artistic.'

'That's a shame. I would have enjoyed instructing you.'

'I'll come and watch.' I pause. 'Did Evie learn?'

'She did,' Iris says, but her tone is hesitant.

I look around me. 'Are any of these her work?'

Iris shakes her head. 'She only tried on and off, and

even with my help the results were a little less than sat-isfying. I think they might either have been thrown away or put out of sight.'

Although Edward has made it clear that he does not wish me to discuss his previous wife, I am com-pelled to continue. 'Having both Evie and Jacob die so suddenly must have been very hard for you. And Jacob so young. Edward told me he only had seven years.'

Something passes between them, so fast that I almost miss it – a wariness – and I think that Edward must have requested that they too refrain from this subject. Iris bows her head gravely in acknowledge-ment but says not a word. I search her for signs of how she might feel but she is unreadable.

The conversation moves quickly to other things. Iris's attention is earnest and I decide I like this sensi-tive, modest creature; her eccentricity is interesting rather than off-putting. She will be entertaining com-pany and with a manner so directed towards pleasing, it will be hard to find anything to dislike.

'And what hobbies did you pursue at home?' she asks.

'I was too occupied with helping my mother, but once, a long time ago, I learned a little piano and did some drawing – neither with any great natural skill.' I gaze out to the white landscape where here and there a patch of moorland emerges from its icy cast.

'Walking is what I love most and I plan to explore the moor as soon as there's a thaw. I hope you enjoy walking too, Iris. I'd be delighted to have your company, and you can educate me as to the flora and fauna and show me all the best places for hiking.'

She falls silent and lowers her eyes.

It is Mrs North who speaks. 'Miss Stonehouse doesn't leave the house. The spirits have warned her that to do so would result in calamity for her.'

Iris turns scarlet with embarrassment. 'It's true, Annie, I have a terror of it and have had for many years. Even the thought of opening the front door and going down the steps is enough to set me in a panic. I'm sorry but I'll make a very poor walking partner for you.'

The strength of her shame stirs me with pity and suddenly my perspective of her changes: with no outside entertainment her gifts must be everything to her and the future ahead must stretch bleakly with little hope of change. No wonder she is so keen to make a friend of me.

'I'm sorry to hear this, but you'll be no less of a companion for it, and I believe that fears can be tackled by doing the very thing we're afraid of. Perhaps I could help you if you'd let me.'

'I thank you, but the spirits are very clear that to go from Guardbridge would bring disaster.'

'But surely no such thing awaits you.'

'I tried once, a long time ago, and when I returned fell almost instantly ill with a stomach complaint that kept me in bed for several weeks.'

'That sounds like bad luck.'

'As you get to know me better, you'll learn that the spirits speak the truth, even if that truth is not what you want to hear.'

'And so you can never go to town, or visit friends?' I ask.

'I have no friends. I don't go anywhere, Annie, but I'm happy enough here. I have Southy and Edward, and now I have you.' Iris looks through the panes to the woods and I wonder if she hears with how much longing she uttered those words.

'When you go walking, though,' she says, 'I urge you to take a stick. Some of the moorland is dangerous – there are swampy areas. Every year people lose their lives to them.'

The conversation moves quickly on, but as we talk, I begin to notice a hesitancy in Iris, a lack of sureness and how she often turns to Mrs North as if seeking approval. Edward had once described Iris as timid, but I sense something more – something fragile. Her manner is almost childlike.

When the clock chimes twelve, I rise to return to my quarters. Iris looks to Mrs North, her mood light, and clasps her hands. 'A new baby, Southy, and a new sister. My happiness is complete.'

Leaving their rooms, I ponder Iris's unusual character. I realize that as well as gaining a sense of her
frailty, I have also come away with the notion that she
is not entirely well in her mind – it is more than her
horror of leaving the house and her claim to hear the
dead; it has come from some other source: the constant looks to Mrs North and the way, at times, she
would stop mid-sentence and drift in her thoughts. It
strikes me that she, like me, has suffered from some
event from which recovery is not entirely possible.
Instead of making me feel deeper empathy, it makes
me a little uneasy – as if Iris's damage might throw
light on my own.

In her workroom, Iris picks at the end of her thread
and buries it into the eye of her needle.

'I'm so glad for company and Annie is everything I
hoped for. Her manner is so charming and she has an
easy temperament, I think, although there is a look of
fear about her too. I wonder what her life was like
before. She's evidently very keen to learn more of
Evie and Jacob, but that's not surprising.'

'It'll be difficult to know what to say given your
brother doesn't want them discussed,' Mrs North
says.

'It's better Annie knows as little as possible.'

'Indeed you're right. I thought it a shame that she
didn't show more enthusiasm for your gifts.'

'It's clear she doesn't believe, not yet anyway, but I'm grateful she's not repelled by them. She's even agreed to attend the séances.' Iris gazes out to where snow slips across the window. 'Evie and Jacob are close today; the spirits have stirred at her coming – did I tell you that?'

'You did.'

'She's interesting, I think. Did you gain the impression that she's keen to resist examination?'

'She seemed open enough to me, but I'm sure you're the better judge in these matters.'

'I felt it very much; there's something in her that she's anxious to hide. But I expect we'll learn what that is in time. And if she doesn't tell me, the spirits will. I'm pleased Edward found her. He must be happy. I want him to be happy.'

Suddenly Iris gets up from the chair and walks to where Annie had been sitting. 'This was not here before.' Iris bends down to retrieve something from the floor and turns it to the light – a feather, small and black. 'Well, well,' she says.

'What is it?' Mrs North asks.

'This is curious, Southy.' Placing it on her palm she shows it to Mrs North.

'She must have picked it up on her dress.'

'She may have, but feathers don't usually just attach themselves like that, Southy.' She goes to the window to observe it better. 'Of all the tokens a

36

spirit might leave to signal interest, there's none more potent than that of a black feather.' She rubs it thoughtfully between her fingers and puts it in her pocket. Her expression is reflective. 'What a strange sign, Southy.' And she pulls her shawl closer to stifle a shiver.

3

After a solitary lunch, I seek out Agnes and spend time with John. On every occasion we are together I notice some new thing: a dimple in his cheek or how his thumb curves a little back on its joint. But too soon I am conscious of my deficits, that instead of joy and love this most precious of responsibilities brings guilt and confusion. I cannot help but think of you and all the minutes, all the hours, I have been denied. As I cradle John now, I think: is this how you looked at two months? Was your hair as dark, your eyes as bright, was your smile as wide? And with each year John will grow and stand in that space where you should be and remind me, even more forcibly, that you call someone else *mother*. It is a relief when John grows fretful and Agnes declares it is time for a feed.

I go to the drawing-room fire and do not feel the pleasure I expected at the empty hours ahead – only restlessness. The idea of so much time to be spent at my own leisure had been one of the things I antici- pated most keenly, but the reality is thin. Through the window the moor glitters with ice; the frosted ferns are like cut-out paper things through mist. I take out the glass beads we bought in Bath and set them out, but although engaged, my attention constantly goes to the wild golden sky and the half-hearted flakes that drift and flurry outside.

In spite of Edward's insistence that I need more time to recover, I ring the bell for my coat and boots and tie up my skirts.

Once in the garden the air bites and the bogs and hummocks are swept to the smooth lines of snowfall. Somewhere a creature barks. I tread the new snow to the edge of a lake where the reeds and rushes are crusted white. I gaze into the water that gathers the blackness of its depths and spits it upwards against the ice. I imagine the sluggish tail of salmon or carp stirring the mud below, but as I look my mind is filled with an image – Evie, her face, sculpted by Edward's brushes, pushing through the water to death. I shiver and blink it away.

A wind comes down from the hills and breathes through the oaks. Behind me, Guardbridge throws a series of flawed shadows, creating patches of darkness where none should exist. And as I stand there I feel suddenly watched.

I twist round and my eyes go up to the house, and there, at one of the windows, a person is looking down. Counting back from my own chamber, I realize it is the one that belonged to Evie. The room is too dim to make out more than a silhouette, but the figure is too small to be either Iris or Mrs North. An under maid who I have not seen? I do not know why but I give a shudder and direct my gaze purposefully away.

The hours elapse and the milky coldness of night begins to seep into the house through mismatched joints and whispering gaps. It brings with it the wildness of the moor and the wind that is never still so that the trees are bent to it like creatures grown with faulty spines and arthritic stoops.

We sit at supper where, once again, the candles flicker in their silver stems.

'I enjoyed meeting Iris today. You kept her abilities very secret. Were you afraid I'd object?'

He pauses. 'Do you?'

'No, but you know already that I'd never believe she could possibly speak to the dead.'

'You think she's mad? Or lying?'

'Of course not – many people claim such things. I think she wants to believe it very much and perhaps imagines she can.'

'But if you'd known, would it have influenced how you felt about coming here?'

'Not at all. I find it intriguing.'

He gives a dry laugh. 'Your father wouldn't agree.'

'I'm not my father. I've agreed to attend her next séance too.'

'Good. I was planning to ask if you would.'

'Why does it matter to you?'

'I worry about Iris; it's a comfort knowing there's someone there to witness what happens.'

'Why me? If you wanted to know, wouldn't you go yourself?'

'Men aren't welcome; we don't bring the right energy apparently.' His smile is tinged with humour. 'Can I rely on you?'

'Yes,' I say, 'although I don't like the idea of spying.'

'It's not that. Iris is my sister and I worry about her. I only want to know whether you think they harm her at all.'

I ponder that. 'How could they harm her?'

'From a child she's suffered with fugues and trances, but they're getting worse. Mrs North tries to hide it, but I'm not fooled. She sleepwalks too. I often work late into the night and witness them and they too grow in frequency.'

'And you suspect it's the séances that cause this?'

'Without a doubt.'

'Poor Iris,' I say. 'I'll let you know if I see anything that concerns me. Do you think she talks to the spirits?'

He pauses. 'I don't believe the dead return at the full moon and roam Guardbridge like guests at a Christmas party. But I have to concede that Iris occasionally demonstrates an uncanny ability to pluck a truth out of nowhere.'

Surely if Iris has done this, it is from some developed sense of her understanding for people and she has made a lucky guess, but I cross my arms over my belly as if it were possible to see what I conceal.

Edward smooths a napkin on his lap. 'Thank you. I wasn't sure how you'd react when you heard. It's important you become friends. In a household as small as ours, alliances make the living so much easier if they go well.'

I sense pressure here and I recall Iris's hesitant responses regarding Evie. I reflect on whether relations between Iris and Evie had not been smooth, which would explain why Edward is so keen to promote my own camaraderie with his sister.

'I'll enjoy her company very much,' I say. 'You also failed to tell me about her fear of leaving Guardbridge.'

'My poor sister. I'm so familiar with it now that I forget.'

'Such afflictions can be helped, you know, and if Iris is willing, I'd like to try to persuade her outside, a little at a time.'

'Good luck with that. None of us have succeeded.'

'But it's such a tragedy.'

'She's happy, though, don't you think?'

'Maybe,' I say. 'I sensed –' I pause, wondering how to frame my words – 'I sensed she's suffered some trouble that's made her fragile.'

'What made you think that?'

'I'm not sure exactly. She's delicate somehow.'

He regards me as if he had discovered something new in me. 'Our mother died when Iris was twelve and Iris took it particularly badly. You're right. I don't think she's ever fully recovered. Perhaps you're psychic too, Annie.'

I laugh. 'I can assure you, I'm not. Your mother's death must have been a difficult event.'

'It wasn't so much for myself, but it changed Iris.'

'And how did your family feel about her claim to talk to spirits?'

He spears a piece of meat. 'My father just about tolerated it – our mother, however, hated it, and Iris learned very young to be secretive about her talent, at least until she died.'

'Why did Iris feel able to pursue it when your mother died if your father didn't entirely approve?'

'He was away often before her death and more so afterwards. He preferred the company of his club in town and took scant interest in the affairs of his daughter.'

A silence falls between us that says many things, of children left to the care of servants, of one particular child, whose company appears to have been that of the dead.

For a moment he is pensive and there is a melancholy about him that I have witnessed often. I consider how strange and sad that, for both of us, we have such painful things in our pasts. I imagine opening my mouth and talking of you, but even the thought sends a whisper of fear through me.

It is then, cutting through the noises of the room, that I hear a baby's cries. I put down my fork and listen. Then, folding the napkin, I stand.

'What is it, Annie?'

'I can hear John.'

'There's nothing.'

I listen again and discern a far-off wail and the pattering of footsteps. 'Yes, did you hear that?'

'Sit down, Annie. We're too far from the nurseries for sound to carry. I thought I'd married a sensible woman. You're much too anxious about John; if he needs you, Agnes will bring him. That's what she's for.'

But my attention is now elsewhere; I pick up the knife and put it down again. It is contradictory that even though I remain disconnected from him I cannot think beyond the noise of his cry and how the urge to go to him is insurmountable. It comes again and I shoot a look at Edward.

'For heaven's sake, Annie. These unnecessary interruptions aren't good. This is only the second evening we've spent together at Guardbridge.' He shrugs with displeasure. 'I can see you won't settle until your curiosity has been satisfied.'

45

I am too absorbed by the noise to care too much for his reaction and by the time he picks up his glass, I am already halfway out of the door.

The hall is quiet but for the sounds from the scullery. Lifting my skirts, I hurry up the stairs and to the landing where the lamplight swells and dips in the darkness. Pausing to listen, there is only the faint wind.

I reach the nursery wing and realize Edward is right, and that John is too far from the main house to be able to hear him from the dining room. Now, outside his door, there is no sound anyway. Still, I walk in.

Agnes looks up from her knitting and stands, a faint frown between her brows, which she quickly smooths.

No crying. Only the tick of the clock and the hiss of the fire. John lies on his back, his fine lashes curled over his eyes. Agnes puts a finger to her lips.

'I thought I heard him,' I whisper, but Agnes points and shakes her head. I hesitate, awkward now in my foolishness, so I nod guiltily and rush back to Edward, who must be on his next course and pondering my unnecessary absence.

'I'm sorry,' I concede. 'John hadn't woken.'

'I keep telling you. He's in safe hands. I know being a new mother can be difficult but it's time you settled now. I agree wholeheartedly with Agnes's methods. John is best served by her.'

They all see it, I think. John is better without me.

Later, on the way upstairs, I am conscious there is something about Guardbridge that causes me the tiniest disquiet. I stop and examine the idea, unsure as to its cause. The house is not still but then, like most old homes, it has a life of its own and creaks and groans according to the weather and temperature. Beyond my candlelight, darkness hangs along the passageway and the doors to other rooms are set back, leaving rectangles of space; I think how easily they could contain a person hidden from sight.

I come to a portrait of Evie and Jacob and stop, a little out of breath. As I gaze at their likenesses, I am aware of the faint impression they leave — as if they were still living. As if, turning on one of the long corridors, I may come face to face with them. There is, about Jacob's eyes, something unnaturally intense that leaves me faintly troubled. He stares out from the canvas with such force that, for a moment, it is as if there is no paint between us.

4

The first week passes quickly and soon Guardbridge
is as familiar as any home might be. I settle in to my
new role and its routines. January passes to February,
yet winter still keeps the house and the moors fast in
its embrace.

One morning, after breakfast, the door of the
drawing room opens. I expect one of the maids but it
is Edward in a loose linen shirt and waistcoat spat-
tered with colour and with numerous pockets and
pouches for the storing of tools.

'Come, Annie,' he says.

In the corridor I take his hand. 'You're going to
paint me?' I can hardly keep the smile from my face.
'Where will you hang my portrait?'

'Where it best looks.' His strides are long and decisive,
and I have to nearly run to keep up.

'Do I need to change?'

'Not today. Later I'll choose a dress for you.'

The studio is bitterly cold.

Edward indicates a chaise-longue of faded yellow
velvet, but I know already this is where he will paint
me; it is where he painted Evie and Jacob so many

times. I recognize its cushioned back and behind are two windows through which sun falls and meets, placing the sofa in spotlight.

His movements are courteous and efficient; for the first time it is not the husband I am with but the artist. He is somehow taller, his movements sparser and more confident. He puts on an apron, gives the ties a sharp pull, checks his brushes and although I am the subject I sense that he has already forgotten me.

The maids keep the fire well stocked and, as the hours elapse and the sky turns to white and finally the colour of corn he grows happier, humming under his breath. At times I want to close my eyes and sleep or hunger growls in my middle, but I do not wish to disturb him.

My mind wanders, finding moments from the past: the burnt cakes Lizzie made that we fed to the pig, how Ellen twisted her skirts in her hands but her face remained immobile from shock as our father stood before her, hand raised to strike. And the happier times: giggling in bed from some silly joke that Ellen told until the boards creaked with our helpless mirth. The mouse smell of the boys' hair as I passed a comb through it or the way Albert tried to stay close to me, wanting always to have some part of him touch me.

Once I had imagined I would marry and settle somewhere near to my family, somewhere where it would be possible to walk only a little way and knock on the peeling front door – to have my sisters and brothers run into my arms, to help my mother at the kitchen table and watch the children grow. How that changed after you, and all that happened.

As my thoughts touch on you, inevitably, I am back on an autumn afternoon of my fifteenth year as a bundle is deposited in my arms – a button nose and wide brow. *Enough*, I think – and my heart bumps painfully.

'Stop moving, Annie. Are you feeling well? I'm nearly done.'

I had not realized that I had stirred. But it is not long until Edward speaks again to announce that he is done for the day. I rise stiffly and move towards the painting.

'Not yet, Annie. Only when I've finished. Only when I'm happy.' There is an assuredness to his tone that leaves no area for debate.

The smell of linseed oil and turpentine stays on me and, as I make my way to bed, I pass a picture of Evie and stop to consider it. As I stand there, two maids approach the corridor and their hushed whispers reach me.

'Is that what you heard?'

'It is. And worse.'

I move back into one of the alcoves and cannot discern what is next said. Then their voices come again.

'Poor Mrs Stonehouse. I don't believe she's been told a thing.'

'Shh, and don't let Mrs Ford hear you say it. You'd be in for a right dressing-down.'

It is a wet day and I find Iris and Mrs North at the drawing-room fire. The spitting rain is syncopated by the crackling of logs. Iris is wrapped in a heavy shawl.

'Miss Stonehouse slept badly last night,' Mrs North says.

'Rats,' Iris says. 'Do you hear them at night, Annie? Guardbridge is a veritable palace for rats. I've told Mrs Ford that greater measures must be employed to rid us of them.'

'You'll never get rid of rats and especially not somewhere like this where there are such easy pickings,' Mrs North remarks.

Iris tries to hide a weary yawn.

'Should you go back to bed, Iris, to catch up with your sleep?' I suggest.

She shakes her head. 'I'm tired of lying down. If I do it too much, my head thumps and the bedroom is colder than ever today. Where is John?'

'Agnes has him.'

'Why don't you bring him down? I'd love to see him.' Her eyes are curious. She must wonder why I do not take more interest.

'He'll be asleep now.' I think of him curled beneath the covers like a comma, knees drawn up, or lying on his back arms flung to the side, palms open, waiting for the world to drop gifts into his hands. I would like him to always feel like that.

Iris sighs wistfully and goes to the window where rain is thickening to sleet on the panes. Even with extra layers the chill is difficult to ignore. After a pause, she says, 'Did Edward tell you about the Guardbridge Glass?'

'What's that?' I ask.

Iris brightens. 'He really hasn't said much about me, has he? I use it at the séances. The first Miss Stone-houses, three sisters, created it to ensure their spirits would always be able to meet and return here after death.'

There is something so naive and delusional about the idea that the dead might be able to return by means of something earth-bound that I feel a sudden pity for her. 'How does it work?'

'I'm not sure I know. The glass is claimed to pro-vide a channel for souls to travel between the two worlds but even between the séances it exerts an influ-ence, allowing the spirits to communicate with me. Perhaps, without it, I would have no psychic gift at all.'

'So, you call the sisters back at your séance?'

'I don't specifically call them, but I like to believe they use it to return and talk among themselves as they once did. Spirits do come, but I don't always know who they are.'

'Do you use the glass between séances?'

'The glass is not to be touched between sittings. It is designed only for that night and it is said that to use it at other times will diminish its effectiveness.'

'And it has always been here since it was created?'

'The glass belongs to Guardbridge. To remove it would be to rob it of its power.'

I think of Evie and Jacob. 'Do the spirits of those who have died most recently come more often than those long passed?'

She gives me a shrewd look. 'Perhaps.'

'When they come, do you mean they come back as ghosts?'

'Oh no, they're not so material as that. It's hard to explain, but I feel them.' She presses a palm to her heart.

'What do they say?'

'Many things, of things past, of things related to now and sometimes I believe they come to mourn their deaths or even their lives.'

'Evie and Jacob died so young; they have much to regret.'

She smiles but it does not reach her eyes. 'They do.'

Mrs North watches us with interest, for once her hands idle. 'Why don't you show Mrs Stonehouse the glass?' she says.

Iris turns bright eyes to me. 'Do you want to see it?'

I feel a burn of curiosity for this possession in which Iris deposits so much faith.

'Very much,' I say.

With a flurry of energy, she takes my palm and leads me away. There is something playful about our pilgrimage to the mysterious object that inhabits Iris's world. From the hall we traverse more passageways. In the first week I had made a cursory investigation of this part of the house but was repelled by its neglect. The temperature is icier, and, left to its own devices, the walls have lost panelling, the rugs thinned to scraps of faded fabric, and ceilings and corners are draped in cobwebs as if they wore widow's weeds.

'The glass has always been kept in the blue room but, as you can see, we don't upkeep it now.' We follow a corridor, doors missing to show empty, echoing spaces beyond and windows grimed with dirt. Drifts of dead leaves curl across tiles and are blown into nooks. All this is glimpsed fleetingly, but I pull Iris back when I see a music room. 'The piano should not be left in such conditions. Does nobody take care of the instruments?' I say, aghast at such negligence.

'I don't play. My mother was always too ill to teach me and I didn't have a master.'

I walk in and note the dust-filmed lid. 'I had always hoped to continue. Perhaps here I could.'

'Come away,' Iris says. 'It's too cold to dawdle.'

'But this looks like a fine instrument. I must ask

Edward to get a tuner in and see if we can heat the air a little. It may be useable.'

I lift the lid, but Iris takes my arm firmly and pulls me back. 'He won't like it; it belonged to Evie, you know, and I believe it's not so very fine and too badly out of tune to be repaired now.'

For an instant, I imagine Evie's figure upon the seat, her fingers running over the keys as Edward listens in delight. 'You're right,' I say with a sigh, 'I can't ask if this belonged to her.'

'Come on, let's find the glass. I always think coming here is like an adventure,' Iris says, bringing an end to the discussion.

We come eventually to a door and Iris guides me in. The duck-egg wallpaper hangs damp and peeling from the walls. All the windows look out on to the back of the house, showing the river and woods.

'The view is one of the best,' Iris says.

'Your parlour is above it – you look out this way too.'

'Sometimes I stand in the middle of my floor and imagine, through timbers, the glass waiting for me below.'

We move to the centre of the room where a silver filigree box sits atop a pedestal. Iris takes a key from her chatelaine and slips it into the lock. She opens the lid, revealing a glass globe that gleams faintly in the pale light.

It is strange but as I gaze down I become aware of

the curious atmosphere – the blue room has an energy that is all its own. I look about as if I will find the source of this impression but it is not something that is moored to the décor; it is something else. It is not a quality that is easy to evaluate, and I think that this must be because the glass itself claims its powers are supernatural. Soon, I think, I will find out if it can do as it professes.

Suddenly a pair of ravens come squawking out of the trees and fly just outside the window, making me jump.

Iris laughs.

'It's a beautiful thing,' I admit, returning my attention to the glass. Even in the dull light it has a faint iridescence.

She nods reverentially and I observe her fine profile and the neat lines of her face and I sense a change in her. When she smiles at me she exerts a confidence I am unfamiliar with.

'In spite of the fear you feel about leaving, don't you long to be away from Guardbridge sometimes? You're so young. Life could still bring you a family and I can see how much children mean to you.'

She does not flinch and I consider that she has been long armoured against this question.

'That's not to be.'

I open my mouth to say more but the tone of her reply is final. She closes the lid and locks it once more.

We begin walking away, our skirts gathering dust. Just as we leave, I turn; the room is oddly still, strangely shadowed, and there, on a branch, outside the window, one of the ravens remains perched, its black eye gazing in and fixed on me.

It is a relief to be back in the relative heat of the drawing room and the comfortable sight of Mrs North, needles tapping. Iris sits and gathers her shawl; her thoughts are far away.

'The glass is a lovely thing, isn't it?' Mrs North says.

I agree, although there remains with me a sense that I have been brushed by something unearthly. I take the tip of my cotton and slick it with beeswax before threading it through one of the glass beads.

'I hear Edward has begun painting you,' Iris says.

'He has. I had to keep still for so many, many hours.' I glance at Evie's portrait above the fireplace. 'The task is more arduous than I anticipated.' I think of the portraits in the house and my sense that the sitters were less than happy. 'How did Evie enjoy it – and Jacob too? Edward painted him very young.'

'I don't recall that Evie complained,' Iris says.

'And Jacob?'

There is a pause that is just a little too long.

'I suppose,' Iris says, 'that it's harder for any child to

sit still for a protracted period; they're not designed for such patience.'

So Jacob struggled with it. Is that what Edward painted – Jacob's dislike of being forced to adopt a stance that he could not break? I think of John and wonder how he will be when that duty falls to him.

It is Mrs North who changes the subject. 'What did he have you wear?'

'At the time I was in a blue silk we bought in London, but he said he may have me wear something different.'

'Blue looks well on you, I think,' Iris says.

Mrs North nods vigorously. 'It goes with your emeralds too.'

Iris gets up from her seat and reaches out to the chain where the pale jewels are strung on gold links from my neck.

Our eyes meet and when Iris's fingers brush my skin I feel, for the briefest moment, something stormy.

Edward has left me for the night, but I cannot sleep.

As the room holds me, there is a faint but persistent whining that comes from somewhere close. It is a different sound from that of the wind; there is something mechanical in its tone that suggests it is not manufactured by nature. I light a candle and circle the floor, following the noise until I come to part of the panelling near one of the windows.

The sound makes me uncomfortable – it draws on unfamiliar senses as if Guardbridge were imbued with something of the supernatural. I put an ear to the panelling where it becomes clear that it emanates from somewhere just beyond.

In the corridor I track the passageway to the adjacent chamber, to furniture swathed in protective sheets – the bedchamber of some ancestor. I disturb a mouse nest in the fabric of a sofa and wait for the scuttling to cease.

There is no noise.

Back at the bedroom, I return to the wall and this time detect a catch buried in the panelling, almost invisible to the eye. I pull it to discover a cupboard. The motion of the door sets what is hanging there into a greater spin. Fixed high up is a diorama of stuffed animals attached to a hoop such as the one I saw in Iris's parlour.

It turns to the movement of air, eliciting a hum. I hold up the candle. Birds hang from its frame. I draw closer and the candle catches the gleam of their eyes. Though not eyes; instead of the glass beads I expect, these have shells pierced in place, giving the impression of both blindness and sight. It is utterly obscene and I shut the door quickly, leaning my back against it until my pulse stops racing. It cannot stay; I will take it down and find a new home for it first thing in the morning.

I lie back in bed and attempt to put it from my mind, but even behind the wood their spiralled gaze swings in the air as if they could watch me. Closing my eyelids, I try to ignore it, but it is as if my discovery has imbued it with more energy because now the pitch is higher as if it were spinning fiercer and fiercer.

When I eventually sleep, I dream of Guardbridge. Shadows leach to the walls and take unnatural shape from my candle. I know that I have lost something, something precious, but my progress meanders and my desperation to find it presses with more urgency. From room to room I go, the sense of loss propelling me ever more fervently. As I fly through the corridors in anguish, the house about me darkens, then a light grows out of the blackness itself and I know I must follow. Through nameless passageways and corridors I pass, and in and out of rooms until, eventually, I am standing in Guardbridge's main hall and gazing up to the first floor.

Holding the chamber stick high, I throw light to the curling banisters and flaking walls. Up I look to the top of the stairs where a small figure crouches in the blackness.

'I see you,' I whisper. 'I see you now.'

5

Light leaks in from the curtains. Although it is over a year since I left home, half of me still expects to wake to the cottage and to my sisters beside me and outside the sleepy sound of the hens and dissonant screech of gulls. I recall the diorama and listen – nothing, but the air is soured by its memory and a troubled dream which is now growing distant.

I rise from the bed and open the cupboard with the intention of taking it down but in daylight it is more innocuous, and I decide to ask Iris about it instead. It is then that I realize that Iris's séance falls tomorrow.

This morning the aromas of the house are brighter and more distinct. I am now accustomed to Guard-bridge's scents and noises, from the way steps sound on the servants' stairs and passageways to the flare as lamps are lit and the smell of wax and polish.

It is mid-morning when wheels sound on the drive. It is Bessie who informs me that Edward's uncle, Mr Forster, has come to pay his respects.

'Will Miss Stonehouse be joining us?'

'She's just this minute taken to her bed, ma'am.'

'That's a pity,' I say, and go to the mirror to adjust my hair. It will be me alone who meets him, Edward having gone early to town. He has warned me that his uncle would come soon to find something to gossip about and will be pleased to have missed him. But, despite his warning, I find myself keen for new company.

Bessie shows in a small red-faced man with a fuzz of greying hair that sprouts from a tight-fitting velvet cap. His suit is speckled with ash and he brings with him the scent of pipe smoke and whisky.

After his wily eyes have scoured me and he has given a quick sharp smile that displays no warmth whatsoever, he seats himself in the chair closest to the fire and begins to recount his journey in relentless detail.

Bessie comes in shortly with hot drinks and food from the kitchen but he gives the coffee a sour look and asks for a glass of porter.

When she has gone, he turns his eyes to me, 'Well,' he says, taking his pipe and rummaging through his pockets for tobacco, 'Edward has proved yet again that he's a man of good taste. And what do you think of this great lump of a house?'

'It's impressive. Did you ever live here?'

'No, no, not me. I was Edward's mother's brother – but I've stayed here more than once. And, of course, I come to visit my nephew and niece as I did your

64

predecessor. You must wonder about the first Mrs Stonehouse, what with Edward marrying so soon after she died. I told him to wait or, even better, not to marry again. That's what I said. Of course there are good reasons for marrying, to gain an heir, but you wouldn't have me wedded at any price. I said to Edward, at the very least put more time behind it before embarking again, but would he listen?'

The only reply that comes to my tongue is a sharp one, and so I say nothing.

He gives a dry laugh and crumbles a piece of cake between his fingers. 'We were good friends, Evie and I.'

'You were?'

'Oh yes, such class and manners she had, and, of course, she brought a generous dowry.' He casts his gaze over the walls. 'Guardbridge isn't cheap to run and Edward's painting has always been more of a hobby than a profession, in spite of his prestige. Edward struck very rich when he met her.' He pauses and takes a draught from his glass. 'Are you from a wealthy family?'

A hot flush rises to my cheeks. 'We were not poor, but I would not describe us as wealthy.'

'Later, though –' he sighs – 'well, it wasn't all so good then, but I expect Edward has told you this?'

'Of course,' I lie, but believe he had said it guessing full well he had not.

'I don't agree with what they said of poor Evie.'

Poor Evie? I try to hide my growing interest. 'What did they say of her?'

He gives me an artful smile. 'Well, my dear, Evie grew difficult to please.'

'Difficult to please?'

'That's what they said.'

'What didn't please her?'

'The more pertinent question might be: what did please her? And, you know, she came to hate Guardbridge, or maybe it was only those within it.'

Hate Guardbridge? 'Why?' My voice is a whisper.

He rubs his hands together and gazes around as if seeing it for the first time, then gives an uncertain laugh. 'I don't know – maybe the fact it's so remote out here on these lonely moors. If you wanted to run away, it would be hard, wouldn't it?'

I say nothing.

He refills his pipe, raining tobacco strands upon his coat, already liberally smeared with what looks like a considerable portion of his last meal. 'Nerves. That's what I say. Why are women so prone to nerves? Give me a man any day. Yes, we were good friends, but Evie had too many nerves.'

My eyes drift to her portrait and I imagine her now as a woman unhappy and dissatisfied and wonder again about their marriage.

'In that respect she was not unlike my unfortunate

niece.' He pauses and puts his head to one side. 'Or perhaps –' his eyes spark with a hungry gleam – 'it's Guardbridge itself that brings out the worst in its women. It has a reputation, you know.' He gives me an assessing look and I think about Mrs Breach and those solemn words spoken to me so long ago.

I shrink deeper into my skin with dislike.

He leans back in the chair, brushing his waistcoat, and fiddles for his pipe again. 'Pour me another glass if you would be so kind. There's a good girl.' His lips are red and shiny.

'So, you must be well acquainted with Iris by now?' He does not wait for my answer. 'I see by your expression that you are.' He tips his chin and gives a mirthless chuckle. 'What do you think of her? I recall her as a young girl, a babe. Always a rum one, was Iris. I said to her mother that it was so. Generally mothers can't fault their children. But –' he grows reflective again – 'her mother wasn't enamoured of her daughter. Edward was the apple of her eye, but poor little Iris didn't please her.'

Poor Iris, indeed, I think. How much we have in common. 'I like Iris very much,' I tell him.

'Well, that's good, as I'm not sure that she and Evie got along and, in a house as lacking in company as this, that must pall.' He empties his glass and looks morosely at the jug. 'Yes, poor old Iris. She's harmless enough, I suppose.' But his eyes narrow and he rubs at his sleeve nervously.

'But what are you made of Mrs Stonehouse?' And there is something unsteady in his look. 'You've brought Guardbridge what it needs, of course – a new child and a boy for the entail.' He sighs. 'Poor Jacob. It's a great tragedy that he and his mother died quite so young.' Then he looks at me slyly and pauses before adding, 'But not so much for you, my dear.'

I blush. 'The scarlet fever is a cruel disease.'

'The scarlet fever, eh?' But there is an inflection that catches at me. He watches me carefully now and this time there is no humour or sarcasm, but something else.

I think back to that overheard conversation by the servants. 'That's how they died,' I press.

He grimaces. 'In a place as isolated as this, we can only believe that what we are told is the truth.'

I am flooded with misgiving but then I consider how Edward told me that this man's sole intention in coming to visit would be to fill me with doubt and discomfort, and I am angry.

As if sensing the change in my mood, his eyes slip away from me and he fiddles with his pockets, pulling out pipe tobacco and matches and then returning them and checking that they are securely packed away, then he rings the bell for his coat.

'I must be off, my dear. I have a meeting with Mr Oakley at Abbeydale today where I believe Mrs Oakley is to give me a good lunch. The food here, of course, is always excellent, although Guardbridge replaces its staff more than anywhere else in England, but Mrs Oakley has a special flair.' His tongue passes over his lips in anticipation. 'Her roast potatoes are the work of a magician.'

He reaches over suddenly and places a smooth palm over my hand, his expression almost apologetic. 'You be a good girl, now, Mrs Stonehouse.'

He stands with a groan of discomfort. 'I really must be off. At least it's stopped snowing.'

At the door he turns. 'Do you hear me, Mrs Stonehouse? Be a good girl.'

For a few moments the impact of his words leaves me motionless. He is everything Edward warned me against: opinionated, tactless and with a desire to cause mischief. I think of what he has said, suggesting, albeit obliquely, that I have not been told the truth regarding the deaths of Evie and Jacob, and that final statement – *Be a good girl.* And for all his bluster and roguishness I cannot shake the impression it has left: not a suggestion, not a plea. A warning.

6

By lunchtime the rain has turned again to snow and a storm is blowing off the moors, sending spindrift whirling at the windows; smoke coughs from the chimney flues and taints the air. After visiting John, I try to settle with some needlepoint, but my attention is constantly drawn away and back to my conversation with Mr Forster. Around me Guardbridge creaks in the gale and, beyond that, the house echoes back my unease and, with it, a sense that Guardbridge has suddenly become elevated from its material realm.

As wind comes blowing through the passageways I am reminded of whispers. I think of the glass and its claimed channel between the living and the dead and realize that if I allowed myself to dwell on such ideas it would be too easy to imagine some truth in them. It is Mr Forster who has unsettled me, that is all.

I get up to stretch my legs, taking the corridor towards the music room, but the air is too cold and my uneasiness does not pass. I imagine tomorrow's séance and see Evie and Jacob, silent and ghost-like, nosing their way along the passageways to where Iris cups the glass.

Mrs North comes with an invitation from Iris, who is now fully recovered. She directs me up to their quarters and to the workroom dedicated to her taxidermy. I wonder if her ailment was manufactured to avoid meeting her uncle; I would not blame her if that were so, especially after his cutting remarks.

Iris is wearing a fetching jacket of red. 'You look lovely,' I say, and she smiles. 'I wish you'd been there earlier when your uncle came. I missed your company very much.'

I can see she is pleased but her eyes are rimmed with anxiety.

'Your uncle's very happy with the sound of his own voice.'

'He likes to gossip too,' Iris says.

'I neither listen to nor impart gossip.'

Her narrow shoulders sag with relief and I feel an urge to put my arms round her. 'Your uncle can say nothing to me that will affect my regard for you.'

I look about me at the labelled drawers of fleshing knives, scalpels and T-pins. There are jars of chemicals and glass cabinets containing more of her work. A tray of beaded eyes of different sizes and colours sits on a table and the shelves sag under the weight of manuals. There is a strong smell of carbolic that does not fully mask the faintest scent of decay.

'I found a diorama in my room – hidden in a secret cupboard behind the panelling.'

'Which cupboard is that?' Iris asks. 'I don't know of any such cupboard.'

'It's by the window opposite the door. The animals don't have eyes, only shells in their place.'

Iris frowns and turns to Mrs North with a shrug. 'Do you recall such a thing?'

'You don't keep all your work. Was it one made a long time ago, perhaps?'

'I'm sure I'd remember.'

'Maybe it was one of Evie Stonehouse's,' Mrs North says, 'though I don't know what it would be doing hidden where you say.'

I wonder if it was made by Evie, why she did not use beads to give it sight; perhaps, I muse, it is unfinished.

Next to Iris is a stuffed linnet, its beak half open as if felled in song.

Mrs North sits beside Iris ready to pass scissors or a particular knife.

'What do you think of my workroom?' Iris asks.

'I'm impressed,' I say. 'What are you doing now?'

Iris lifts her palm and holds it out – it's a tiny brown lizard.

'Although I usually only do birds, other animals are interesting to work on. I'm in the final stages now.' She reaches into a box beside her and takes out a piece of paper that opens to a ball of hair, undoubtedly human.

'When I'm at the point of closing the animals, I put

something from the living of Guardbridge inside them too – a nail clipping or hair, a token. In this way the spirits are drawn closer to Guardbridge by the souls who once owned them.'

I think of the diorama in my cupboard and am further repelled. 'But I thought it was to you that you wanted the spirits to come?'

'I do and they will, but this gives them passage to all who are here, not just myself. This hair,' she says, 'do you recognize it by its colour?'

I know it instantly – wiry of texture and already flecked with grey. In spite of my resolve not to think ill of Iris, my feelings find sudden empathy with Mr Forster's opinions of his niece.

Iris beams. 'Of course you do. It's Edward's.'

'If you intend to draw spirits to somebody, you couldn't choose a less susceptible subject than your brother,' I say teasingly.

Mrs North looks up. 'You never spoke a truer word, Mrs Stonehouse.'

Iris laughs. 'It doesn't matter that Edward is sceptical. It's not for his benefit that it's done.'

There is seemingly no answer to this. 'Why a lizard?' I ask.

'They have a quickness of movement and are masters of disguise.'

What does she mean? That Edward is a master of disguise?

Iris must sense my alarm and she gushes, 'That is, they are flexible and quick and . . .' She trails off awkwardly.

Mrs North says, 'There's no meaning in the lizard, I assure you. Iris loves and respects all creatures equally; she just expressed herself wrong.'

'Did my uncle tell you how odd he thought this pursuit? He's had plenty of opinions over the years,' Iris adds.

'No,' I say.

'I suspect he remarked on my character, though.' Iris's brow grows heavy and her knife slips, nicking the edge of her finger where a spot of blood appears.

Mrs North frets immediately, but Iris throws her off with: 'Don't be such a fusspot, Southy. It's nothing, nothing.' She puts the finger to her mouth and sucks at the wound.

'Did he speak much of me then?'

'Hardly –' I begin.

'But I expect he took the opportunity to make unjust remarks as to the state of my mental well-being? Yes, you look apologetic, Annie. The truth is that he has no regard for me at all. He doesn't trust my gift and thinks I'd be better off locked away – sent to an asylum. He said as much when I was a child. It's just like him to come so soon and try to turn you against me.'

Mrs North says, 'Now, Iris. I'm sure that's not what he thinks at all.'

But Iris snaps at her. 'You know it is. They didn't want me, did they? It would have been an easy way to get me away from Guardbridge. If it weren't for you, Southy, and Edward, that is probably where I would've ended up. Sometimes I think I would've been better off.' She slams the knife down.

I think of the comment Mr Forster had made regarding her mother's lack of feeling for her daughter and feel a stab of pity. Even so, Iris's outburst has shocked me and I glance at Mrs North whose face is stricken.

I reach for her hand. 'Iris, you must believe me when I say that I could see your uncle's character immediately and nothing he could say would influence what I think of you. You have Edward and Mrs North to support you and now you have me. You never need believe that you're not wanted here.'

Her eyes become wet and when she looks up at me it is with such gratitude that it spurs my compassion further.

Then the moment passes with the righting of the knife on the table. 'I'm nearly finished now. Get me my message box, Southy.' And it is as if the calm had never been breached.

Mrs North opens a cabinet, bringing out a box inlaid with mother-of-pearl. From her chatelaine Iris takes another key and opens the lid. The box is filled with bits of folded-over waxed paper.

'What's that for?' I ask.

'I also slip a message into the body cavity so that the spirit animals will take it to the person for whom it's intended.' She picks one out then relocks the box carefully.

'You send messages to particular people?'

'To those I've loved and to those that I wish to speak with.'

Messages to the dead in the bodies of the dead? The idea is so macabre and disquieting that I look away to hide my reaction.

'You can do this too, Annie, if you like. Is there someone who has passed away who you would like to send a note to?'

My aunt comes to mind, the thinning yellow hair that lay greasily on her sallow crown, the blue eyes sucked of colour and the lines of pain that creased around the once plump mouth. A burn of tenderness and loss, for when it was clear that I was with child it had been she who had sat me down, her arms about me, and told me, woman to woman, how it was to be. My aunt, who did not blame me as my parents had, who believed so much in me that she had portioned out her money to give allowance for my dowry. My throat thickens with grief but I shake my head – if she were able to receive any message from death, and I do not believe she can, I would not want it to be in this way.

With a pair of tweezers, Iris puts the paper carefully inside the lizard's skin. 'This missive will find its way to the other side as surely as a carrier pigeon does to any living recipient.'

And for all my liking and sympathy for Iris, I think how easily she has made herself the subject of derision. But when I look up, she is watching me with a splinter of something cold in her eye – and I gain the strange sense she has heard my thoughts.

The shadows grow early. By the time the hall clock chimes three light has already failed and wind is blowing in hard from high places – draughts scurry through gaps in tiles and casings as if they were seeking the warmer climes of the house. In attics and walls, rats scratch at their quarters and bats fold and unfold wings in ripples of darkness. Footfalls are softer as if holding off attention.

Through the window, under a louring sky, the moor is cast in monochromes. The leafless willows creak over the surface of the lake that is as black as an eye's pupil. We all shiver in our wools and my mind keeps returning to Mr Forster and the inflection in his voice when the subject of scarlet fever had been raised, but he was clearly so keen to unnerve that I resolve not to waste further energy fulfilling his intentions.

As the afternoon progresses, the house grows strangely quiet. Usually I am conscious of all those sounds of human habitation, but as I prepare for dinner I feel the odd sense of the house having gathered up Iris's energy in preparation for tomorrow's séance.

Edward and I are taciturn over a dinner where the wine gets spilled and sauces either have not thickened enough or grow lumps. I eat with little appetite. Edward's cheeks are already flushed from wine and I try to remember the bridal tour. Did he drink too much then? Because he certainly does now. Tonight Edward lifts the carafe more than usual and still cannot quench his thirst. I watch on uneasily and realize that we are changing at Guardbridge, that, for all his longing to return, for all his love of his home, I believe he would rather be somewhere else – or is it me? Do I no longer please him? I recall Mr Forster's words, *Be a good girl*, and my eyes slip to his fingers on the glass's stem, and for an instant I see them not like this but curled into a fist.

'I'll be leaving early tomorrow on a commission.'

'How long will you be gone?'

'It's hard to say; one week perhaps?'

'I will miss you. Your uncle was here today and he came to gossip just as you said he would.'

'Mrs Ford told me. He's a ridiculous man, isn't he? What did he say?'

'Do you really want to know?'

'Why not?' He says it lightly but there is an edge to his voice that makes me consider twice about how much to reveal, but my curiosity is too pressing. 'He wanted me to know that Evie wasn't happy. That she hated Guardbridge or those within it.'

His skin flushes. 'I should have banned him from visiting.' Although he does not raise his voice, I sense the reservoir of anger that lurks behind his calm demeanour.

I think of what Iris said about the lizard. I should stop. 'Why did she hate it?'

He pours more wine but his hand is unsteady, dripping spots on to the cloth. 'It wasn't what she wanted, so it seems.'

'But she chose it,' I say, 'just as I have. Why wouldn't she be satisfied?'

When he looks up his eyes shine with anguish and I sense that I have dug out something from his core that he tries to keep buried. He leans towards me and strokes a finger across my collarbone. 'That's true. Like you, she didn't make the choice for love.'

I look down uncomfortably; his tone suggests to me that he had thought, at least at one time, that love had been part of it on her side.

'Did you love her?' I dare to ask.

He pushes the food away and pours more wine. 'I told you before and I'll say it again: I won't tolerate discussion of it.'

I cannot stop. 'But even under these circumstances, it doesn't mean that someone would not be happy with Guardbridge. It's a fine house and a good living. Enough to make any person content, I would think.'

'You've been open, Annie. At least with you there's no duplicity between us. When you and I talked of marriage, we both understood what it was we wanted and what it was the other offered. You've never led me to think that love was part of it.' His tongue rolls the words thickly. 'Evie was not so honest.'

So she lied; she told Edward she loved him. He has neither confirmed nor denied what he felt but if he loved her, and I think, given his response, that he must have done, her lack of it must have been deeply wounding.

'She had other secrets too.' His voice is calm again. 'I particularly don't like secrets, Annie.'

I shiver and pull my shawl closer round my shoulders.

'Why aren't you wearing it tonight?' His eyes are on my neck and my hand leaps to my throat for the necklace, but it is not there. Frantically I search the floor and inside my clothes.

'I'm sure I was wearing it – it must have fallen.'

He looks away with disgust.

I get up for the bell.

'Not now, for Heaven's sake. The staff have better things to do than look for lost jewels in the dark. If

81

they're not in your room, let Mrs Ford know tonight and a search must begin as soon as it's light. A piece of jewellery that valuable cannot be lost. I hope to God it's found swiftly. What a day.' He runs fingers through his hair in a gesture of impatience. 'But come on, Annie, I can see you have more on your mind. We may as well have it out. What else did my esteemed uncle tell you?'

I pause. The clock ticks. The fire spits an ember to the hearth. If they died as Edward claimed, then the question is not a dangerous one and of course there is no mystery there; why would he not have told the truth?

'When I mentioned how sad it was that scarlet fever had killed Evie and Jacob, your uncle's response . . . well, to be honest, it was almost as if he believed that I'd been told a lie.'

'Nonsense.' He slams his glass down and throws his napkin to the tabletop. I shrink back with alarm. 'I'll see you in a week.'

And then he is out of the door, his heels rapping the hall tiles, and I am left stunned by the strength of his reaction. *Of course it was nonsense*, I think. Yet Edward had not been able to meet my eyes when he denied it.

He does not come to me later and I am grateful. I lie, my thoughts weaving convoluted paths that arrive at the same unsatisfactory conclusions. I am interrupted by the rattle of light footsteps. No doubt some maid in a hurry to answer a call or to return to an unfinished duty, but I wonder what would bring a maid to this part of the house so late.

I close my eyes, the eaves creak and groan — then the diorama begins to turn and it is like the cry of voices far off on the moor.

In the parlour of her suite Iris stands in the middle of the floor and with the closing of her eyes feels Guardbridge's open. Like a web, her mind captures the house in all its secret detail: how wind shivers in the garret spaces, the scratch of rats' claws on stone and the damp moor air that is sucked into hallways to sour on the already musky aromas. But it is the glass's energy that wings its way to her, its messages already pressing to be heard, and the house shifts and adjusts.

When Mrs North comes in, rubbing her sore knuckles, she finds Iris pale and anxious.

'There you are, dear,' she says. 'I was thinking it was time you should be in bed.'

'The spirits, Southy,' Iris says. 'They're more restless and urgent than I've ever known.'

'That's nice,' Mrs North says abstractedly.

'I don't think you understand. Something has changed with the coming of Annie.'

'I'm sure it will be fine.'

But Iris shakes her head vehemently. 'You're wrong. It's just as the spirits told me all that time ago — something is afoot that will alter Guardbridge forever.'

7

It is the day of the séance and when I wake to Flora preparing my clothes it is clear she is agitated.

'Mrs Ford has had us up for hours and no one can find your necklace.'

A feeling of dread settles on me when I recall how angry Edward had been. It had not occurred to me that it would not be quickly found.

'Is there anywhere else you think you might have been yesterday that you've forgotten?' she asks.

'Mrs Ford and I went through everything I did last night, but I'll keep thinking,' I say.

She lowers her eyes. 'I hope it's found soon.'

'You have no need to worry, Flora. It's my foolishness that's responsible.'

'With an object as valuable as that the staff soon come under suspicion, and I'm one of the newer maids.'

It had not occurred to me that there could be consequences such as this.

'Flora, I hope you know that the idea you might steal from me is not something I'd ever consider. I'll be sure to tell Mrs Ford how highly I regard you.

Between you and me, is it possible that someone here stole the necklace?'

'I don't think so. I know everyone so well now and there's not one person who I'd consider capable of such wickedness.'

After breakfast I call for Mrs Ford and I assure her that Flora could not be guilty.

'Flora's a good girl, we all know that, but your missing jewels are a serious matter.'

When Mrs Ford has gone, I lie back on the chair. The sky is clear and, although still cold, the snow only lies heavily on higher ground.

I spend the morning writing letters, leaving my mother's for last. Outside, the fast white clouds remind me of home, of the smell of the sea and the fine sand that gathered in the cracks of the stone steps, of Lizzie and Albert playing ball on the terrace as my mother and I stood at the kitchen table, peeling prawns or kneading bread.

I look down at the blank paper and do not know how to begin, because the things that I want to say are all those that I cannot. I want to ask her advice about the necklace, tell her of Guardbridge, of the good and the bad: of Flora whose kind administrations mean so much and of Iris and her strangeness and how I have come to like her. I imagine telling her of other things – the diorama with the blind, seeing creatures, the baby I am too afraid to love and hold at such great distance from my heart. Mostly I want to say how I still feel when I think of you, my first precious son, how it has cut me in two and pressed me back together in some way that is wrong.

I clench my teeth hard to hold back emotion and think of the questions that have received no answers and my fingers tingle to ask again. Where is my son, Mama? Who did you give him to and how does he fare? I wish now that I had listened more closely during those months before your birth, to all those conversations that I pretended were not happening. In truth, I could not be rid of you soon enough. And as I lay in my bed, out of sight of the world with a fictitious illness, I dreamed only of life returning to what it had been. How naive I was. If I had known then what it would be like to hold you and how little time we would have, I would have fought harder to keep you. But your arrival and departure were as swift and final as the opening and closing of a door.

I scrub the tears from my face and reach the end of the letter. I wish I could send messages of love but I have been rebuffed too often.

Anne, I write at the end, just *Anne*.

The task of letter-writing has left me tired and after lunch I pick up a book but only turn a few pages before I fall asleep. It is dusk when I wake and the sun is low in the sky. I tie up my skirts and set out for the moors. Sound drifts as wind passes over the crags. The air smells of ice and the cold clings like a gauze. Even in my hat and coat I soon shiver.

I walk a rough path through the frost-rimed gorse towards the sloping hills and pause to take in the wild beauty of it; my boots sink in the snow and are soon cold. I look across to where Guardbridge sits, heavy and resolute against the landscape.

Slowly light ebbs away and I make my way back, my boots slipping now and then on an icy patch until I reach the flat. Twilight is falling fast and the trees cast spidery shadows. I walk quickly and reach the gate that marks the boundary of Guardbridge.

Mist has come down about the house like the film of an eye, but high up a moon, blown to fullness, emerges behind the chimneys. There is a drumming of wing beats and the sky darkens as a swarm of birds descends to the copse with muffled caws, settling on branches and knocking flakes of whiteness to the ground. They gather on the roofs and the oaks shudder with their calls.

At the corner of my eye another bird flits just beyond my vision and from its colour and beak I believe for a moment that it is a linnet. But when I turn there is nothing but the limbs of a birch moving in the breeze.

Inside Guardbridge, a strange stillness has settled on the passageways; the corridors feel changed as if the dimensions are flexible, as if the house itself is no longer anchored within the limits of its physicality. I think about the night that lies ahead, and the séance it will bring. For all my lack of belief up till now my chest tightens with a sense that I am about to turn a corner – one that I can never retrace.

When it is time to dress, I climb the stairs and there is a faint noise, a ringing, as constant as a bell's chime. It is a sound that sits on the edge of other sounds – thin and yet, as it grows, it draws every other noise to its heart. My head begins to throb. I meet Flora at the top of the stairs. 'What's that?' I ask.

'It's Miss Stonehouse.' Flora's voice is barely a whisper.

'What's she doing?'

'It's her glass, ma'am.'

'You mean the Guardbridge Glass?'

Flora shakes her head. 'Miss Stonehouse has glass bowls. She passes something round the rim to make them ring.'

'But for what purpose?'

'I think it clears the air for the séance.' She gives a little shrug of bewilderment and we smile at each other in the near dark.

More strange, unsettling behaviour. Lying on the bed is the outfit that Iris has instructed I wear – a black high-collared dress with matching gloves and hat.

Flora brushes my hair and braids it over my scalp,

pinning on the cap with ebony-headed pins. I gaze at my reflection, at my dark eyes and pointed chin. If Edward died now, this is the widow I would make. Flora's movements are quick but uncertain and in the reflection her lips are pulled tight.

'Did you know about Miss Stonehouse's ways before you came?' I ask.

'It's well known hereabouts.'

'Did it make you afraid?'

'No,' she says carefully and glances at my reflection as if to gauge whether or not her mistress is.

'And Miss Stonehouse, is her reputation outside Guardbridge bad?'

'It's not worse than some, ma'am, although there are plenty of those who think what she does wicked in the eyes of the lord.'

'Is that what you think?'

'If you don't mind me being so forward, I would say it's ungodly, but it's not for me to hold an opinion.' Her fingers play with the brush handle. 'Will that be all?'

'Yes, Flora, thank you.'

She leaves, her eyes a little anxious, her lips parted as if she has one further thing to impart. And now I am alone again with the strange ringing that swings in the air like a carousel, it catches the whine of the diorama and they work in tandem.

The clock strikes eight. I stand.

The candles flicker, sending shapes that are too long, which move too slowly as if they too were caught in the sound. I think of spirits moving through the house, passing through the corridors, up and down, up and down.

The ringing sings in my bones and something moves within my blood and calls deep within me.

As I make my way to Iris's quarters, the lamps, for once, burn steadily as though they were awake, and I am fully alert, as if some sleeping part of me has opened its eye.

The sky is opaque but for the moon and my steps are softer on the worn carpentry; the candle I carry nearly unwavering in the draught crafted by my progress. The lamps watch, unblinking, from their holders. Even the blackness seems to have eyes. But I stand tall – after all, the dead cannot be called.

I knock gently at Iris's door and enter. I pause as it is so ill lit as to render all landmarks nearly invisible. Eventually, out of the gloom, I discern a table has been placed in the centre of the floor and laid with an ebony-coloured cloth. On the surface, under a glass globe, is a diorama of small creatures and next to it, swathed in linen, is what I assume is the glass. Scented smoke drifts from a dish filled with oil and herbs.

The air hums with the sound of the bowls. Iris looks

up. Her eyes are bright, skin flushed. If I had ever imagined her fragile, there is no evidence of that now.

Like me, Iris and Mrs North are both dressed entirely in black. Mrs North hands me a cup.

'What is it?'

'Drink it, Annie. Drink it,' Iris urges. 'It will help.'

I sip the hot tincture and frown at the bitterness. 'What's in it?'

'Mugwort, rosemary, a few herbs and brandy – it will make you more able to hear and see beyond the curtain of this life.'

I regard it dubiously, but Iris is so grave that I know not to do so would greatly offend. I put it to my lips and the strange stinging liquid slips down my throat. Now the ringing has ceased, I hear a whine from above and look up to a diorama of birds that spin in a draught, their heads slightly upturned.

Mrs North takes her place in the circle and there is suddenly a stillness inside my head as if I had momentarily stepped outside myself. Iris removes the linen, revealing the glass, and my fingers twitch to touch the surface.

'You must not,' Iris says, reading my thoughts. 'It's only for those women, like me, who are born of Stonehouse blood.' A ripple of delight spills across her face.

Mrs North quenches all but one of the candles.

'Remove your gloves,' Iris says.

Then both of my hands are taken in theirs. The shadowy corners seep closer and the ring of our palms gathers energy. I feel empty but then it happens: a connection runs through my veins, some of Iris's intensity fusing to my own. Above, the diorama spins harder, marrying the last resonance of the bowl's song, and I am drawn to the way the darkness pools across the cloth, the cool dryness of our hands and the strange urgency that is released.

Iris's eyes flicker and burn with inner fire. My skin grows hot and the diorama spins faster, humming with higher sound. Then, in an instant, my fingers are released.

Iris lays both her palms on the globe and takes a shuddering inhalation. She remains like that for some minutes until I am convinced that nothing more will happen, then she casts her breath on to the animals that sit at the centre of the table and it is as if the birds, even within their casing, flutter and stir inside their feathers. *A trick*, I think. Iris begins to murmur in a stream of jumbled sound.

My head thumps and I pull my gaze away to look through the window, but the moon has gone. Something in the air has changed too – more subtle – as if someone had just passed through it.

Iris's eyes open; her arms spread wide. 'They're coming,' she whispers.

In that moment, like a wick ignited inside a lamp,

the atmosphere blooms. Sweat breaks out on my neck. *It is not true*, I tell myself. This is just as my aunt once told me, how, as any good actor demonstrates, we can be persuaded to believe things that do not exist. Not true.

The drink sits on my tongue, and I wonder what was in it and if it has cast me under a spell. I know too well the ability laudanum has to make waking dreams.

The dioramas fall still. Iris is silent too. Her eyes are glazed, her lips now moving without sound, and I think of the stories of the saints and the possessed.

Suddenly Iris turns her head and looks to me with both surprise and something accusatory. '*You*,' she whispers.

For how long we are locked like this I cannot tell, but eventually she shudders and gazes once more upon the glass. 'They're gone,' she says. 'I'm so cold now, Southy, so cold.'

Mrs North rushes for a blanket.

Iris stands slowly, pressing her thin wrists to the chair to lever herself out as if she were a woman with forty more years. She walks up to me slowly and strokes an icy finger across my cheek in a gesture that should convey affection and yet about her eyes is a look of suspicion and hostility. '*You*,' she rasps again. '*You.*'

'What do you mean?' My voice is husky.

But she does not answer and continues to stare at

me, past skin, beyond bone and to the soft and vulnerable parts that lie inside.

Mrs North returns and guides Iris away. There is no sound of wind or spitting fire, but my senses sharpen to applewood smoke, lemon oil and the far-off aroma of yeast proving in jars.

Before me, the glass's surface seems to smoke in the candlelight. My fingers tingle with the urge to touch it. The door to Iris's chamber closes behind them. My heart gives an uneasy twist and then I am reaching out and clasping my palms about it as Iris had. Nothing, just the polished smoothness of it, but then a tug somewhere behind my navel as if something has pulled at my guts and heat rushes through me.

I wrench my hands away with a gasp and search the room. It is empty and yet I feel in my marrow that something has changed. I regret my action, and then chide myself for imagining that anything can be altered by the mere touch of an object.

From above, as slowly as a dream, a single black feather falls from the diorama and settles on the table before me and there is a noise from behind, a small exhalation. *Enough*, I think and, standing shakily, I make for the door.

The passageway outside is too dim and unfamiliar. I lift my skirts to move faster, thinking only of the comforting familiarity of my own chamber.

I take a wrong turn not once but twice and find myself in the west wing. *How did I get here?* I retrace my steps and am once again at the oriel window by Iris's quarters. There is a sound in the silence – something in the places where the lamps do not reach. My mouth dries and I hear Iris's accusation again, as clearly as if she stood next to me: *You.*

Suddenly I cannot move, my breath harsh in my ears, and then from the darkness at the end of the corridor there is a smudge of movement.

'No.' The word in my mouth does not move on my lips nor for an instant does it dispel the sense of a presence but even as I stare there is nothing to see but a shadowed wall. Even so, I am running, horror smothered in my throat.

At times I stop and believe there is an echo of steps behind me until, finally, reaching the end of a long corridor, I recognize the servants' stairs in my own wing and, sagging with relief, steady myself with the newel post. *Nothing there*, I think, *nothing there, nothing there* – only the sound of my own heels played back through the hollowness of the passage.

At my own room I fumble with the handle, then close the door firmly behind me. I think I discern a quick soft movement outside. With trembling fingers I light candles and ring for one of the maids.

But it is Mrs North who eventually knocks, her expression stretched with concern. 'Mrs Stonehouse? I came to see if you were well. Look, you're shaking.' She takes a shawl and wraps it gently round my shoulders.

'Try not to let your imagination roam too much. It won't help to take it to heart.'

My teeth chatter so much I can barely speak. 'Did you hear what she said to me? She said, "*You.*" What could she mean by it?'

'I'm afraid to admit that over the years I've heard her utter many strange and inexplicable things and I've no idea what she means.' Mrs North pats my hand.

'You don't think Iris has psychic power?'

'Well, I wouldn't say that exactly. In fact, I believe her to have some talent. Miss Stonehouse has demonstrated too often that she can fall upon a truth that has never been uttered aloud; perhaps it's the spirits who tell her, I don't know. Iris certainly believes it.'

Edward has said the same, but surely it is only fortuitous guesswork.

'But as to calling back the dead, I've never seen anything to convince me.'

'I thought that I saw something. Out there in the corridor.'

'What did you see?' Her tone is surprisingly solemn.

But even as I recall the vague movement, I know that it must have been a trick of shadow and light. I do not believe in ghosts. Mrs North is right.

'It was nothing,' I say, and she shakes her head chidingly.

'That's right. There was nothing there, Mrs Stone-house.'

There is so much comfort in her steady assurance that, for a moment, I long to lay my cheek against her and tell her everything. Tell her of you, of home, of my distant marriage to Edward and my curiosity about Evie. I want to tell her that I do not know how to love John. But she has turned a little away from me and is studying the bed.

'What's that?'

I follow her gaze at something caught in a crease of the counterpane. My eyes widen.

'A feather,' she says, and now the smile she wore has gone and is replaced by something else. 'Did you put it there, Mrs Stonehouse?'

I shake my head.

She withdraws a little and her manner is less assured. 'A black feather.'

I do not like the chilled tone in which she says that. 'It could easily have found its way there when the maids came and aired the room,' I say.

She does not answer and something in her expression strokes me with a finger of ice.

'Why, what circumstance do you think accounts for it?'

'Miss Stonehouse has not discussed her beliefs with you about such things?'

'No.' And for all my desire not to hear something

that might cause more dismay, I cannot help myself. 'Tell me.'

'According to Miss Stonehouse, a feather is the token left when you've been visited by a spirit.'

I think of the cats that saunter from the barns and hunt for mice and scraps in Guardbridge's grounds.

'A feather anywhere in Guardbridge would surely come from a more temporal cause —'

'And this is black,' she continues, ignoring me.

'What of it?' I say.

'A black feather is left by a particular kind of spirit. One who has suffered an early death.' Her gaze shifts to the corridor and she takes a sharp breath and draws herself in. 'A black feather is left by a child.'

She takes my hand. 'Now, Mrs Stonehouse, it's time you got to bed. I recommend a glass of brandy to calm you.' Ringing the bell, she stands, all warmth dissipated, and I feel her urgency to be gone; before I can utter a goodnight the door has closed behind her.

I sit, frozen, and when Flora comes I request a brandy, as suggested, and ask her to light more lamps, but even lit I know that sleep will not come easily. I will not attend another séance, I decide. Once is enough. A draught whips in from the sashes where the curtains are not fully closed. Going to the window, I draw them back further. The round moon lights the garden, spilling on to the shape of the lion statues and licking the top of the wall, but its very brightness is alarming.

As I reach out to close them, my candlelight catches the nearest pane. There, on the glass, someone has written three words. From the way they run with condensation they seem new. I search behind me and consider ringing the bell again. My pulse ticks. The words swim behind my eyes. Too easily I could succumb to all that the night has brought. I must resist. Surely, I reason, this was executed earlier in the day by a playful hand. Before I can reconsider, I place the tip of my finger to the glass and smudge the words through.

Yet as I climb between the covers and lie back, eyes wide, I see those words again and again, as clear as if they were still before me.

I am here, they had said. *I am here.*

8

I wake, feeling as thin as paper and so insubstantial that a mere brush of air could blow me away. My skin in the mirror is blotchy. The previous night is distant – the words on the window, the séance itself, even Mrs North's visit and the explanation for the feather. How could I have allowed myself to become so affected? And yet there is something new in the atmosphere – something changed, something I cannot name. My head is woolly as if I had taken too much wine.

Flora comes with tea and when she has gone I check the window, but all the panes are now frozen. Back in bed, I sip the tea and my palms tingle from the memory of their touch upon Iris's glass. A wave of dizziness and weakness forces me to lie back momentarily. There is something dreamlike that has pushed the night into a place of uncertain recall.

Flora's step sounds from the end of the corridor and grows louder. I try to sit up and fail. I consider again whether the drink I had been given contained laudanum or some other drug – it would account not only for my flight of fancy but also the depth of sleep that followed.

Another footfall outside the room. Flora again? She pauses and I call out. There is no response and after a few seconds she moves past, until there is silence but for the patter of rain that echoes in the high-up spaces.

At breakfast Flora informs me that Iris is too weak to come down and so I make my way once again through the corridors to her quarters. As I reach the oriel window, I recall the previous night and pause. A draught comes up from one of the stairwells, bringing the stale scent of damp and distant decay. I notice a portrait of Jacob there. I have not seen it before – when I pass this way I generally turn the other way, towards the window and the view.

The portrait is unusual inasmuch that in it Jacob is alone. He sits on a stool, straight-backed, his slender arms resting on his lap. In one hand he holds an ivory elephant.

Thinking of the feather and Mrs North's unsettling explanation, I study his face with more attention. In most of his likenesses Jacob appears impatient or sullen, but not in this one and I step back as if bitten. Even at the age of seven, the father has painted his son with a look of malice in his eye. And now I recall the words on the window and am angry with myself that I am so easily perturbed.

Is this a true representation of the moment Jacob

was painted or Edward's doing? There is no portrait of Jacob in the house in which there is an expression of ease or pleasure. Surely if Jacob was bored or tired from sitting, Edward could have painted a smile from memory. Why render his son with such an unfavourable countenance?

As I stand, a cold waft of sourness is drawn from the deserted stairwell and I sense that I am no longer alone.

I take a breath. 'Hello?'

Nothing comes in return, save a shifting of the air. I walk to where the stairwell curves down to the lower floor and stare down into the shadowy space, to the worn stone steps and to where the stairs take a turn and disappear from view. There is nothing there, yet I find myself hurrying more quickly to Iris's quarters.

Mrs North and Iris are in their customary seats, Iris hunched, smudges beneath her eyes and a blanket laid upon her lap. She seems, as she sits there, older than Mrs North who has a band of worry at her own brow. I regard Iris with slightly altered feelings and recall that word on her lips: *you.*

Iris shifts and glances at the blue of the sky and I soften. If I were her and did not have friends or company, I too might spend as much energy on my beliefs. I go over and kiss her cool cheek.

The table on which the séance had been conducted is now in a window position decorated with a vase of flowers. The hanging dioramas are gone too. I think of how I touched the glass and am relieved that Iris will never know.

'How are you?' It is hard to visualize this frail creature as the one who burned so vividly only hours ago.

'She's always under par after a sitting,' Mrs North says.

'Do you recall much of the séance?' I ask. Although what I really want to know is does she remember what she said and what was meant by that uttered word?

She shakes her head. 'No, most of my recollection is gone by the next morning.'

Although it cannot be true, in less than twelve hours, it seems to me that Iris is thinner, the gloves wrinkle on her fingers and there are hollows in her cheeks.

'Do the séances always leave you so ill?'

'They do, don't they, Southy?' There is sadness in her voice.

'They do, Miss Stonehouse, indeed they do.' She gives me a pointed look. 'If I had my way, Miss Stonehouse would not conduct these communions at all.'

'You know why I must. You say too much. It's not your place.' She puts her cup down heavily, causing the saucer to rattle, and gets unsteadily to her feet.

I move to follow but Mrs North gestures me back down. 'Stay where you are, Mrs Stonehouse. I will assist her.'

When Mrs North has returned and adjusted herself back into the chair, she shakes her head. 'These séances do nothing but harm for that young woman. But how are you, may I ask? Last night you were a little shaken, I think.'

'I hadn't known what to expect. Today I have no ill effects but I'm reminded by something Mr Forster said: that Evie hated Guardbridge. Was it the séances?'

'He told you that?' She looks at me curiously. 'It's true. The séances affected her deeply. She felt they were ungodly.'

'Is that the reason Evie came to dislike it here?'

'It would have been part of it, I think. I hope you don't come to feel the same as time passes.'

'My views are not as strong as hers,' I say. 'Mr Forster went on to say that Evie had been difficult. What did he mean?'

She sighs and puts down her work. 'Mr Stonehouse hasn't told you much about his previous wife?'

'Barely anything.'

'We're not supposed to gossip.'

'I wouldn't break your confidence, Mrs North, but it's hard to come to a place with so much unknown to me. I would ask Iris if it was appropriate, but her loyalty is, quite rightly, with her brother.'

Her eyes flick to Iris's door. 'Very well –' she lowers

her voice – 'I understand why Mr Stonehouse would be reticent, but I also appreciate your interest.' For a few seconds she gazes back into the past. 'You see, Mrs Stonehouse was not a happy woman. I don't believe that living so far from town suited her. She liked company and, of course, we are a long way from that and at Guardbridge there is only us.' She gives me a grim smile. 'Miss Stonehouse and her ways soon stopped being acceptable, if they ever were, and that became a cause of conflict. I think now that the tolerance she showed at first was only a show for her husband.'

'Evie and Iris didn't get on?'

'No. She disgusted Mrs Stonehouse too much with her ways.'

A stab of pity for Iris. 'I learned too that Evie had a secret.'

Her look becomes guarded, 'We all have things we like to keep hidden.'

'I mean a particular secret?'

She reddens uncomfortably. 'I'm not saying you're wrong, but if she did, it's not my place to say it.'

'Of course.' With disappointment I resign myself to not learning Evie's secret from Mrs North, at least not today. 'I hope you'll forgive me these questions, but I gather that her marriage to Edward was not successful.'

'You must have wondered about this from the

beginning. To walk in another woman's shoes when those shoes have barely grown cold. At first they appeared happy. Mr Stonehouse was very in love, but after twelve months the union soured, but then I know from personal experience that marriage is often not the happy affair we imagine. It's not until we live with someone that we learn their true nature.' She gives me a penetrating look.

What Mrs North says confirms what I have learned. And I wonder if that is why when Edward married again he did not do it for love. At least we do not have the power to hurt each other in that way.

'When I look at Jacob's portrait, he too is unhappy,' I say.

'Children are often the greatest victims of a bad marriage.'

'It was very bad then?'

'I won't lie to you, it was, and it took a terrible toll on Mrs Stonehouse and their son.'

'In what way?'

'As the marriage deteriorated so did her well-being. She grew angrier and more miserable; her behaviour became quite disturbing.'

'What do you mean?'

'She had no control over her temper and would often express it when it would have been better not to.'

'But that's not an unusual trait. What was disturbing about it?'

'Mrs Stonehouse was highly strung and it seemed every day there was something to complain about or something that she didn't like. When I say "disturbing", I mean that she lost control of her unhappiness, becoming increasingly abject. It was painful to watch how she altered, how, at Guardbridge, she was reduced to a scrap of misery.'

I am assailed with a creeping sensation of uneasiness at these words. 'Was she the one who had the most care for her son?'

'No, thank goodness. He had a nurse, as John does. A Mrs Cavanagh.' Her voice becomes clipped. 'I didn't approve of her, mind.'

'For what reason?'

'Not least because she was careless with him – she neglected her task and left him to his own devices. Miss Stonehouse and I did our best, but Evie Stonehouse discouraged Jacob from visiting us on account of Miss Stonehouse's séances. I think she made Jacob afraid of coming here and towards the end we saw little of them. I hope that makes your understanding clearer.'

'I thank you. I'm very grateful,' I say, and turning the conversation, remark, 'Iris seems very ill today.'

'She's worse after every sitting.'

'What is the reason, do you think?'

She leans forward conspiratorially. 'Because the one spirit she seeks never comes.'

'But I didn't think it was any particular spirit that Iris tried to summon.'

'That's what Miss Stonehouse claims, but let me tell you otherwise. There's only one she ever searches for.'

'Who's that?'

'It's her mother, Mrs Stonehouse.'

'Her mother? I'm confused. I thought Iris was not close to her mother and that Mrs Stonehouse was not fond of her daughter?'

Mrs North's lips tighten. 'You've heard correctly.'

'And yet she seeks her?'

'Oh, she seeks her with increasing fervour; it's always her mother to whom she sends those messages and I conclude it's for the very reason you state – she didn't gain her mother's love or approval in life and now seeks it beyond the veil of death.'

I press back how macabre I find this idea. I say, 'What did Iris do that made her mother so hostile? Was it her claim to see spirits?'

'The dislike was set well before that. Mrs Stonehouse was very ill after her son's birth; it's my belief that she never wanted another child and from the very first she pushed her daughter away. The less attention her mother paid, the more Miss Stonehouse sought it. Miss Stonehouse spent hours crafting gifts – handkerchiefs sewn with her mother's initials and embroidered table pieces – and she took them to her mother like little offerings. But later they would be cast aside and either given to servants or burned on the fires. I'm only glad that I could be there to comfort her.'

'Did it worsen as Iris grew older and her strangeness became more apparent?'

'It did and every rejection was a new wound for Miss Stonehouse, but as she aged Miss Stonehouse's love became full of anger too.'

'Iris was twelve when her mother died?'

'She was a month or so under thirteen, the very worst time of life in many ways – a time when we women experience so many changes in our bodies. This age was not kind to Miss Stonehouse and she suffered badly from moods and rages, more so than most young women.' She pauses in reflection.

I remember then that moment in the drawing room when Iris's finger had brushed my neck and my sense of the stormy nature of her emotions. 'The relationship with her mother must have been very bad when she died.'

'You have no idea. It took all my effort to keep her from doing or saying something she might regret; her moods were a cause of great contention within the household.'

'I know that Iris's mother was ill for most of their childhoods, but what was her illness?'

'She had many over the years, but it was cancer that she suffered from at the end.'

I think of my aunt. 'I'd wondered why Edward never spoke of it, but it makes better sense now; cancer is such a cruel and painful death.'

'Oh, it wasn't the cancer that caused her death, but I'm not surprised Mr Stonehouse is silent on the matter – a death such as his mother suffered was a particularly difficult one.'

'What was it, if not cancer?'

She pauses. A breeze rattles at the sashes and sends a shaft of cold air into the room. When she speaks again, her voice is grave, almost reverent. 'It wasn't any illness that took her. It was a fire, Mrs Stonehouse, the very fire that damaged the wing of Guardbridge that is no longer used.'

For an instant I see smoke curling into the wind, hear the roar as flames tear at the building.

My feelings must show themselves for when she speaks again her voice is grim.

'Indeed, it was a truly terrible way to die.'

9

Iris gazes at the glass one last time, then wraps it in a silk cloth to return to the blue room, careful that her skin does not touch the unclothed surface. She does not remember much of last night and Mrs North has said little.

The main room is empty; Annie and Mrs North have gone. Mrs North's knitting sits neatly on the table, its weave increasingly uneven, and Iris feels a stab of love and pity for the pain she suffers. The cushions where they sat are dented from their weight and the antimacassars adrift from their usual precision.

Sun streams in and falls on to the fading rugs. Far off is the sound of wind and birds. In a corner the table she used for the séance is now covered with a white cloth. Iris lifts the cloth and runs a finger along the place where Annie had been and has a sudden clear memory of her, rigid and pale-faced, and another of Annie's palms flat upon the tabletop, shock engraved about her eyes.

At the stairs Iris takes a detour to Annie's door and knocks. There is no answer but Iris can feel already that Annie is not there. She turns the handle and goes in. The room is tidy; an open book and glass sit on a table. All the surfaces have been dusted and there are the scents of soap and woodsmoke.

She wanders through the room but finds no answers. Leaving, she makes her way downstairs. It is as she is walking towards the blue room that it begins: the glass grows suddenly warm in her hands and the air is restless. A ringing begins in her ears and she senses that the glass is reluctant to return to its box.

The blue room is icy and Iris is uncertain as she turns the key and lifts the lid, preparing to lay the glass down. Carefully she places it in its velvet nest; yet still there remains the certainty that something has altered.

Iris is preparing to lock the glass away when she does something she has never before dared – she reaches down and places her finger on the glass. The door behind her bangs shut with such force that the sashes clatter. The windowpanes darken and behind her, in a strange and sibilant tongue, come the words:

'*Iris, beware.*'

10

The sky is heavy with cloud but I leave the oppressive gloom of the house to seek refuge among the wind-flattened trees. The air is warmer and the undergrowth and hedges shimmer with melted snow and the smell of damp bracken is in the air. A mist has sidled down from the peaks, veiling the moor in grey.

As I pass the north wing, it is clear to me that it was never the fire that caused the evacuation but the fact that Edward and Iris's mother died there; the damage itself was never enough to justify its abandonment.

It begins to rain, so I turn and hurry back.

As I reach the main house, something catches my attention and I look up; once again there is someone at Evie's window. If the door is largely kept locked, who is in there? Do maids still come to clean it?

Inside, I take a button hook, remove my boots, then rush up the stairs, hoping to find whoever it is still in residence, but the door will not open. Surely not enough time has elapsed for the person I saw to leave? I give the handle another futile push and remember that there is another entrance – the one that links it from Edward's room. From my own chamber I pass through Edward's dressing room to his bedchamber and then to the door between his and Evie's. It is open.

I enter cautiously, only to find it empty. The curtains are now drawn again against the afternoon. I pull them open, flooding the space with light. A film of dust lies across the tables and chests; whoever was here had not come to clean. Iris? But according to recent accounts they were not fond of each other. Edward is not back so it is not him.

I study my surroundings for more clues to Evie's character or for a hint as to her nature, but there is nothing. Had I expected disarray? Her things flung to the floor in an act of rage? But everything is calm and ordered. At the dressing table I pull out drawers, causing the rattle of trinkets and hair clips, pomades and lotions and various cosmetics.

Edward loved her, and even though I do not love Edward, my feelings are complicated. I lower myself to a chair and sit at the mirror where she must have sat so often. In the reflection behind me is their marital bed — that place where they lay together, where she bore Jacob, where she died of fever? And I am grateful that Edward provided new furniture for my own arrival.

Is it Edward who has instructed that the room remain locked — as a guard against his grief and the sad memories their marriage evoked?

In one corner sits a desk set with inkstand, a pounce pot and quills. I open it with interest. Inside is headed notepaper and envelopes. I wonder who she wrote to and what family or friends she may have had.

A shaft of light glances across the surface of her notepaper and reveals the imprint upon the top sheet – faint dots of ink that have gone through to the next page. I take it to the window to examine it and find indents from the scrawled loops of words. This may have been Evie's final letter.

Recalling a trick I was taught as a child, I wipe my finger along the back of the chimney breast and smear charcoal across the paper, but the sound of wheels and hooves breaks my concentration. I stand up to see who has arrived. The coach door is already opening and Edward is staring up. Why is he back so early? Has he seen me at Evie's sashes? I imagine him discovering this indiscretion and am horrified. I retreat from the pane and stuff the sheet into my pocket and return hurriedly to my own bedroom.

At my dressing table I adjust my hair and pinch colour to my cheeks.

Downstairs, Mrs Ford and a maid I do not recognize are already in the hall and I go outside to greet him. There is nothing in his face to suggest that he saw me in Evie's chamber and then, in a burst of rebellious feeling, I think, so what if I were to look? Would that not be something any woman might do in my position? But just as I decide that any anxiety on my part is redundant, I catch his eye, and before he is able to conceal it there is a narrowing of his gaze that sets my heart pounding.

We walk together in the fading afternoon, back up the steps, the horse's heels clacking on the driveway behind us. When we are in the drawing room, he refuses coffee and food, asking only for wine. He sighs inelegantly and leans back on the sofa, closing his eyes briefly in fatigue.

'Why are you back so soon?'

'My model took ill. I'll have to return.' He pulls off his gloves impatiently and puts his hands to the fire. 'Why, are you disappointed to see me?'

'No,' I say. 'No.'

He smiles then, and I think I must have mistaken that momentary coldness.

'You look tired. Did you have a comfortable night?' In all my actions I feel the urgency to promote a sense of warmth between us that I cannot claim.

'You would think it would be an easy thing to get good food at a half-decent house.'

'I would have thought so, Edward,' I say.

He stretches, pushing his legs out to the grate with a sigh. From his pocket he takes a cigar. 'The lady of the house wouldn't stop talking and her tone was high and sharp. What is it about those who chatter too much? Why is it that they so often have the least to say? My ears are still ringing with it. What news have you here? Have you had any visitors? Letters from friends? Or lost a servant?'

I cannot imagine who he might think I have entertained.

'Nobody,' I say. 'Although there is a new maid I just saw in the hall. Mrs Ford needed to replace one of the staff but that's not very newsworthy. The most exciting thing is that one of the farm cats brought in a rat, which then proceeded to run riot in the scullery before Bessie, who is the only one not terrified of them, caught it and dispensed it with a bang to the back wall.'

Edward smiles. 'I've missed you,' he says.

In that moment his expression suggests that it is true and for an instant we hold each other's eyes as if seeing each other for the first time in some new light, or perhaps, I think, we are searching one another for the depth of our deceptions. I do not know.

'And Iris's séance. How did that go?' His look is keener now.

I laugh to hide the rise of feelings. 'It was unsettling,' I say. 'I have to confess that Iris is a persuasive medium. Perhaps I agreed to go too easily.'

'I hope she's not convinced you? One medium in the family is quite enough.'

'I'm not influenced, no.'

'I'm glad to hear it. Iris is my sister, but as the mother to my son it would not be acceptable if you adopted her beliefs.'

'You're quite safe,' I say, but I am aware that I do not express it with as much certainty as I once had.

'You look unsure. Did you mind attending?' he asks.

'I was interested to see what happens, but I don't think I'll go again.'

'I'm grateful you did. You know I worry about Iris and that's why I very much wanted you to be present.'

'Well, I can report back that nothing happened to concern you.'

'I'm relieved. Let's hope she displays no signs afterwards. As I've already said, I believe the séances are the source of her troubling behaviour and so I'd be gratified if you continue to take part and let me know if she does anything to cause anxiety. I don't ask much of you, Annie, do I?'

How can I refuse? But I am shocked at the dismay I feel, having assured myself that I will never attend again.

'The necklace, I can see that it hasn't been found.'

I shake my head. 'I'm so sorry, Edward.'

His jaw tightens. I sit back as if his hand might suddenly lash out. 'Something like this causes so much trouble among the staff. The police must be informed, not that they will do much, but at least if it turns up there's a possibility it might make its way back to me.'

Evening drifts in without notice and I am surprised when the maids begin lighting the oil lamps. It has grown cold too, a cold that comes after a warmer sun has left the sky and the moor and Guardbridge prepare for night. And in me this ending of the day is not a happy one. I am conscious that something has altered; I cannot rid myself of the memory of the black feather and Mrs North's explanation.

I am here, someone had written on the glass – *I am here*.

Wind chases across the moor and batters at the house. Edward is quiet and distracted, turning over the pages of *The Illustrated London News* with listless fingers. It is a relief to climb to the bedroom and slip between the sheets and listen to the wildness.

Edward comes to me but even with his mouth on mine, I know his thoughts have drifted elsewhere, and when he is gone I lie restless under the covers. Sleep is just pulling at me when I recall the paper I had taken from Evie's desk.

I sit up and light a candle, then retrieve it from the drawer. Carefully I flatten it out. It is hard to read as the charcoal has not taken cleanly to all the indentation, but her script is smooth and fluent and I study the shape of her letters, filling in here and there where necessary.

As the meaning emerges, I begin to wish that I had not indulged my curiosity. God, how I wish I had not. I screw it to a ball and throw it to the embers as if fire might erase the memory of her words.

If I do not leave here soon, I fear I shall die.

11

Iris sits at the window where, through the sashes, the smell of the river and first hint of gorse flower lay a sweetness over the nuttiness of oak. Mrs North has left early for town with a list of items for purchase. The snow has gone and the landscape glistens with its melt. Patches of early snowdrops have pushed their way out of the earth and are picked out by the morning sun.

Through the panes, the blue of sky is a mockery to the papered walls, the stuffiness of rugs and ornaments, of heavy tables and mantels. And this first breath of spring pulls deep within her to that part that has never fully relinquished the promise of it or the feel of the moor beneath her boots.

Guardbridge broods and derides her and she is beset with a sudden hatred for all that it is – for all that she is. When Annie knocks at the door and enters, Iris feels a pinch of resentment for everything that Annie possesses but does not appreciate.

'Hello, Iris.' Annie moves towards her, her brow creasing. 'What's the matter?'

Iris puts a hand to her cheek and finds wetness. She had not known that she had been crying. She wipes at her skin but cannot quite summon an expression of cheerfulness.

'Where's Mrs North? Have you argued?'

Iris shakes her head. 'No, I'm well, truly.' Her eyes drift again to the snowdrops. 'This time of year always brings melancholia.'

'Let me join you. I would welcome company. It's such a beautiful view you have from here.'

'It is,' Iris says.

'Do you suffer melancholia frequently?'

'Frequently enough.' Iris sighs and turns her back on the taunting beauty beyond the panes. 'But spring is the worst and that can only be a month away.'

'How many years have you endured it?'

'Since I was . . . since my mother died.' *Everything,* Iris thinks, *stems from that.*

'The house is gloomier on a day such as this.' Annie pauses. 'Iris, come outside with me. Would you? I understand your reasons for not leaving, but part of me believes that, if not a disaster, it's already a great misfortune that you are forced to remain in. Shall we try?'

'No.'

Her response is automatic and well rehearsed from years of protest.

'Surely the prediction doesn't necessarily hold.

Perhaps what happened before is already the fulfilment of it. Have the spirits warned you again?'

'They have.'

'What have they said exactly?'

'Of catastrophe that will befall me.'

'Your stomach complaint wasn't a catastrophe.'

Iris studies Annie's earnest expression; it is clearly not her intention to cause distress, and she is right: the stomach complaint was unpleasant but not bad enough to earn that description. Iris ponders this. In fact, it would be more true to say that disaster came before that, on the night her mother died. Although seldom far from her mind, the memories simmer and add agitation to her already troubled thoughts. But she recalls those recent words of warning.

'You don't believe me when I say that the spirits can predict, do you?' Iris asks.

Annie shifts uncomfortably. 'I suppose it's hard for me to grasp and it's not me they speak to.' She hesitates. 'Although I know you value it. It can't be easy to learn of things that haven't happened, particularly something like this that has affected your whole life so cruelly. Perhaps the glass and the spirits have reasons to not want you to leave. After all, if you were able to go, wouldn't you end up living elsewhere? I think you told me the glass only works at Guardbridge?'

'The glass belongs at Guardbridge and is not to be moved.' But what Annie has said stirs something deep within her. For an instant she imagines her life without the glass, imagines the passageways empty of whispers, empty of the spirits who come to its call. She looks down at her hands, too small and pale to summon things of such enormous power. The glass and spirits only have existence if she remains in the house. If she left – her heart skips a beat – if she left, the spirits would be forever tethered to that other world.

As a child she had never envisaged this life; she would have been horrified to know this was her destiny. The glass had never foretold that. She dreamed of a house and family of her own – a future the glass could not follow. She has not considered the glass in such a way before and now she questions whether she should trust it as fervently as she does? *Iris, beware.* What if the glass saw this very moment and sent a warning – not because Iris is in danger but because the glass itself is?

Iris is surprised to hear the words she utters next; she had not known that they were there or conceived that they would ever leave her lips.

'Take me outside.'

'Are you certain?' Having proposed it, Annie's voice is suddenly unsure.

Iris turns to the window again. 'I can't bear it. This morning I cannot bear it.' And with the declaration, each missed day trapped inside Guardbridge comes and fills her with loss.

'Here.' Annie takes Iris's hand and pulls her to her feet. Then, leaving no room for a change of mind, she hurries Iris through the house and to the hall where they go to the boot room to find suitable footwear.

As Iris buttons the leather, the swell of hope and courage begins to diminish and is deluged in a tide of fear. *What am I doing?* The button hook defeats her fumbling attempts. But Annie takes the hook and completes the task. With that done, Annie bustles her quickly back to the hall before Iris can decide she has made a mistake. Iris's skin is now more white than pale and only a frown of fierce determination remains of her earlier impulsive daring.

Annie opens the front door and Iris is assailed by the scents of the moor and the twitter of birds that weave in the sky above. She gives a gasp of love or fear. She does not know which.

Annie propels her to the top step, Iris shaking so violently that she wonders how she will manage the descent. 'Just one at a time,' Annie says, leading her carefully down. 'You've nearly done it.'

And she has, Iris realizes. She has crossed the threshold between the house and garden. She gives a tremulous laugh, the fear both paralysing and exhilarating.

At the bottom Iris sways and Annie holds her, and now with the endless blue above and Guardbridge behind the yawning space swallows her whole with the terror of what she has done – for surely she has succumbed to a moment of foolishness and sooner or later calamity will strike. She begins to scrabble for breath, her heart hammering so hard that her chest bursts with pain. *I'm dying*, she thinks.

She pulls away from Annie and half falls, half scrambles up the steps in desperation for the safety of the house. Annie is in close pursuit and finally Iris is in the hall again and slamming the great door behind them. Even then, behind her ribs, the agony remains and she gasps over and over.

Then she feels Annie's arms about her, strong and warm, and hears a gentle stream of words and gradually Iris's body retreats from panic, leaving her weak with shock. Carefully Annie guides her up the stairs and to her quarters where she pours brandy and urges her to drink.

Annie is nearly in tears. 'I'm so sorry. I didn't know it would affect you like that.'

When Iris is calmer she says, 'You meant well. All I ask is that you don't tell Edward or Mrs North.'

'Of course not, if you wish. Do you think that something will happen as a result? As the spirits told you?'

'I don't know, but I didn't go far and did not, in truth, leave Guardbridge's grounds. It's not clear if the statement refers to the house or estate but once is enough. I know now that I'll never try again.' The bitterness of it sours on her tongue.

Annie stokes the fire. 'Shall I call for tea and cake? We could play cards or talk until Mrs North returns?'

'I'm tired now. I thank you for your kind intentions, but I think I'll lie down for a while until Southy is back for lunch.'

Iris watches Annie go and shudders. What madness made her do it? Slowly she gets up and closes the curtains against the day. At least she can spare herself the pain of that.

I am grateful to be distracted from my thoughts of Iris and the pain I caused her by Edward calling me for a final sitting.

This time, as he works, he is distracted, dropping tools and knocking over a pot of brushes. Twice he jerks my head so forcefully that I wince and cry out, but he barely notices.

It is not only the words on the window that haunt me now but what Evie penned – why did she believe she would die? Was it the ramblings of a troubled mind? And I return again to what Mr Forster had said and his intimation that Evie and Jacob did not perish of fever. I watch Edward and feel the cold spread of suspicion – but, no, I must not allow my thoughts to travel in that direction. If I do, I will surely be lost, and I have seen nothing in his behaviour to give me reason to believe that Evie should have been afraid of him. If she was afraid, it was of something else.

But my thoughts will not be stilled. I remember the evening Edward told me that Evie held a secret. Was this plea written before Edward learned it or after? I have not wanted to consider this, but is it possible that I have badly misread Edward? My instincts when we met were that Edward was not a man who would demonstrate violence, but I have learned that such flaws of character can remain well hidden. Anyone who knew my father would not have imagined that behind closed doors he was capable of such brutality.

I watch Edward now as if the signs might be there in the way he stands or mixes paint on the palette. If violence was in his nature, wouldn't I know it? I think of his mother's necklace and how in my carelessness I have lost it. My father used his fists for sins far less serious than that.

I consider what Mrs North said about Edward's first marriage, how it had soured, and I wonder if the words that Evie wrote were a figure of speech. According to Mrs North, Evie was highly strung and I imagine her, overly dramatic, penning those words in a fit of pique. That was it surely.

Darkness is creeping up the walls when finally Edward stands back from the easel and presses fingers into the muscles of his back. 'Come, Annie.'

I rise stiffly and join him. The canvas is almost as large as I am. I gaze with surprise and then pleasure; surely I do not look like this? I lean in to examine each detail of my face, from the lighter flecks in my irises, to the way he has moulded my lips and the smooth lines of my forehead, but it is my hair that is the glory, springing from the scalp like an ebony fire, and my neck so white with shoulders that look as if they could bruise just by looking at them.

'Are you pleased?' he asks, his manner restored to good humour, and I cannot keep back my smiles.

We wander back through the house for tea, but in the hall he turns up the stairs.

'I must change, and then I have estate work until supper.' He looks past me now as if, having captured my image, I no longer signify.

He does not join me for dinner and when it is time I go to bed alone.

When I wake the house has fallen into that pre-midnight slumber – the clock is at half past eleven and the curtains, open to the moor, show the moon's bright eye and I am wide awake.

I have a sudden urge to see my portrait again, to study myself as Edward sees me, or is it to reassure myself that I am solid? Because tonight the edges of me feel insubstantial.

Taking a candle, I walk the passageways, aware of the way my slippers scrape the floor with a soft slur of sound and how the lamps burn into the dark like beacons.

Clutching the candle tighter I find my way to the studio door. Inside, the flame is swaddled by the profundity of darkness. I move towards the portrait when suddenly the wick blooms and I take in, once again, the reality of my own countenance and marvel that I am something of form. But even as I admire it, I am conscious of something else; there is about it something that recalls all the portraits of Evie. I examine each feature until I realize it is not the characteristics that are the same. No, it is the expression of uncertainty I wear. Is that how I have always looked to Edward or is it something new?

I stand further back and inspect it from a distance, gazing from the face down to the white hands, to the detail of the dress and finally to the shoes with gold buckles. Then my eyes are drawn to the wall that he painted behind me — faded nearly to grey and patchy with shadow. Somehow, by brushstroke and colour, he has manufactured a form out of that flatness and there appears to be the outline of another sitting beside me. No sooner have I seen this than once again only the plain backdrop remains.

I blink hard, look once more, and there it is without doubt sitting beside me: the unmistakable shape of a child.

My hands sweat and I draw further back and catch sight of something on the floor. A piece of paper torn from a sketch? Somehow I know it is not. When I lean down I discover a feather, black and smooth all the way to its silky point. I recoil. It means nothing, nothing at all. But I think of Jacob's early death nonetheless. Shivering, I pick it up and hurry back to my chamber, apprehension churning inside me.

Inside, I throw the feather to the fire. The atmosphere is too chilled, too silent — the flame of the candle trembles in some semblance of my anxiety. I light another. My chest is tight, my lungs compressed and surely now, through the silence, there is some sound, something breathy.

I cast my gaze about me but see nothing and then through my horror comes the sound of the diorama twisting on its wire over and over until my blood sings with it.

12

Even the brighter weather does not dispel the uneasiness last night has caused.

I am on my way back from a consultation with Mrs Ford when I am stopped by the new maid, who bears a silver tray on which there is a letter.

'This is addressed to you, ma'am,' she says.

'Thank you, and what's your name?'

'Marsha, ma'am.'

'I hope you'll be happy with us.'

Once in the drawing room I pull the letter excitedly towards me; it is the only correspondence I have received, and I assume it must have come from my mother or Mrs Breach. As I handle it, I realize with dismay that it has already been opened. For a moment I am hot with anger and recall my father's inquisitorial invasion of my privacy, raiding my letters and diaries to discover evidence of the lover he was convinced I had lied about. He never believed the truth. I hope Edward is not that way inclined.

The letter is from my mother and I pull it out quickly to see if it contains some piece of bad news.

An appraisal reassures me that no harm has come to any member of the family and then I sit back more comfortably and read it slowly to relish each line.

Dear Anne, it begins.

The letter is so filled with trivia of the everyday that was once familiar that I have to fight the impulse to gobble up each titbit too greedily. Every word is of disproportionate interest: Lizzie fell and broke the best milk jug, Robert has ringworm, Albert burned his mouth on a spoon he dipped into a pot of stewing fruit and the rats are worse than ever. And all the while I hear the sound of hens in the yard, the smell of the parlour and the rush of waves on shingle. But it is at the end that my heart leaps to new joy. They are coming. They are packed and Albert and Lizzie will be leaving to visit on Friday.

My delight is equal to none. I imagine showing them John and the house, giving them as much fine food as they can eat and spending time in their company. With no work, we can play games and walk as much as pleases us. Suddenly Guardbridge is full of happy promise. I go in search of Edward, discovering him in the library.

'A good friend of my mother's is coming this way next Friday and bringing Albert and Lizzie to Guardbridge, as requested.'

'Slow down, Annie.' He is not pleased. 'You should

have asked. I must return to London today and won't be back until at least the following weekend.'

'I didn't know. We've discussed this, Edward,' I say. 'A week or so back and you said it would be fine.'

'We didn't discuss it, Annie. I would've remembered and I would have deferred my trip for later, at least until after their arrival.'

I falter; I think I recall the conversation but under the weight of his displeasure my confidence falters. 'I'm sure I did,' I say. 'If not, I must apologize. It's too late now to change things.' I pause. 'You didn't tell me you'd opened the letter, Edward.'

He looks up with a mixture of incredulity and anger. 'Do you think I did that on purpose? You've received no letters since you came and I therefore don't expect them. Furthermore, Annie, if I'd opened it with the intention of reading the contents, then I would know already what they were – and it must be obvious that I don't. It was a careless mistake.'

I flush with shame. 'I'm sorry. I should have trusted you.'

'You should. It seems to me that you're becoming increasingly absent-minded and suspicious. First the necklace and now you imagine conversations that didn't happen, and I see the way you look at me sometimes, as if I were your enemy rather than husband. Why would you think that? Aren't you happy here? Haven't I provided for all your needs and more? You don't even have to worry about John. Don't look at me like that. Do you think I don't see it? You barely spend any time with our son. You have your whole life to spend at leisure and still you're not happy.'

I flinch. 'I am happy,' I insist.

'You don't appear so.'

But the gulf that has now formed between us feels too great to surmount. I cannot admit how I truly feel. I think of John and my heart twists with guilt and shame.

'Your reaction to the letter was too strong.' He studies my face. 'You make me think you have something to hide.'

'I don't,' I lie.

'Well, so be it.' But his eyes regard me doubtfully.

In the afternoon I begin arrangements with Mrs Ford and make my way to the nursery quarters that Lizzie and Albert will use. The main room is hung with cheerful curtains and there are various chests and tables displaying toys. Pictures of animals line the walls in faded frames and lead soldiers stand in orderly fashion on a shelf. In one corner is a rocking horse with a frayed saddle and a neck stained from generations of sticky fingers. A box of wooden animals sits on a table and I think of John a few years from now, cross-legged on the hearth rug to play.

By that time I will have overcome whatever it is that holds me back, will I not? Is it fear of losing him that makes me like this? Fear that if I loved John as I love you, and something happened, I could not bear it? Or perhaps it is guilt – guilt that I let them take you away and which punishes me in this cruellest of fashions by denying me access to my heart. Surely time will heal me, I think, and in the future I will sit beside John and pass him a soldier and we will line them up and fill the cannon with ball bearings. When they shoot across the floor we will look at each other and laugh and begin all over again. I pause and try to take comfort in this image and tell myself it will happen.

On one of the chests is a box made of yew. Drawn by its prettiness, I open it expecting to find a toy or game, but instead it holds a robin, its breast dulled by age or wear, feathers collecting mites. Iris's work. It does not have beads for eyes; in fact, on close inspection it does not have eyes at all – instead there are two small holes – and I drop it in disgust. Did Jacob take this or was he given it? Was he the one who plucked them out? I am assailed with an impulse to open the window and throw it as far as I can. I will not have John or my siblings find it. I wrap it in cloth and put it in my pocket, intending it for the fire, but in my room I pause. I am not sure why but I secrete it under some notepaper in the desk.

It is then that horses sound on the drive where Edward is getting into his coach. He does not even glance back and I am assailed by a further sense of failure and disappointment.

But my thoughts turn swiftly to the visit and I remember Lizzie and her long-held desire to play the piano; perhaps I could show her the rudiments while Edward is away.

The air is as chilled as it was the day Iris took me to see the glass. In the music room I pull out the stool and sit where Evie must have sat; I run a finger across the cold surfaces of ivory and ebony. A piece of sheet music remains on the music shelf, curled at the corners and foxed from damp.

I imagine Evie's slim white hand and press down. I try again, harder this time, but all that comes back is the dull thunk of ivory hitting wood. With surprise I test more keys but they all come back dead.

Curious now, I kneel on the rug and ease out the front panel of the piano. Then I stare unbelievingly into the depths of the instrument where the strings have been slashed, rendering the instrument mute. I stand, shocked, and wonder who would have executed violence on such a lovely thing, a treasured thing – not Evie, surely, but then I recall Mrs North's comments that as time went on Evie's mind became more disturbed and that she did not have good rein on her temper. I wonder if perhaps it was Evie herself who did it in an act of childish rage, albeit one in which she would be the chief victim. It is then that I revisit Iris's manner when we first came here. She knew. I am convinced of it. Why did she wish to hide the fact?

I hurry back to the main house and although I have already seen them I have a sudden desire to look at every portrait of Evie and Jacob. If I chart their images I could make a map of their short lives; I will see the deterioration in Evie and how unhappy she was.

I make my way through the house beginning with the pictures that I believe are earliest. In these she is alone; Edward did not paint Jacob until he was four or five. In each likeness I study Evie for clues as to her state of mind, yet I do not discern anger or misery but, rather, something else that is more like apprehension.

In the later portraits it is Jacob who steals my attention; there is often a bruised look upon his countenance as if he had been crying and an uncertain set of his mouth and brow. Did Edward force him to sit under threat of punishment? But I do not believe that – in all probability Jacob had tried to avoid the task, and I imagine him now, eyes on the bright sky and the lure of the moor, Edward telling him just ten minutes longer and Jacob fidgeting until his father shouts out in impatience, causing Jacob's tears. I see Edward lifting his son up to apologize, not having realized the harshness of his tone.

The painting by the oriel window gives me most unease. There is too much anger in Jacob's eyes for me to be comfortable – it is, if not the final portrait of him, at least one of them. Here his face has lost some of its youthful roundness; the man that he would have grown up to be is shadowed in the lines of his jaw and brow.

After I have viewed them all, I go downstairs, but it is to one particular image that my memory goes again and again, which is mounted in one of the little parlours that is seldom used. I have been to look at it often enough; it is the one in which I think Evie appears the most beautiful – yet in it she is oddly without expression. Edward has rendered her detached, almost frozen. Beside her, Jacob is equally removed, as if they were both made of stone. But this time, as I studied it more closely, my eyes drifted down from their faces all the way to their hands and it transfixed me – Evie's and Jacob's are clasped to each other – clasped so tightly that Evie's fingers are white.

I know that what I have seen in Evie's face is not the acceleration of a troubled soul. What Edward has painted is fear. Fear of Guardbridge? Fear of him? And now I think of the piano with a shudder.

The sun has gone from the sky, leaving baleful clouds that sink to the moor. I think again of Evie and know something was wrong, something beyond her state of mind and her wretched marriage – something real and menacing that haunted her. It has been here from the first, but I have not allowed myself to believe it.

It is as if the house itself has sucked on something poisonous, sucked it into the very timbers and stone and then that poison has leaked back into the air and into those who breathe it. My head is full of questions and when I see Flora coming in from the scullery, I say, 'Flora, do you know which of the staff who are here now were at Guardbridge when Evie Stonehouse was ill? When she and Jacob died?'

The question catches her and there is something about her eyes that tells me she is surprised I have not asked before — that perhaps this very question is important. And part of me withdraws, as if to another room, far enough away that whatever she says will not touch me.

She does not answer immediately and as I wait, the air cooling about me, she meets my gaze. 'None,' she says finally and there is a chill in her tone. 'Not one of us was here when they died. All of us came after.'

13

Evening is drawing across the moor when I make my way to Iris's quarters to tell her about the visit from Albert and Lizzie. At the oriel window I stand and rub my cold fingers and think how much I have begun to dislike how night alters the space within Guard-bridge, distorting it as a faulty lens might bend an image to its own imagination.

I knock at Iris's door and when I go in, I smile and utter greetings with a warmth I do not feel. I want to ask her — who was it who destroyed the piano? Why was Evie so afraid? But I am apprehensive to hear the answers. What if it were not Evie who did it? What if it were Edward himself? At my news Iris appears genuinely delighted and I am pleased that I have been the source of joy when so recently I was the cause of such distress. I catch some of her happiness and my mood lifts.

'But what if they don't like me?'

'They will,' I assure her.

'Won't they hate the taxidermy?'

'Not at all. They'll both be fascinated in that way children are with animals. Albert spent hours trying to get close enough to the wild creatures by our house and once tamed a mouse in secret, although my mother discovered it and it was banished. But it would be best that they don't learn of the Guardbridge Glass and your other gift, Iris. It would be too easy to get back to my father, and if he heard about it, he would surely stop them returning.'

Iris nods in affirmation.

'When I was inspecting the nurseries, I came across one of your crafts – a robin. You must have given it to Jacob.'

Iris frowns and looks to Mrs North. 'I recall every creature I have ever worked on and I have not used a robin, I'm sure.'

'Ah, now, I think perhaps that was made by Evie. Do you remember, Miss Stonehouse?' Mrs North says.

'I do now you mention it. She loved the robin over all birds. She continued her interest in taxidermy long after she refused to come to my sittings.'

At this mention of the séances, I am curious. I remember how on the night of the séance Iris had mumbled and seemed to fall into a trance but not said anything meaningful. The only intelligible word that had been spoken was to me. There had been no sign of actual communication.

'How do the spirits talk to you?' I ask.

Iris's face flickers with animation. 'Of course. I

haven't told you. Come.' And getting up she takes me by the arm and leads me to her bedchamber. It is colder here and the weak light does not breach the shadows. There are no cheerful pictures or ornaments, only those dead things that Iris has moulded into some imitation of life.

She pulls out a drawer in a Japanese cabinet from which she produces a leather-bound book and passes it to me. 'Open it,' she says.

I peel the covers apart and study the pages where the writing is haphazard, at times frenzied.

'They speak through my pen,' Iris explains.

'I don't understand.' I try to pick out the words and read a sentence here and there, but they are like the ramblings of a drunkard and the handwriting difficult to decipher. 'Do they write in your book? It seems to have been written by more than just one person.'

She laughs. 'No. After a séance, and at other times too, I go into a trance and then the spirits enter me and write through my hand, relaying their messages here. The handwriting varies because it's different spirits who visit.'

'And you are in trance when this happens? You don't recall afterwards?'

'I never recall. I know you must think me strange.'

'I may not understand but it doesn't follow that I think you strange, though I admit there are aspects of what you do that have given me a little discomfort.'

147

Iris reddens and I cannot tell if it is in anger or embarrassment. 'Do you want me to go from Guardbridge, sister?'

I feel ashamed that I have prompted this reaction. 'No,' I say. 'I would be lonely without you.'

She blinks away a sudden tear. 'I'm so glad for you, Annie. I would hate for us not to be friends.'

'What do the spirits say?' I ask.

'They speak sometimes of things in the past but also of things that have not yet happened. We don't possess that eye, but they do.'

'What future things do they tell you?'

She is silent and then she looks up slyly and whispers. 'They told me about you, Annie.'

My face burns suddenly hot. *She cannot know*, I tell myself. *She cannot.* But even so it takes a few moments to gather my voice. 'What did they say?' I search her expression for clues to knowledge of that most secret thing. But instead she is watching me intently and there is a shimmer of interest that makes me wonder if I have unnecessarily given myself away.

'The spirits predicted your coming to Guardbridge and that you would bring a child with you.'

This, although true, is not any great revelation. Many a new wife falls with her first baby on their bridal tour. However, I am unsettled. 'Shall we return to the fire?' I say, but Iris grasps my wrist with fingers that are unexpectedly strong.

'I can see that you still don't believe me. Why is it that my word is not enough? They speak the truth, I tell you.' The vehemence of her tone gives me pause, and once she has reclaimed my full attention, she says, 'I will prove it; they showed me the little square where you met Edward. The clock chimed eleven and you had a stone in your shoe.'

I recoil as I remember that first encounter in the pinched winter sunshine. Edward in his top hat, his chaise standing idle in the thin shadow, steam rising from the horse's nostrils. Almost, I think, as if he had been waiting for me. He had stopped and allowed his gaze to rest on my face and I had felt the swell of his interest. I too had paused and turned so that he would see my profile that was so often praised. And somehow I had known, even as I walked away towards home, with my baskets and parcels, that it was a beginning.

As I crossed the street a discomfort began in my shoe, something that pressed upon the soft arch. The desire to bend down and slip it from my foot had been nearly irresistible but I had not wanted to be caught in such a task while observed. Until this moment I had forgotten this detail. I remember then that through the noises of the town came the chime of the church clock and the awareness that I was late returning. The thought of my mother's disappointment already robbing me of pleasure.

Cold creeps up my spine. How could Iris know? Something in me stumbles, but, wait, yes, I had not been the only one there – and I am sure that I had told Edward later of the object wedged in my footwear. I am certain because I had walked on and hidden the pain of it and by the time I left the main street and could finally investigate it was to discover it had cut the skin and drawn blood. This very fact had seemed so dramatic that I shared my anecdote with him at a later point.

Iris's face is guileless, and I wonder if she had been told it by Edward and then forgotten – because told it she must have been. Surely Iris cannot truly have predicted the future? Edward must have described it and later, in a trance, she had recorded it on paper and imagined that the spirits had imparted it. And yet both Mrs North and even Edward acknowledge that she demonstrates some skill, though she has not fallen upon my secret, and, given its significance, I reason that surely she will not.

As we return to the fire, I recall the rest of that first encounter, how Edward had gone to the shop and discovered my address and then found a way into our lives out there on the seafront, where there was no road to lead his horses. He made his way down the sandy path swinging his cane and knocked on the door. Our maid invited him to the parlour, where my mother was working in the kitchen in her morning dress and had not had time to tidy her hair, and my father was in his shabby smoking jacket dusty with ash.

But despite all this I had seen how Edward watched me, studied me, and thrilled. In him was a means of escape and when he talked of Guardbridge and its location I knew, I knew that I would come here – that this was where freedom lay.

'It's exactly as you said.' And she nods slowly, accepting my answer for the truth.

When we are sitting once again, I can no longer put off the question. 'I went back to the music room and discovered that the piano there has been vandalized.'

There is an uncomfortable silence.

'Who did that?' I ask.

'I don't know,' Iris says, and Mrs North nods in agreement, but I do not believe them and feel a bolt of impatience.

'By all accounts Evie was very fond of her piano. Surely accusations were made when it happened? You once said that Evie complained a great deal.'

Iris looks sour. 'There were, of course. Evie blamed Edward at first and when he denied it Evie blamed me; she said I did it in revenge because we had fallen out over her disgust of my mediumship.'

Mrs North shakes her head angrily. 'That was such a cruel and unjust charge. I wouldn't be surprised if it was Mrs Stonehouse herself who did it. In that final year she was beside herself. Miss Stonehouse and I often discussed how concerned we were she would lose her mind altogether.'

'Was it in those last twelve months when the piano was damaged?'

'It was indeed, according to my recollection. There was a lot of bother all round that final year, but Mr Stonehouse was just as capable as his wife of temper if you don't mind me saying,' Mrs North remarks. And there is in the following tense silence the suggestion of many things.

I turn to Iris. 'I thought you and Evie fell out fairly soon after the marriage?'

'We maintained a courteous enough relationship, although I knew how much she really disliked me.'

'And who were the staff who were here when Evie and Jacob died? I was told that not one who is in residence now was serving then?'

'It's true. They all left before,' Iris says.

Although I have already heard this, the knowledge punches me once more. 'But why?'

'There were some financial matters that reduced the staff, but scarlet fever is guaranteed to empty a house of its inhabitants,' Iris says.

'And that's how Evie and Jacob died?'

'Why do you think otherwise?' she asks.

'It was something that Mr Forster said.'

'You should pay no attention to him. He's nothing but a troublemaker.'

If it was scarlet fever, it would make sense of the empty house. But later, as I make my way back to my quarters, I feel the shifting sense of deceit – and I find that I am not entirely reassured.

The day sits like a stone. I cannot shake the alarm that there was no one here to witness those deaths but the family. I imagine Evie and Jacob on their sick beds being cared for by Mrs North and Iris, their maids and nurse gone – the brooding silences and hushed expectancy that precedes a death, Guardbridge's unsettling arms opening in anticipation of a new embrace.

The diorama begins to turn and whine in its cupboard. I see again the blind white eyes and in a fit of anger I light a lamp and drag a chair to the cupboard. I avoid looking too closely at those creatures as I reach up and take it down. Leaving the room, I enter an empty one further down the corridor and bury it out of sight beneath some sheeting.

I feel immediately better, though Iris's premonition of mine and Edward's meeting still sits uncomfortably with me. As well as liking Iris, I am aware that she also causes me disquiet. I remember what Edward said of her sleepwalking – is it possible she was the one who wrote on my window? I shall keep the door locked, but when I try to turn the key it sticks.

Flora comes up with wood for the fire and I say, 'Can you try the lock for me? I cannot make it work.'

She nods and tries the key herself, then shakes her head. 'It won't. I wonder if it's the right one.'

'Would you see if there's a spare with Mrs Ford, please?'

'You would like it tonight?'

'Yes, please.'

She gives me an assessing look and leaves.

A little later there is a knock and Flora returns out of breath. 'We looked, Mrs Stonehouse, but there's no spare key for this room.'

'Oh.' I regard the door nervously. 'When you go down again, would you ask Mrs Ford to find a locksmith?'

'Yes'm.' She does not leave but moves awkwardly from foot to foot. 'I think you ought to know that Marsha's been spreading rumours about Miss Stonehouse. I don't know if you were told but her mother worked here in the days when Mr Stonehouse's parents were alive.'

'I didn't know. What is she saying?'

'It's a serious accusation. I think it best that you speak to her yourself.' She hesitates. 'I'd like you to know that none of us believe her. Miss Stonehouse is well liked and Marsha is quite the gossip.'

I sigh, too troubled to hear more. 'Thank you for telling me. I'll speak to her tomorrow morning.'

14

Marsha must be tackled as soon as possible and after breakfast I ring the bell and call for her.

As soon as she enters, I sense that she knows she is in trouble.

'Marsha, I understand some things have been said about Miss Stonehouse.'

Her cheeks redden.

'I would like you to tell me what you said, please.'

She shuffles awkwardly. 'It was no more than I was told by my mother.'

'That's understood, and staff will always gossip about their masters and mistresses, but I believe this accusation is serious.'

'My mother was maid to Annabelle Stonehouse, Miss Stonehouse's mother, and tended her body after the fire.' She swallows uneasily. 'Well, my mother said there were bruises on her.'

'Bruises? What sort of bruises?'

'They were bad, my mother said.'

'Are you saying that Mrs Stonehouse had had an accident?'

'My mother said it wasn't an accident.'

'You'd better tell me exactly what your mother said, Marsha.'

She flushes deeper. 'She said it was her daughter did it – Miss Stonehouse.'

'What evidence did she have for thinking it was Miss Stonehouse?'

'She witnessed it.'

'Before her mother's death, she saw Miss Stonehouse hurt her?'

'Not just before but over the years. She said Miss Stonehouse was often angry with her mother and would pinch and hurt her.'

I reflect with sympathy on the troubled, neglected girl Iris was – perhaps she did lash out, but I find it impossible to imagine that she carried out much, if any, real harm.

'She was a child, Marsha. If Miss Stonehouse occasionally pinched her mother, I'm sure she would have grown out of it. And that is very personal information; it's not something you should have talked about in this house.'

Her lip trembles.

'So this is what you have said. Is there more? We may as well have it out now, Marsha.'

'A few days after Annabelle Stonehouse died, it was necessary to change her dress. A photographer was to come and take a final picture.'

'I see.'

'When my mother disrobed her, there were bruises about her neck.'

'Bodies discolour after death. Could she be mistaken?'

'She said they were very serious. She said that she thinks Mrs Stonehouse was murdered and the fire set to cover it up.'

I shake my head with bewilderment. 'If they were so very bad, why didn't your mother show someone? Tell someone?'

'I think the family just wanted to put Mrs Stonehouse to rest.'

'You do know that Miss Stonehouse had not yet reached her thirteenth year when her mother died, and it would take a great deal of strength to kill someone in the manner you're suggesting. I don't believe a girl that age is likely to do such a thing. It's a terrible allegation.' My voice is cold. 'And I'm astounded that your mother let you come here if she believed one of the ladies of the house capable of such violence.'

She does not reply.

'If you were my daughter, I wouldn't put you in danger. Not that I believe a word of it.'

She begins to cry.

'Marsha,' I say more gently, 'this is a truly grave charge that should never have been made without proof. For such a rumour to become known would grievously affect Miss Stonehouse's reputation.'

'I'm sorry,' she gasps between sobs.

'Does Miss Stonehouse frighten you?'

She shakes her head.

'Does she seem to you like a person likely to murder?'

Again she shakes her head.

'Go and dry your tears. On no account do I want what you have said to get back to Miss Stonehouse. Can you imagine how upset she would be?'

'Will you send me away?'

'I don't know yet,' I say. 'Please get Mrs North for me.'

She nods, wiping her nose, and hurries away.

I sit with my head back and close my eyes. Surely Iris's rages did not escalate to murder, but the facts I have learned leave me uncomfortable. I think back to all that Mrs North has said about Iris's relationship with her mother: the unnaturally strong affection that was constantly thwarted.

Mrs North comes in a little later.

'I heard something deeply alarming about Annabelle Stonehouse,' I say.

'What is that?' Her eyes are bright with interest.

'I was told that at her death her body was badly bruised. It was suggested that she was killed before the fire and that it was Iris who did it.'

'Who told you that?' she snaps, immediately flushing at her abrupt manner.

'It was Marsha.'

'Well, I knew her mother well and she was a gossipy flibbertigibbet too, as I recall. Mr Stonehouse will be livid to hear such a thing.'

'I didn't believe it, of course, but I want to know what happened. You were there.'

'This is many years ago now.' She pauses in thought. 'It's true that Annabelle Stonehouse often bore bruises, but what Marsha did not say was that in her last years Mrs Stonehouse's cancer caused easy discolouration. There was no foul play, I can assure you.' She takes an outraged breath. 'Poor Iris. As if her reputation were not already sullied. As if she could or would harm anyone, leastways the mother she adored.'

'But you said once she had terrible moods.'

'Don't we all? Oh.' She all but stamps her foot. 'This is so unfair.'

'Of course,' I say.

She exhales heavily and her high colour recedes. 'Forgive me if I've been too strong. I've always had to fight for Miss Stonehouse.'

'I was told it was her throat that was bruised.'

'Indeed. She frequently had marks there, and do you know why?'

I shake my head.

'Mrs Stonehouse was rather a vain woman in her day. I helped her dress when need be and there were often bruises to her ribs from tight corsetry and to her neck from the high collars she favoured. They did not hurt her, the bruises, and so I suppose she thought no more about it.'

I am weary now. 'Thank you.'

'Right, I will call Marsha and Mrs Ford. This matter must be put straight immediately and the staff satisfied as to what a wicked untruth has been told. I'm afraid we cannot keep such a girl here.'

'I agree,' I say.

'A girl like that will have us all taking part in thievery and any manner of skulduggery before long, and let the whole world know it too. I dread to think what Miss Stonehouse would say if she heard this wicked, wicked rumour. Please forgive my vehement manner. I hope that I've not spoken out of turn.'

'Your defence of Iris is admirable. I would give a lot to have that sort of loyalty.'

Her expression softens and she pats my hand. 'I hope you know that you have all our loyalty here. There, we will say no more of it.'

She gives a great sigh and shakes her head wryly. 'For so small a household it always astounds me how much drama is generated. Every day, one thing or another.'

After she has left, I gaze out of the window. Mrs North had certainly defended Iris convincingly, but it is not that which now comes back to me again and again but a tiny moment, one which passed so quickly that I am still not sure if it was there or not. It is the fact that when I told Mrs North that Marsha believed that Annabelle was murdered it was not shock I saw but the sort of horror that comes with the recognition that some truth, well hidden, has been discovered.

The days pass, Marsha leaves and a new maid is employed, and all the while my thoughts are distracted by Albert and Lizzie's imminent arrival, but it is not until Friday evening that the carriage finally steers on to the drive and I rush out to meet them.

Lizzie and Albert are being helped down, Albert rubbing his eyes and Lizzie gazing up at Guardbridge with sleepy awe, and I had not known until now how much I had missed them and there are tears even as I smile.

'Albert, Lizzie.' I take them in my arms and inhale those well-remembered scents.

Then I step back, noting Albert's greater height and how the bones of his face are more defined, sharper, his cheeks losing the plumpness of youth. Lizzie has grown too, her features more angled. I study them both, watchful for change, particularly Albert whose sensitive nature fared badly under the crushing will of our father.

'Are you well? I've missed you so much. So much,' I say. 'Did you leave the family in good health?'

Lizzie pours forth the latest news from home. Albert is shy and withdrawn, time apart having rendered him more hesitant. As I usher him in, he turns wide eyes to the lavish hallways, but once in the drawing room we fall into that familiar pattern of old as he sits close and focuses on me with his earnest gaze.

'Can we see the baby?' Lizzie asks.

'Of course.'

Both Albert and Lizzie talk excitedly and comment on the house as I take them up the stairs and through the many passageways.

'It's like a castle,' Albert announces.

'He's a long way away,' Lizzie says, giving me a curious look.

But when we finally arrive at the nursery it is empty.

'Where is he?' Albert asks.

I have an inexplicable knowledge that he is with Iris and I pause to take a breath. 'He might be with his aunt.'

'Shall we go? I want to see him,' Albert says.

'Not now,' I insist. 'He will be nearly ready for bed.'

'Will you put him to bed?' Lizzie asks.

'I have Agnes, his nurse, for that.'

'Does John mind?' she says.

'No.' My heart gives a contraction. 'I'll show you where you're to sleep and the playroom. There are lots of toys.'

This knowledge is enough to draw their attention

from John. They circle the nursery with excitement. Albert is immediately drawn by the rocking horse, Lizzie to the farm animals.

Perching on one of the beds I watch them as if I can never watch them enough. 'Is there any more news from home?' I ask.

'Ellen now has the work that you once did.'

'And she's not as nice as you,' Albert quips. 'She boxes my ears and doesn't like me around. She called me a 'noying bug.'

'Oh, Albert,' Lizzie puts in. 'She's not that bad and she has so much to do she doesn't need you in the way.'

'And have you messages or a letter for me?' I ask. 'From Mama or Papa?'

Lizzie brushes out the hair of a doll she has found and buttons it into a dress. 'Papa said he hopes you're being a good girl.'

'And nothing from Mama?' What had I expected? I had thought perhaps a gift for my son – her legitimate grandchild.

'It's better than you deserve,' Albert pipes up in an imitation of what my father might say.

'Shh,' Lizzie says.

I regret asking.

'Are you being good?' Lizzie asks quietly when Albert is occupied.

'Of course,' I say and wonder why I do not protest

163

at the assumption that I am bad. A wave of despair and anger passes through me. I will never please them, not now.

'Is your husband kind? Has he painted you yet?'

'Yes,' I say, 'you must let me show you.'

We make our way back through the house, Albert with a soldier in each hand.

There are oohs and aahs over the studio. 'Oh, Annie!' Lizzie cries. 'He's so clever. What is it like being married to an artist? Have you shown him your drawings?'

I laugh. 'No, I'm afraid my skill is very poor beside Edward's. He's the very last person to whom I would show them.' I walk them to my portrait. 'There,' I say with pride.

They both gaze with awe.

'I wish I was as pretty as you,' Lizzie says. 'It's not fair.'

'Maybe you'll be prettier when you're as grown up as Annie,' Albert says.

'Shut up,' Lizzie snaps.

I fold a stray hair behind her ears. 'I think you very pretty, Lizzie. I'll look out some clothes for you to take home. You'll be able to adjust them to your size.'

The rest of the evening, even in the company of my siblings, passes too slowly and I am relieved when it is time for bed.

Flora brings hot water, but it is me who sponges

Albert's face, combs through his hair and gets him into his nightshirt; the smell of him takes me back home and presses on something tender.

Lizzie changes in the night nursery with the help of Flora and finally they are both tucked into bed. I light candles and move about the room, folding Albert's discarded clothes while he and Lizzie talk in whispers.

'You don't need to whisper here,' I say. 'No one can hear you.'

Leaning down, I kiss his cheek and feel a swarm of love. 'Goodnight, Albert.'

'You baby him, that's what father says,' Lizzie jibes, and I cross the rug to kiss her too, tucking the covers round her chin. She makes a pretence of wriggling away, but I can see she is pleased.

At the door I turn. Albert's face is very small against the pillows. He says, 'Can I sleep with you in your room?'

But if Edward returned early and came to me, he wouldn't be pleased. 'Don't you like it here? With a lovely fire?'

Albert gazes up at me. 'No,' he says.

I laugh. 'Isn't it warmer than home, and the bed more comfy?'

'I don't like it,' he insists.

'Shh,' Lizzie hisses.

'Well, it's true.'

'What?'

'It's . . .' He exchanges looks with his sister.

'What?' I repeat.

'I looked in the mirror and the boy who looked back wasn't me.'

My gaze flies to the mirror. 'What do you mean? Who was it?'

'I don't know.' His forehead rucks with anxiety.

I draw back as if his words have scalded me. 'No, Albert,' I say calmly, 'you're mistaken.' I take a swift look at Lizzie who is chewing the end of her braid, but she does not comment.

'Can you tell Lizzie to leave the lamp on?'

'I'm sure it was just a trick of the light, but, yes, leave the lamp on, please, Lizzie.'

The only illumination now comes from the fire and one lamp. The soldiers that Albert has lined up along the surfaces of chests and tables throw thin shadows and for a moment I imagine Jacob looking up at me, his dark hair falling over angry eyes. *Stop it*, I tell myself. *Stop now*. And, forcing a smile, I say, 'Sleep well,' and close the door.

In the hall I pause – the wall lights flicker capriciously, wind whips across the moor and the doors, shrunken in the chill, tap-tap in their frames.

What Albert has said bears down on me, more so with the force of my denial. *It is not so*, I tell myself. I remember the night of the séance when I thought, for

166

a brief instant, that there had been a figure at the end of the corridor. It is not as Albert said. If it were . . . If it were? And I sense that if I acknowledged it, the rush of fear would be more than I could contend with.

Around me blackness pools and makes anomalous shapes. My heart beats faster than walking can account for. At Evie's door I pause. There is a clatter from beyond. I place my palm on the handle and try it. There is another sound – but now I do not want to face the possibility that the cause is something other than an object knocked from a table by the wind.

I enter my room and as I go about readying myself for bed, the diorama begins to hum. But I had taken it down. Surely, a few days ago, I had pulled a chair to the cupboard and removed it to the next room.

But when I look, it is worse than I imagined. The space is empty. I listen, my hands curled so tightly that the nails dig into my palm – and still my ears cradle the sound of it whining on its hook. How can that be? Is there another secreted within the walls? I go to the window. Outside, the wind rises and hurls rain at the glass. The trees are bone white, the lake a glitter of water with the moon's eye shivering on its surface.

It is then that I am aware of something in the air. I cannot move. If I turn, Jacob will be standing in the shadow watching me – his skin as bleached as birch bark, dead eyes gazing into me with hatred. With all my courage I snap round.

The room is empty. There is nobody there. I ring the bell then take down my hair and, sitting at the dressing table, begin to brush it through. But the candlelight picks out the edge of something on the surface of the mirror – more words, executed with a grease-smeared finger. Fear begins to writhe inside me. I pick up the chamber stick and pass it across the glass; if I do it swiftly, they will be gone. But they do not disappear. I sit back and something in me withers.

See me, someone has written. *See me*.

15

Weak sunlight filters in through the panes. I think of Albert and Lizzie and the joy I should feel. But I cannot quell the feelings that were stirred last night. Flora combs out my hair and begins pinning it up, chatting about my siblings and how much Cook is looking forward to treating them with 'something special', as she calls it.

'Flora, are there any maids in the house who would play a trick?'

She looks shocked. 'Not on the family. What sort of trick?'

'Someone wrote on my mirror.'

'A lot of the staff cannot write, Mrs Stonehouse. What was there?'

'*See me*,' I say.

She chuckles. 'It's a harmless enough statement and very apt as that is what we do when looking in the mirror, but I don't think it's one of us. Could it have been Lizzie?'

I ponder this and wonder if she is correct but I cannot quite imagine Lizzie in the task. Flora's explanation should ease me, but I cannot forget what Albert said and already the day is sullied.

When dressed, I go immediately to the nursery where John is lying on his back kicking his legs with glee.

'Good morning,' Agnes says, rising. 'This little man will soon be rolling over.'

I drop a finger into his fist and he curls over it and pulls it to his mouth. I open my lips to ask about her absence the night before but do not want my suspicions confirmed. I do not want to think of them all together – myself elsewhere.

'My brother and sister have arrived and we'll be coming to visit John after breakfast.'

'I heard. It must be lovely for you, Mrs Stonehouse – and, of course, come whenever you wish.'

Next, I find Albert and Lizzie. The mirror is turned to the wall.

'It was the only way he'd sleep,' Lizzie says.

'And did you, Albert?'

He nods but his eyes look bruised, and I suspect he did not sleep well, if at all.

'He looks so tiny,' Albert says and wants to hold him. Albert and then Lizzie both sit as John is placed on their laps under Agnes's supervision and both are inordinately pleased.

'I'm an uncle, you know,' Albert announces impressively. 'And I'll always be much, much older than John.'

'You will,' Agnes says, laughing. 'It is a very important position, as is being an aunt.' She smiles at Lizzie.

I glance at Lizzie and wonder what she recalls of the time I bore you. She had been but three years, and I comfort myself with the knowledge that she would have been too young to have known or understood what was happening. I am certain my parents would not risk the shame by telling her — lest she pass the information elsewhere. It is for her own good. But as I watch my siblings with John, I feel a deeper denial of you.

At evening's approach wheels turn on the drive. Getting up, I leave the children and make my way to the front entrance and, seeing it is Edward, go out to meet him. Although disquieted, my happiness at Albert and Lizzie's arrival makes me more generous in my welcome than I would have been and, noting his drawn face, I put my arms about him.

Briefly he holds me and for an instant there is a warmth in his eye, which too quickly dissipates. 'Are your sister and brother here?'

'In the drawing room,' I say.

Bessie takes his overcoat and hat.

'Now all I need is brandy and something to eat, something hot — the food at the inn was dreadful.'

In the drawing room Lizzie and Albert rise from their toys to greet him. Lizzie blushes and curtseys and Albert gives a little bow. Bessie follows shortly with brandy and hot savouries.

'So, good fellow, what do you think of your sister's new home?'

'I like the garden and the food is good.' Albert studies the tray that Bessie has brought with interest and Edward tells them to help themselves.

He turns to Lizzie. 'I hope you've been made comfortable?'

Lizzie answers that she has.

'What have you done today?'

'We met Miss Stonehouse and Mrs North,' Lizzie says.

'And she showed us the skull of a blackbird and lots of bones.'

Edward laughs at the unconcealed glee in Albert's tone. 'Apart from studying bones, what have you planned for your visit?'

'We're going to town and Annie is giving us something to spend,' Albert says.

'When you do, remind me and I shall add to your bounty with a few coins of my own.'

Edward and the children lighten the house and all its uneasy spaces and I imagine the years ahead, when we will have more children, children who I do not have difficulty loving, and Guardbridge will become a place of joy.

*

That night, Albert, settling into bed with a pile of soldiers beside him, shows no alarm, although the mirror remains firmly in its new position.

'What do you think of your new brother-in-law?' I ask them.

'I don't want to marry but if I do, I hope I marry as well as you, Annie,' Lizzie says. 'Apart from your husband most men are horrid.'

'I would hate to marry,' Albert says. 'Unless it's you.'

I give him a hug. 'Are you jealous of Edward?'

He shrugs. 'Will we have beef again tomorrow?'

'We'll definitely have it before you have to return. Now goodnight,' I say with mock severity.

I hum a tune as I make my way downstairs and when I enter the drawing room I am ready to be pleased and to be pleasing. But Edward is pacing and when he turns to me his expression is severe.

'My work was near Helmsworth and I stopped by to pay my respects to your parents.'

A shiver of misgiving. 'Nothing was wrong, was it?'

'Nothing was wrong. They were in good health, Annie.' He pauses. 'It struck me again how, when they speak of you, it's with some disrespect.'

I protest but he waves it away. 'I don't mean that they are openly rude; it's more the sense I gain. I'm not stupid; they don't like you. What is it that causes the rift with them?'

I feel the danger of this conversation, feel the

danger of confession when what I must do is deny it. 'It's obvious to you that I'm not greatly loved?'

'It always was. I supposed, like my sister, you didn't please them.' He comes close to me and I can feel the warmth of his breath. 'But it's not that, is it? I sense . . . I sense you've disappointed them. Is there something I should know? As you are aware, and for good reason, I dislike secrets above all things.'

The lie is too great, too momentous. My throat hurts with the force of deception but refute it I do. 'What reason was there for your parents to feel as they did for Iris? Why do you think it might be different for me? My father is keener on the boys than the girls and my mother –' I pause – 'my mother has never taken to me.'

He considers and shrugs his acceptance, but then he looks directly into my eyes and lowers his voice. 'I told you about Evie. She was not the woman I thought I'd married. If I thought the same had happened again. If I thought that . . .' He lets out a shuddering gasp and looks away, but for an instant there is an expression that chills my marrow and I know – I truly know – that this is a man whose nature I have not fully learned.

The next week passes with surprising speed. There are so many things to show Lizzie and Albert, and Edward takes them fishing more than once. In the evenings we play games until, yawning, it is time for bed. The weather, as if determined to play its part, summons a spring-like spell of warmth.

One morning a headache has me remain in my chamber, leaving the children in the care of Flora. I stand at the window and observe Albert and Lizzie as they play in the copse. Too soon the time for them to leave will come and part of me wants to go with them. Am I always desiring to run from those things that are uncomfortable?

In and out of view they go, behind birch and cherry. They are holding hands and swinging in a circle. It is a game I remember and suddenly I am not twenty but nine, with the children from the house next door, their sticky palms in mine and how I leaned back and watched the sky turn above me.

They are set so deeply behind trees that I catch only flickers of them – now Albert, now Lizzie. Shadows fall between them, darkening on their faces but something is wrong. I lean closer – now Lizzie, now Albert – and I grip the sill because they are not alone. Every now and then there is a child who is neither of my siblings, standing a little way back, half hidden between trunks. I am assailed with a wave of such dizzying anxiety that I lean on the wall for support and now it is only the two of them again. I stare until my eyes burn and although I see only Lizzie and Albert, my memory holds that image as if it were a photograph — a boy of slim build with black and piercing eyes. *See me*. And now those words no longer feel so innocent and I lie back on the bed, a pulse beating fast in my throat.

Flora knocks and comes in with my laundered clothes. 'Mrs Stonehouse? Are you ill?'

Do I look that bad? 'No, I'm well,' I lie.

'You're too pale. Let me bring you a cup of chocolate.'

When Flora returns, I wait until she leaves before I take a sip, lest she witness the trembling of my hands. I try to understand what has just happened — could it have been a visiting child of one of the staff? I will not ask. I know the answer already — if that was the case, I would surely have been told. There could have been nobody there and if that is the case, then I conjured that figure myself. As I conjured the sound of the diorama? I will not believe in ghosts.

Doubt empties out all other feeling. What will happen if I cannot trust my own senses? What creature would I be? There was an afternoon, I recall now, one after you had gone and I was lying on my cot near the stove, drugged into submission. I had looked across to where sparks from the fire turned to butterflies that settled on the range. I had tried to get up to save them from burning but my limbs had been too uncoordinated to achieve their objective and I had begun to cry and it had not been for the helpless imaginary creatures but for the butterfly inside me that was flying too close to the heat.

The remains of the day pass listlessly, my head still throbbing, and after supper I take myself to bed and curl beneath the covers, restless with anxiety. I wake from some nightmare in a sweat of dread. All but one of the lamps have gone out and it flickers only unsteadily. The curtains are drawn back, showing the shape of a moon. I am not alone. God, I am not alone.

I turn over but it is no ghost. Iris leans over me and my nostrils fill with the sourness of her breath. Her eyes spark dangerously. Something like a growl escapes her.

'You touched it,' she spits. 'You touched the glass.'

I draw away. 'I didn't, Iris. I didn't.' But she leans closer and traps my wrist under her hand.

'You touched it.' And it is clear now that she is not herself, that she is in that unwaking state that Edward told me about. She does not see me at all — she is sleeping but in sleeping learned what I did.

I pull my arm away, desperate to be free of her fingers. Her face alters — it is twisted and suddenly it is not Iris's expression there but one that my own father wore. The voice that comes from her throat is deeper.

'You're wicked,' she rasps, 'a wicked, wicked girl, and you will be punished.'

Instantly the memory unfolds behind my eyes: the shock of my father's fist to my belly, how I had creased under it, the sound of my sleeve ripping as he dragged me over the tiles. *You wicked, wicked girl.* I begin to shiver. I try again to wriggle away but I do not wish to wake her – what if in waking she recalls what she is saying now?

Her muscles slacken. She becomes vague and uncertain. Limply her hands fall to her sides and she turns and makes her way out of the room.

I lie in shock, the draught from the corridor sifting staleness into the air. I want to cry from anger and fear, then the low whine from the diorama begins and I clamp my hands to my ears.

It is not there, not there, I tell myself. *Not there.*

16

George brings the coach to the front of the house. A grinning Flora busies herself taking rugs and furs to the carriage. Albert and even Lizzie fidget in their excitement. I am grateful that we leave before the need to see Iris, relieved to distance myself from the events of the previous night.

Lodging, with increasing anxiety, is the fact I can no longer deny that Iris has some form of second sight — how else would she have been able to say what she had as she sleepwalked? But there is not only that. I recall the boy standing in the copse and twist uneasily in my seat.

We are soon settled and on our way out of Guardbridge. Albert sits by the window rocking his legs back and forth and even Lizzie gives my hand a squeeze and kisses my cheek. But I am waiting until we are away, on the winding moor road, and then I turn and view Guardbridge — a black shadow against the leaden sky.

I feel a loosening of emotion, as if I had been holding my breath for a long time. Lying back against the cushions, I gaze out to where wind sweeps the moor, rippling briar, and buzzards glide high in the cloud on their broad flat wings.

The journey passes quickly in talk of what we shall do, and Lizzie and Albert take out their purses more than once to count their coins and measure what they might buy, and it seems only an hour when the carriage pulls into an inn and we are helped down with our baskets. Tipping his cap, George takes the horses to rest and we walk to the town square and to the babble of noise and smells.

It has been many months since I have been among such crowds, and after the solitude and uniformity of Guardbridge, my senses do not know where to settle — on the women in their smart attires and colourful hats, the costermongers shouting wares or the faint smell of the sea, roasting meat and breads.

'I must go to the dressmaker for a fitting,' I say to Flora, 'but I'll find you later.' I check the clock. 'We could meet in the town square in an hour?'

Flora gathers the children and baskets and I watch their retreat — Albert gripping Flora's hand and Lizzie, basket swinging, face upturned to Flora as she talks with enthusiasm.

The dress shop is situated on the main road, its display window lit by colourful lamps. I am excited at the thought of being able to afford a few new garments in the latest fashions and fabrics. The bell tinkles and a young woman ushers me in with a courteous bob, guiding me to a chair by the fire and offering food and drink. I accept a glass of wine, taking off my gloves and warming my hands on the heat.

When I have finished, a woman in an elaborate dress of striped pink comes through from the far end of the shop.

'Good afternoon. I'm Mrs Truelove, proprietor. This must be your first visit. I would surely have remembered a woman of such fine features and figure had you honoured us with your custom before.'

I smile and hand her my card.

Mrs Truelove glances down and then her eyes fly back to me with a brief expression of shock, which she quickly disguises with another warm rush of compliments. But as I stand to follow her there is a slight withdrawal of charm and I wonder what has made it so. Surely she knows that Evie Stonehouse is dead, and that Edward has taken a new wife – or is it something else? Mr Forster's words come back to me, bringing a renewal of doubt and suspicion.

I am led to a room where satins and bombazines are displayed in abundance alongside cabinets of lace, buttons and beads. My measurements are taken, then Mrs Truelove shows me round, encouraging me to feel the fineness of one or other material or telling me how well my complexion would look against a certain colour and advising me on the latest styles. We are occupied when I glance up and say in the most casual tone I can muster:

'I saw your shock when you read my card. Did you not know that the previous Mrs Stonehouse had died?'

Her eyes skate mine. 'Yes, we knew. A death of such a prominent lady and son is news that soon makes its way into the community.'

'She was a customer here?'

'Oh yes. You would have to travel a fair way to find the equal of this establishment. How is Mr Stonehouse?'

'He is well, considering. It was a sad death, don't you think?'

She hesitates, assessing me and finally, leaning a little in, she says, 'We were very fond of Mrs Stonehouse. If you don't mind me asking, what exactly was the manner of their accidents?'

A jolt of shock strikes my midriff. I bend to pick up a corner of fabric, behaving as if the question had not startled me.

'Well,' I say, 'Mr Stonehouse doesn't like to dwell on it and I'm afraid I've not been told the exact circumstances.'

She nods. 'Yes, indeed. Poor Mr Stonehouse.' She pauses. 'Perhaps you hoped that I would have the details?' Her eyes are full of eager curiosity now.

I flush but do not reply and Mrs Truelove continues with her tour, although I take in no more of what she says and when the clock chimes the hour it is a relief to make my excuses and step out into the cold, my thoughts reeling.

We arrive home to the first stars over Guardbridge. I wake Albert and Lizzie who have both fallen asleep. I take the children straight to the fire where Bessie brings bowls of soup and biscuits. The conversation grates hard on me. If what Mrs Truelove says is the truth and Evie did not die of fever – then they have all lied. I must know, even if Edward does not wish to discuss it.

'Where is Mr Stonehouse?' I ask one of the maids.

'He was in the studio last time I knew.'

I find Edward working on a new portrait, an empty bottle of wine on his work table.

He puts down his brush. 'The outing has done you good.'

'Edward, I learned something in town that disturbs me. It was about Evie.'

His expression is guarded.

'You told me she died of fever. However, today I learned differently. I heard that she and Jacob met with an accident.' I stifle a shiver.

Blood seeps to his cheeks. 'Who said that?' His tone is sharp.

'It was a casual remark in the dressmaker's shop.'

I cannot tell if he is angry or upset but eventually he sighs. 'You would've learned sooner or later and I've often wondered if I should have told you the truth from the beginning, but rightly or wrongly I found the facts too painful and didn't want to talk of them. I forbade Iris from telling you and insisted that if rumour came the way of the staff, it was not to be discussed. A death such as Evie's brings shame upon us all and for me a burden of guilt.'

'What do you mean, Edward? What happened to her?'

I cannot read his expression, only feel the force of his emotion. 'Evie died by self-murder, Annie. She killed herself. Now do you understand?'

Dismay. Of all the things I had imagined this had not occurred to me. I feel a wave of pity but if only I had known, I would have been spared many hours of doubt. I go up to him and put my hand over his. 'I can see why you've kept it from me, Edward, but, yes, I believe you should've told me.'

'Evie's manner of death will be a blight on the Stonehouse family name and my reputation for as long as I live.'

'It's a dreadful thing to have happened. But why? Why would she have undertaken such a terrible act? I've gathered she wasn't happy but this is extreme.'

'Evie? How would I know why she would go so

far? I realize that I had very little knowledge of the woman I married. And at the end ... I had even less.'

And yet I know she hated Guardbridge, know that there were tempers and arguments; there must be things he is not telling me. And the secret she held that I still do not know. A sudden image comes to me of Edward leaning over Evie, fury in his face.

'Were you there?' I whisper.

He shoots me a look of shock. 'What do you mean?'

'I mean, when she killed herself, were you here at Guardbridge?'

His shock turns to anger. 'I was not.'

Relief and now compassion flower in me. I reach across and touch his cheek. 'I'm so sorry, Edward, so deeply sorry.'

It is dark and he has not lit many lamps; the studio is cold. 'Can I call for a hot drink? And you should build up the fire. You'll catch your chill here.'

'I'll ring myself if I need anything.' His eyes go to the glass. He picks up his brush again, impatient for me to leave him to his work and perhaps his thoughts. For a moment I am hurt but another part sighs in relief – for surely I have heard enough and need time alone to think over what I now know.

But as I move to go a chill of realization has me pause and I face him in horror. 'Edward, if Evie died by self-murder, how did Jacob die?'

His hand falters for an instant, then he continues what he is doing. He does not look at me now.

'Evie drowned Jacob and then she threw herself into the river and died too.' His voice is thick with emotion. 'Now you'll understand more than ever why I never wish to visit this subject.'

17

I am grateful Edward does not come to me tonight – my mind is too full of feeling and conflict. I cannot grasp the enormity of this new information and the tragedy that takes an individual to the point of desiring death, and yet was there not a time when I too found the pain of living almost too much to endure? But why would she take her child with her? I think of Edward's portraits and the uneasy atmosphere of the house. Evie had hated what Iris did, and her relationship with Edward had deteriorated – had she killed Jacob in the belief that she was protecting him?

I feel a burn of pity for Evie and Jacob – no person can be deserving of such misery. And Edward. How does he bear it?

My thoughts move to Edward's decision that the portraits of her remain. Why would he want an image of someone he is so keen to forget to constantly nudge his thoughts back in that very direction? Does he blame himself and keep them as a reminder of how things can go wrong? Or something else?

I remember now that he talked of Evie's secret – and how his anger showed. Did he punish her in the way my father did me? I have not seen sign of any violence in him and his manner has been courteous and gentleman-like but I recall when his eyes glittered dangerously and I had felt . . . I had felt afraid.

The room grows colder and the lamps throw spectral shadows. Guardbridge seems to hold all the dreadful occurrences that have ever played out here — as if to live at Guardbridge is to become infected. I recall seeing another child in the copse and the words on the glass, the moments when I do not feel alone and how I hear what is not there. And Edward, why does he begin to make me afraid?

My body starts to tremble and my heart races. I cram my fingers into my mouth to smother a scream. The memory of your beginning starts to squeeze itself out of that terrible space in my mind, that space I try so hard not to revisit but it is as if one horror must lead to another and now I am walking back from town and *he* has stepped out of the wood. I do not want to remember. I do not but the images come like bullets that my will cannot hold back. The confident swagger, the way I knew even before he put his hands on me what was to follow — the startling cloudburst of knowledge that I would not escape him. Terror has a clarity all its own and carves the remembrance deep within the flesh like a tattoo. And afterwards what was to become my life was left torn and forever bloodied.

As I had stumbled home, I had not really been inside myself – he had driven me out. And later, much later, when you had been taken from my arms, what little that was left went with you.

The next week gathers speed and leaves February behind. The moon is now on its way back to fullness and I will have to attend Iris's next séance. When the day of Lizzie and Albert's departure finally arrives, it is clear that both children are not sad to leave Guardbridge.

As much as I try to enjoy the final morning with them, my thoughts remain constantly distracted. I stop often at one or other portrait to fathom what might have been happening to Evie to cause such desperation of mind and action, but I cannot learn by imagining.

It is raining as the brougham is packed with gifts and food from the kitchen, and Lizzie and Albert take a final cup of chocolate. Mrs North and Iris wish them well and demand promises that they will soon return.

I recall the joy of their arrival and cannot fathom why their going does not make me more desolate. I lift Albert into the carriage and, for a moment, we hold each other close, then I hug Lizzie until she pulls away with a grunt of annoyance and straightens her hair and hat.

Albert leans down. 'Can you come home with baby John?' he asks.

'One day. I hope you tell Mama and Papa that you had a good time with your sister and that all is well.'

'I will,' Lizzie says.

'And you, Albert? Will you? You've had a good time, haven't you?' I ask, because I am no longer sure.

He regards me with a serious and contemplative expression that I would expect on a child much older than his five years. 'Why don't you come home with us?' he says again.

'Shhh,' Lizzie hisses.

'What is it?' I ask him. 'You know this is my home now. I can only visit Helmsworth as a guest.'

He leans towards me. 'Lizzie said I shouldn't say, but I want to know who he is.'

Lizzie makes a noise of impatience. 'It's his imagination,' she scoffs.

'What do you mean, Albert? Who who is?'

The coachman urges that they must make haste as poor weather is predicted. The door slams shut and I stand at the window.

'Who, Albert?' I urge. 'Tell me what you mean.'

He slides the window open a fraction. 'The other boy,' he says. 'The one in the house. It's not my imagination. Why can't you see him, Annie?' He is close to tears, his brow puckered with worry lines. Beside him, Lizzie has lowered her head and I can only stand and stare as the carriage rattles down the drive, its coach lamps throwing beams of light cut by rain, and out of the grounds.

I watch the coach's departure for as long as it is in sight although my collar grows wet and my face slick, and even when the crunch of distant wheels is no longer distinguishable from the sound of the downpour I do not move. It is a while before I turn to Guardbridge.

Water gushes from gutters and drainage pipes to the worn terrace. The surface of the lake jumps with droplets and I can hear, even through the wind, the fierce cry of the river.

I take a deep breath and try to pull back a wave of abhorrence – *the other boy*. But a door I have fought to keep not just closed but locked creaks open and now its contents leak into me like a tide. I think of the other murmurs, the other warnings. *It is a bad place*. And I walk back to the entrance as I might into the cave of a hungry bear.

I spend the rest of the day only wanting the solace of my bed and my own company but there are household matters that need attention. I walk through each action unconscious of myself until finally, after dinner and coffee, the clock reaches an hour by which I might reasonably excuse myself.

Edward looks up from his book. 'It's early.'

'I'm tired,' I lie.

191

He gives a small shrug. 'I can see you miss Albert and Lizzie. You must invite them again.'

But I wonder what they might say.

When Flora comes, I ask for a bottle of sleeping draught. I know I will not rest without it and when I finally put my head on the pillow, despite my feelings, sleep comes quickly.

I dream. It is night and I am walking barefoot past the north of the house in the blaze of a full moon. A thin layer of snow silvers the ground. In my hands is the Guardbridge Glass and I hold it up to catch the light. In its reflection Guardbridge behind me is on fire; smoke spirals into the ether and orange flames illuminate the windows.

I walk past the house and towards the wood. Ahead, the river runs and a stream of mist rises from the surface and meets other branches of cloud. As they move towards me, they gather momentum; they are spirits of the dead.

Snow begins to fall and, as it does, each flake becomes a bird that takes to the sky and circles above me dropping feathers. I clutch the glass tighter and open my mouth. 'I am wicked, wicked,' I say. Moving closer to the river I take the glass and hurl it into the water. Then I look up and into my open mouth the feathers fall and fill my lungs – and I wake in choking horror.

*

The covers have slid to the floor. I am freezing. Far off, a whine that I force myself to ignore turns in the air. I fumble for matches and light a candle, then lie back and search the dark corners of the room. My thoughts drift back again to Evie and it is then that I remember the robin I found in the nursery, the one made by her, and I wonder whether she, like Iris, placed a message inside its breast. I sit up.

I go to the desk drawer and retrieve it from under the notepaper. Unwrapping the cloth, I lay it on my palm, small and perfect but for the cavities where there should be eyes. Taking scissors, I rip at its chest, showering feather and dust to the floor, and there, just as I had hoped, is a piece of folded paper.

I open it and gaze down. The words burn before my eyes, bringing a wave of nauseating horror.

I take the creature and the message and throw them to the embers, adding more wood until they are buried beneath a blaze. Then I return to bed and gaze unseeingly at the ceiling.

Help me, Evie had written and reiterated: *Help me, help me, help me.*

18

The day starts softly with a grey-blue sky and watery light that speaks of ordinary things. But high up in a patch without cloud is the outline of the moon, as round as a marble. Flora dresses me and I gaze at my reflection in the mirror and at my face, sharper than it was with lids heavy with sleeplessness. I know now that Guardbridge is everything that Mrs Breach had said. And worse, that I am haunted, for surely I cannot continue to deny the evidence of my eyes and my senses. Has not Albert seen him too? But I cannot reveal to Edward that I believe such a thing. To do so would cast me in the same light as Iris.

My feelings for Iris have begun to alter. But I cannot blame her when it was I who touched the glass and who summoned Jacob, and I think of those black feathers.

I am thinner, not only on the outside where my clothes grow loose, but on the inside too. I think back to the weeks of torment and confusion after you were born and a bolt of panic tears through me at the thought of what I am once again becoming.

Now the moon's energy is gathering in the corridors

and weaving through those empty spaces. I envisage later and Iris cramped over the glass – at least she has made no mention of what she said on her night visit. I wonder at the book in which she scribes the spirits' messages – is it written there that I touched the glass, that my father cast me as a wicked creature?

I seek out John and spend an hour in the drawing room. When he reaches up and clings to me, the guilt for my coldness is almost unbearable. I look at John but see only you. Are you inside by a fire? Does someone hold you when you are sad and wipe your cheek to remove a smear of jam? Does someone tuck you into bed and place a kiss upon your brow?

When John begins to grow restless and hungry once more I am grateful to pass him back to Agnes. At my writing desk I pen a letter to my parents and to Lizzie and Albert, to Mrs Breach and then to a friend from long ago and all these things feel important – they hold off the night and what is to come. It is only as shadows begin to steal across the passageways and the ringing of Iris's glass bowls sound in the air that I know I will not escape it.

Edward has taken again to town, and I wonder if he chooses always to be away for the séances. I dine alone, although I cannot summon an appetite for the woodcock or soup and eat so little that when the maid comes to clear away she asks me if I am quite well.

Flora helps me into the black gown and I pull impatiently at the high neck and uncomfortable cuffs.

'Can you hear that?' I ask.

She cocks her head. 'The ringing has stopped.'

'Not that,' I say. 'The other noise.' Because, quite distinctly, there is a faint whine.

'I only hear the wind.'

'Yes,' I say, unconvinced. 'It makes such a ghostly noise.' I wish I had not used that word.

Out in the corridor the lamps do not fully light the passageways and each step is taken with forced calm. *I am not afraid*, I lie, but at Iris's door I pause for so long that I wonder how I dare enter at all.

The room is lit as before, the glass on the table, and Iris's complexion whiter for her black attire. Mrs North wears a look of anxious submission, but Iris is alive in the way I recall from the previous moon as if someone had threaded lamplight beneath her skin.

The candles are extinguished and Iris looks down upon the covered globe. My back is rod straight against the chair, my hands clasped tightly in my lap. From the window the moon appears above the treeline.

'Take off your gloves.'

And as before they each take one of my hands — Iris's cool and dry, Mrs North's with a faint sweat upon the palm. I glance at her. A line of worry is on her brow and she regards me with something like pity.

This time I resist Iris. I resist the force of her

intensity. I try to keep my gaze fixed on the sky but when her hand drops from mine I am compelled to observe her.

She takes the glass in her palms and concentrates on it until, once again, she reaches that trance-like state, her lips moving silently to some conversation that only she hears. Mrs North rubs her hands together nervously and I realize that I am biting my lip so hard that I taste blood.

Iris begins to laugh then, almost silently, with a delight that is terrifying. Mrs North shuffles uncomfortably in her seat. Iris begins to rock backwards and forwards, mirth and tears breaking upon her face in a confusion of emotion. I cannot look away. Then suddenly she grips the table so hard the candle holders rattle. Her eyes grow wide. And in this moment she is truly mad, capable of anything.

Iris turns to me. I cannot breathe. She must not speak to me. I will not bear it if she does.

I think I have escaped that fate when her face assumes another – a countenance more childlike.

'See me.' The words are hissed, the tone juvenile.

See me. I think of the mirror. I will be sick.

Mrs North is aghast; sympathy and something else there. Then Iris sighs and droops in the chair, sweat freckled on her forehead. She does not look at me now. It is over. I exhale.

Mrs North rises unsteadily from her chair and

moves to Iris. Iris's gaze grows focused once again but with an expression of bewilderment as if she had returned from some absence and expected to find herself elsewhere.

With gentle hands Mrs North guides Iris from the room and when she returns I am still sitting at the table as I had been, my hands clutched tightly in my skirts. Nothing could persuade me to touch the glass again.

'Are you well, Mrs Stonehouse?' Her voice is gentle.

I shake my head. I am not. I am not well at all.

She rings the bell and advises me to sit by the fire but still I do not move.

A little while later, Flora comes up with brandy, which she places on the table.

'Come now, Mrs Stonehouse. Come get warm.' Mrs North propels me, like a child, towards the flames. 'I have no idea what Miss Stonehouse is talking of. You mustn't let what she says or does affect you so deeply.'

I drink the brandy, grateful for the fierce trail it leaves in my throat.

Finishing the glass, I rise, aware of the distance that I must traverse to get back to my own room, but that is where I want to be. I light my lamp, igniting a faithful flame that will go some way to keep away the night. Part of me hopes that Mrs North will offer to accompany me but I will not ask. To ask would be to admit the degree of my anxiety — not just to her but to myself.

My steps are too slow on the carpets and darkness

dips in and out as I pass lamps. The windows rattle with the growing wind as it whistles over the moor, but, worse, there is a soft step behind me. I pause. *A maid*, I tell myself. I walk on although my legs burn with the desire to run. The temperature even in the short distance from leaving Iris's quarters has dropped and there are spaces of creeping darkness. It comes again, that footfall, and there is about it something stealthy. My heart begins to race. I am at the oriel window now where Jacob's portrait gazes out with such dislike. I dare not look upon his features – this child who I now believe has returned.

I recall again that fateful day, as I returned to our cottage and first glimpsed the man half hidden between trees. I had wanted to run then, as I do now. I paced ahead until his lazy footsteps slid into rhythm behind mine. I felt the hot stab of fear as he approached a little faster. My fear growing but I had turned, better to confront the threat.

Now memory and reality merge, and when that footfall comes again, so quiet it is little more than a whisper, I know, as surely as I had that day, two things: I am not alone and that someone, some*thing* is following me.

I stop, terror bubbling in my chest, and in the semi-silence the walker behind me pauses. Its rage eviscerates the air. I hold my breath and clench my palms that are damp with sweat.

Suddenly the quiet is split by sound. Iris. Her wailing fills my ears with an eerie echo.

'No,' she moans, 'no, no, no.'

I bite down hard on my tongue, flooding my mouth with blood. The lamp slips from my hands and falls to the ground. The flame lives for a second and is then extinguished. I take a gasping breath. I turn.

Nobody there. But at the end of the corridor a faint shadow spreads from the offshoot hallway and is cast to the wall – the shadow of the person who is nearing me, whose slow steps have begun again.

I cannot move. As it nears my own passage, the shape becomes more defined until it is fully revealed, and there – clearly outlined – is a child.

Iris's voice rips the air again. 'No, no, no.'

I have to run, yet my feet remain as if fixed to the floor, and as I gaze horrified a hand creeps round the wall and clasps its corner. Small white fingers curl on the panelling. *See me.* I stumble back, crunching glass with my heel. I flee.

19

When I wake, the room is robed in shadows. The lamps that I kept lit all night are low in their globes and from the window dawn has barely changed in colour since I finally fell asleep not long before sunrise. How long did I slumber? Thirty minutes? Less? My corneas are gritty, my mouth sour and there is a steady thump at my temples.

The ache in my head sends me dizzy and I am gripped by unbearable thirst. I empty the water jug into the glass and drink it down. My eyes swim. *Jacob*, I think. Jacob, murdered by his mother's hand, returned to the home that was his.

I lie shivering under sheets that do not warm me until, finally, there are the sounds of far-off steps, of clatterings and bangings. The house is awake. But night will come again and I do not know how I will bear it.

There is a faint scent of rottenness on the air and I think that perhaps Jacob is here now in this cold dawn, his outline so faint in the morning light that I can no longer see him. Perhaps he is reaching out an arm to touch me. I think of leaving Guardbridge and of how much relief would be gained from being free of its haunting. But where would I go? And surely I could not take John and I have already failed one of my sons. To leave another is unconscionable.

After breakfast I make my way towards Iris's quarters. I know for all the desire I have to tell Iris what happened to gain comfort or explanation, I cannot. For what if Iris told Edward? For him to learn that his new wife believes herself haunted by his dead son would be too cruel, and, more than that, he would consider that I had lost my mind. As it is, I will have to tell him that I will not attend any further séances.

Iris is hunched and miserable in her chair, but as I enter she shows a spark of animation. Mrs North is wrapped in a blanket with a look of shock about her and the smile that forms on her lips is stiff and unnatural. The atmosphere still cradles last night's horror: Iris's hysteria and some echo of those cries that rent the air later.

I take a seat and wait for an explanation – they must know that I heard her.

'How are you, Mrs Stonehouse?' Mrs North's tone is cautious.

'As well as can be,' I say.

'Oh, Southy.' Iris closes her eyes. 'I must lie down; my back aches. Annie, you know by now I'm never fit for company after a sitting.'

Mrs North stands to accompany her to her bed-chamber.

The door closes behind them and I rise too and circle the floor. On one of the tables a raft of photographs catches my attention, but as I look my eyes are drawn to a familiar box – it is the one I have seen in Iris's workroom, filled with the messages she stitches under the skin of her creatures. I try the lid and find it unlocked. Curiously I pick out a piece of paper, unfolding it to read what it contains. *Forgive me*, it says. I try another and then another and finally, I reach deep down to the bottom but they all carry the same words. I remember Mrs North telling me that it was her mother Iris sought and to whom the messages were all sent. *Forgive me*. For what? Her temper, her cruelty, or something worse? It is as if the very quantity of these pleas must carry a greater sin in need of forgiveness. My mind goes back to what Marsha accused Iris of and a chill steals through me.

When Mrs North returns, I am sitting calmly.

She shakes her head.

I want to ask her again about Marsha's claim, to hear her tell me it is nonsense, but her loyalty to Iris is too great for me to believe I would hear the truth. But there are other things that sit heavily on me, and for all Edward's insistence that I do not discuss them I say, 'What was Jacob like?'

She regards me curiously, as if it were the last thing

she expected me to say. 'Jacob, he was – how can I describe him?' The pause is so long I am on the point of prompting her, when she continues. 'He was an independent child, one with a strong spirit. Because of his mother's distaste for all that Miss Stonehouse did, we did not see him a great deal.'

'The portraits Edward painted of him show him unhappy – even, I have thought, angry.'

'I dare say a child of a marriage as miserable as his parents' may well have been angry.'

'Edward told me how Evie died – and what she did to Jacob.'

'Oh.' She flushes. 'I wondered when you'd discover it. Something like that can't remain unknown for long. Did he tell you we were forbidden from disclosing it?'

'Yes, he did.'

'Well, I'm pleased he's revealed it finally. It didn't sit comfortably with me, hiding something so grievous.'

'Do you know the reason Evie would take her own life?'

'Mrs Stonehouse, we're really not supposed to talk of Evie.' She sighs and her eyes go to the window. The conflict she feels passes across her face and then she places both palms on her lap and her eyes grow serious. 'I'll tell you as much of her story that I feel I can, but please don't tell Mr Stonehouse I did.'

I tell her I will not.

'Evie Stonehouse's father was friends with Mr

Stonehouse's and I believe that even from children a betrothal was considered to be beneficial to both parties. The distance of the two families meant that Mr Stonehouse and Evie didn't spend much time together, but Mr Stonehouse fell in love with her all the same and heartily looked forward to their marriage. But as for Evie, I believe that although she professed love she only wed Mr Stonehouse because she was obligated to do so. I never met her family; like yours, they never visited and I have to assume they were not close.

'Mr Stonehouse must have realized early on that she didn't love him and it was a painful blow, as I'm sure you can imagine. When Jacob came, which, like you, happened very quickly, she was not much interested in him either. She went to town regularly and it seemed to me that it was only on these occasions that she showed any joy. I believe Mr Stonehouse . . . well, I believe he still loved her very much, but inevitably their marriage came under stress.

'Even from the first I could see how hard she tried to hide her aversion to Miss Stonehouse's mediumship and only appeared to tolerate it because Mr Stonehouse wanted her to. But as the years went on, she made little pretence of her dislike. She was quite a confident lady and liked to speak her mind.

'Well, for some years she and Mr Stonehouse appeared to manage, although Mrs Stonehouse, as has been said before, was very unhappy and difficult, but in the final twelve months Mr Stonehouse learned that secret you once asked me about. A secret so grievous that it was the cause of the final disintegration of their union. Mrs Stonehouse grew more fraught and challenging and there were financial concerns too. In the end it was not just her. Mr Stonehouse seemed to lose all reason too – his rages.' The worry lines about her eyes become more pronounced and I turn away to hide the swelling of dismay.

'Mrs Stonehouse blamed Miss Stonehouse for much of the conflict and she asked Edward to remove Miss Stonehouse to lodgings in town.' She pauses. 'In some ways I can't criticise her: you see –' she lowers her voice – 'it was the spirits that told Miss Stonehouse the secret and it was Miss Stonehouse who then told her brother.'

I feel sick. 'It was the spirits that discovered it?'

'It was.'

'What was the secret?'

But she shakes her head. 'I can't. If it became known that I'd been even this forthcoming, after being told not to discuss it, it would be bad enough. Please don't ask me that. But going back to her story, once Mr Stonehouse learned the secret he no longer let her leave for town. Their arguments worsened. Everything worsened. And Mr Stonehouse – so much fury. At this point they would have been better off apart.' She lets out a gasp, then lowers her voice. 'You mustn't repeat what I'm about to tell you. Towards the end Mrs Stonehouse ran away with Jacob.'

I am cold. 'When was this?'

'A month before she took her life.'

'Did she come back then?'

'Not of her own accord, no. *He* brought her back.' There is an inflection there that fills me with alarm.

'He?'

'Mr Stonehouse. Once again it was Miss Stonehouse's spirits that did it. They told her where Evie Stonehouse had fled to and she told her brother. He set out immediately and brought them back.' She falls quiet, her expression turning from sadness to anger.

'And those last weeks?' I think of the note in the robin: *Help me.*

'Coming back took what was left of her. She was not the same. If she had been unhappy before, it was clear that now she was truly wretched. Then one morning we woke to find them gone. We thought at first that she had run away again, but even as a search was planned their bodies were discovered a little downstream caught on roots.'

I look out to where the water rushes through the valley, unease pulsing ever faster inside me.

'Did she leave a note?'

She meets my eyes. 'There was no note.'

I rub warmth into my hands.

'I can see how it affects you,' she says. 'It's a terrible,

terrible tale and —' she frowns — 'one that won't have been easy for you to hear, Mrs Stonehouse, particularly after last night, which has clearly alarmed you. Are you quite well now?' She leans over and places a palm on mine. 'I hope you'll forgive me for not coming to your assistance, but Miss Stonehouse needed me.'

'I didn't need assistance,' I lie, 'and Iris clearly did.'

'But we heard you.'

I look at her, puzzled.

'You screamed,' she says, 'not long after you left.'

'No,' I say, 'that was Iris. It wasn't me. Don't you remember her mania in the séance? You were with her. I heard it just after I left. She screamed.'

I do not notice that the door to Iris's room is now open and she is standing in the frame. Her eyes on me are cool and assessing.

'It was you, *sister*. Not I,' she says smoothly. 'You were the one who called out.'

I lie on the bed and pull the blankets over me. Despite the heavy covers I am too chilled. When I close my eyes those cries ring through my memory: *No, no, no.* Me — it was me who spoke those words, not Iris, and now the night has been torn apart and I do not know any longer what truly happened. My world, I think, is disassembling brick by brick. I do not know what or who to believe — not Edward, not Iris and least of all myself.

A smell of rot continues to drift in the air and after lunch I consult Mrs Ford. I ask her to have a thorough investigation to discover the source of the odour and ask again about the locksmith.

'Aye, that's done, ma'am. I think he'll come in the next few days.' She coughs awkwardly. 'I took the liberty of inspecting the lock myself and it's damaged.'

'Damaged? I didn't see that.'

'You wouldn't, Mrs Stonehouse. I took a lamp and stood it on the other side – the breakage is on the inside. It's as if someone has taken a tool and destroyed the mechanism within.'

I'm speechless.

'I can see you're alarmed. I'm sure it was done a long time ago. While I was there, I also inspected the other door to your room.'

She does not say 'the door from Edward's quarters', and I admire her tact.

'Well, that too has been destroyed. In fact, if you look on the side that is in his dressing room, you will see marks that suggest to me that someone has attempted to remove the entire lock.'

'I see,' I say.

The knowledge is yet one more thing to cause disquiet and even though I now know that Evie had her chamber on the other side of Edward's, the fact that the lock to any room might be damaged is not a happy one.

*

Edward returns and joins me for dinner and part of me withdraws. I remember Mrs North's words – *his rages*. Have I assumed too much? Have I made a terrible mistake? I want to challenge him, to demand details. I try to swallow but each mouthful sticks in my throat. As I watch his hands on the cutlery or curled round his glass, I realize it is too easy now to imagine them flashing out in anger. I cannot eat the meat and take only a piece of bread and a glass of wine that sends my head spinning.

Edward watches me. He does not look pleased. 'You're changing, Annie. You're not happy.' His tone is weary as if he has had this conversation before. He drinks the wine as if it were water.

'Iris makes me a little afraid sometimes,' I say, attempting a lightness of tone that fails.

'Did she do something at the séance to alarm you?'

'No,' I lie. 'Perhaps it's my ties to a religious background after all.' Changing the subject, I ask, 'Did you tell Iris how we met? That day in Helmsworth?'

He gazes off into his memory with a sad smile. 'I remember the market square well and that you wore a brown coat with a green collar and green hat. I knew that I wanted to find out more of you. You reminded me of . . .' He shakes his head. 'You reminded me that happier times were possible.'

I recall that morning too and how the breeze touched my cheeks and how certain I had been of fate. 'But did you tell Iris?'

'Of course I told her. Without a wife Iris held the role of mistress of Guardbridge – answerable only to me. My marriage affects her position here.' He finishes his wine and pours more.

'But did you tell her the specifics? Do you recall how I told you later that there had been a stone in my shoe and how I didn't want to stop and remove it while you were watching?'

He laughs. 'No, I'd forgotten that. How like you, Annie. I suspect you'd suffer a great deal rather than show pain.'

His insight is startling and I lower my eyes to conceal what rushes to the surface of my thoughts. I shrug lightly, not accepting or dismissing his verdict. 'So you didn't tell Iris?'

'No, I think not. I've only just remembered myself. Did she tell you I had?'

I cannot answer. She saw it all – the spirits showed her. And so it is certain that sooner or later she will know what I hide.

'Annie?' Edward rises from his chair. 'You're as white as a sheet. Do you need to lie down?' He reaches out to touch my forehead and I flinch. With thinning lips he snaps his hand back. He is about to say something when he turns and leaves the room, slamming the door behind him.

It is not quite dawn. Something wakes me from a dream that has been deep and troubled. I glance down to where the sleeping draught sits on the table and consider a further dose that will keep me unconscious until the night is over. The wind has abated to silence but the odour of rot is present again and stronger. I sit up. There is a patter of footsteps. I turn to the door and am horrified to discover it open to the passageway beyond. There is someone there. I wait, breath held in suspension. Another step and I grip the bedding to my chest.

Something flits past the opening, too fast to catch it with my eye – then again, back the other way. Back and forth, back and forth and the sound of feet on the rug are faster and faster. Then, for one dreadful moment, it passes slowly and he stands there. The atmosphere grows frigid and stills. Time spools and stretches on its reel. From the blur of his face, his glittering eyes meet mine – biting into my very soul. Something wicked charges the air. My belly turns. Jacob.

Then he is gone.

20

The morning brings a pale sky and the sound of sparrows. It is still cold but spring is beginning to touch the landscape. There is assurance in the odours of meat and bread and coffee. I want to rub last night away, to remove the thing in the doorway but my knowledge is beyond doubt. How do I manage what I now know about Jacob's return? How do I continue to act as mother and wife, as mistress of this house, and all the while hide the growing horror inside me?

I know it is my fault. I touched the glass – I called him. It occurs to me that Jacob might visit the nursery and see my son lying in the bed that was his, watching his own father hold a new baby. But a ghost is a passive thing, is it not? It can look. Maybe it can touch and feel but it cannot harm. And Jacob, why of all the spirits who resided here, why him? Why not Evie? I ponder the tragedy of Jacob's life, his world stopped at seven years by his mother's hand; perhaps of all the harrowing stories weaved within Guardbridge's walls, his is the most pitiable.

As I leave my room, I pause outside my door. There is something on the floor, disguised by the rug's pattern: another black feather. I do not need to ponder its source; what Mrs North told me was clearly true.

With each turn of the hour fear is screwed tighter and tighter. When I go to Iris's quarters it is a surprise and a serendipitous one to find her alone. I take my seat aware of the subtle change in our relationship – gone is the easy friendship. How can I be comfortable knowing that at any moment she might discover what I conceal? I sense suspicion on her side too. Does she believe I tried to blame her for the wails that cut the air the night of the séance? The coldness of her tone makes me think she must. My eyes go to her hands and I think of her mother and those bruises about her neck.

'Where is Mrs North?'

'Her joints are sore today. All that rain. She's lying down.' Her voice is flat.

We exchange a few banalities but my thoughts tug constantly to Jacob. 'When the spirits come to you. Are they like ghosts?'

She sits up straighter. 'No,' she says, 'at least not in the traditional understanding we have of ghosts. I don't see them, only feel them.'

'And it's always been like that?'

'Always, and after I began using the Guardbridge Glass they began to write through me.'

'So there've been no ghosts at Guardbridge?'

'Oh, Annie, only those that the flighty maids imagine

on a wintry night in a creaking house, but, no, no ghosts at Guardbridge.'

'What is a ghost then if it isn't those spirits who talk to you?'

'A ghost is a very different thing. A ghost is a restless spirit, one who is troubled, or perhaps it's a spirit who returns to convey an important message. I think a ghost must be a person who in life suffered injustice, unhappiness or violence or perhaps who left this life with something unsaid.'

'So a ghost is unhappy and comes because there is something to communicate?'

'Perhaps, or maybe it's their misery that calls them back, as if they might finally find peace in the place that caused harm.'

See me. 'Maybe to be acknowledged?'

'Or that too. To be seen – to have that life or that unhappiness recognized.' She is reflective.

'Can they harm?' I ask.

'Have you heard of poltergeists?'

'Those spirits that move things around?'

'Yes. Noisy spirits – there are cases of people being thrown out of bed, of objects being flung.'

'And these poltergeists can be seen? As one might a ghost?'

'I'm not sure that the poltergeist is ever glimpsed. I think usually they're witnessed by their actions.'

'And a ghost then? A ghost cannot harm?'

'Oh, I didn't say that.'

Why had I asked? 'What of evil or ill-meaning spirits? Don't you worry that they might come when you use the glass?'

'That's never happened. I trust the glass.'

I do not, I think, and shudder. I have learned enough. To say more would be to give myself away.

'Why do you ask about ghosts, Annie?' Her gaze ranges over me and those dreamy eyes seem to comb inside my skull.

'I'm interested,' I say.

But there is suspicion now.

In a flash she reaches across and takes my hand. I try to pull away but she holds fast. She presses her palm over mine – her hand hot on my cold one – and a shiver of connection passes between us. I try to tug away but it is as if we are glued together and I do not have the power to separate us.

She looks up at me. There is shock in her features and something worse – fear. 'Jacob?' she whispers. 'Jacob?'

I do not answer.

'I hear your thoughts. Jacob came – to you?' She rips her hand away and wipes it on her dress as if my skin had infected her.

The truth is on my face.

Understanding dawns. 'When you screamed after

you left us. You saw him then.' Something else creeps into her expression. It looks like envy.

'You have to help me, Iris. I can't bear his presence. I can't.'

Her eyes narrow. 'He's not come to hurt you. You must open your mind now to the other world that sits alongside ours; you're afraid of what you don't understand, that's all. I tried to help you, but you refused to believe. If he comes to you, it's a privilege – one I would gladly exchange you for.' She frowns, then her voice is hesitant. 'Does he speak to you?'

'No. Can a ghost speak?'

'He could speak to you – yes.'

What would he say if he did? Surely only messages of spite. 'He hates me,' I say.

'Annie, what's this? How could he hate you? Why would he?'

'Because I'm here and he was murdered – this is still his house. I feel it. He means ill.'

'No –' her tone is sharp – 'I won't believe it of him.' She pauses. 'He comes for some reason, but why you, Annie, why you?'

'For the reasons I say – I don't want to speak to him or see him ever again. He can come to you if you choose, Iris – take him. Make him leave me alone. I don't know how I'm to bear it.'

'I can't do that, but I must know everything. Tell me all you have seen, in detail.'

I recount the occasions, repelled by the shine of avidity on her eye. 'You mustn't tell Edward. Can you imagine how he'd feel?' I say. 'Or anyone – not even Mrs North.'

'I won't tell Edward but Southy's a good egg. She won't give you away.'

'I know, Iris. But can I trust you to keep your counsel?'

She smooths her hair. It is clear this kind of confidence appeals to her. 'You haven't told Edward about my . . . about my turns, so Southy tells me, and I'm grateful. I will keep your secret, Annie.'

But suddenly her look turns glassy and her hands fall idle. When she speaks it is in that unconscious way that she does at the séance. I want to put my palms to my ears again. I do not want to hear what she has to utter.

'It's all gone bad. All wrong.'

Flora brings extra lamps, leaving no space unlit. If I sit and read a book, I will manage the night, but the thought of those hours begins to thrum anxiously through me. When Flora has gone I get the bottle of sleeping draught and spill drops to the spoon.

Time passes and the room blurs. My body softens, becomes something of air, and my mind soon follows, floating beyond every concern, every worry. Nothing matters. I know no more.

Something wakes me. With panic I look to the door, but it is mercifully shut. A sound, a cry. Not Iris, a child. John's. He will stop. *Agnes will calm him*, I think, but on it goes. I sit up and swing my legs from the mattress, reaching for my gown. My thoughts are slow, still half drowning. John. I must go to him.

I push my feet into slippers. Carefully I ease open the door to the passageway and listen. Silence then another cry. Holding the lamp high to give the most light, I walk quickly to the servants' staircase.

The floor creaks beneath my feet and a gleam from the skylight paints the landing. There is a quietness now, so deep it is hard to imagine that it has just been broken. I am at John's nursery and I press my ear to the keyhole, expecting to hear Agnes. Nothing.

Easing it open I peer in. The candle flame glimmers on his crib and I see him stir, one chubby arm thrown outwards and settling. I close the door. He had not cried out at all. I imagined it.

Back in my chamber, the stench is back and stronger than ever. A whine cuts through the night – as high and fierce as a mosquito's hungry urgency. Taking the lamp, I pull open the cupboard, eliciting a wave of foul air.

But the cupboard is no longer empty – it is as if my own fear, my own conviction, has materialized it out of nothing. Because the diorama is back, and now it spins, the lamp catching the blind white eyes of the animals – the gleam of feather and skin and the reek of decay. My belly heaves. The birds hang unnaturally – their feathers floating to the ground.

Covering my nose, I drag a chair to unhook it, but the smell is so foul that I am forced to step away. Who could have discovered where I had hidden it and returned it to this cupboard? And I imagine Jacob's small white fingers reaching upwards.

I close the door and open the windows, then dab cologne beneath my nostrils. I get into bed. Then I remember the cry and realize that it had never been infantile. It was not John but a child much older. And, as I lie frozen between the sheets, it comes again and I cover my ears, but even through flesh and bone I hear it, on and on – the cry of a dead child, of a ghost.

I take the laudanum bottle again and drop more on to the spoon, then I lay my head on the pillow. *Help me*, I think, but as I beseech the universe for an end to torment, there comes an ache deep inside me, something bruised and flowering; it is pity for the child who, even in death, makes a sound so mournful it could break a heart.

21

After George has dealt with the removal of the diorama I go downstairs to huddle over the fire. Edward comes in dressed in his travelling clothes.

'I'm going away for a while, Annie.'

He waits for me to say something, to ask about the absence, but I cannot. I can barely summon the energy for an appropriate response. He gives me a look of such intense displeasure that I shudder, then he turns on his heel and storms away without another word. When Iris enters a little later she sweeps into the room with a gaiety that lowers my mood even more and has me turn from her. Has she no regard for how I feel?

When she sees me, there is a fleeting expression of concern that soon passes. Even before I open my mouth she says, 'Listen, Annie, I sent Mrs North to her own entertainment and came to see you. I can't think of anything but what you told me. We must talk of it. Yes, I know you touched the glass, but this means you have the ability to call the spirits back in a way I can't.'

She knows. What else has she learned? How can she talk so easily of something so heinous, so wrong?

'I can see you don't wish to discuss it, but you must listen, Annie, please.'

'I only want him gone.'

She leans towards me. 'But this is a gift. Such a gift. Think, if you can bring back Jacob, you could bring other spirits back. I'd give everything to be able to do what you can.'

'No, Iris. Absolutely no. The very last thing I'd consider doing is that.'

'But you could summon my mother.' She pauses for breath. 'My mother, Annie.' Her eyes glaze. 'You don't know what it's like to lose one; how could you?'

She must be insane.

'Why would you want your mother to return? A ghost is not a person.'

'I've sought my mother since her death. But she never comes. If you brought her back, it would mean everything to me.'

I think of her message box. *Forgive me.* 'What do you want to say to her?'

But she shakes her head.

'I can't do it,' I say. 'And can you be sure that if I touch the glass again, it will be your mother who comes? I didn't call Jacob, but it's him who visits me.'

'I'll be there too and will touch the glass with you.'

'Doing what you ask is the very last thing I would do. I can't be any part of it,' I say.

She smiles a strange smile that I cannot read. 'But you will.'

'No,' I say, my voice rising, 'I won't. If I called Jacob, it's not a good thing, not a kind thing – it's not something that brings pleasure. It's wrong. I know it in my bones.' I recall that night of the first séance and the feel of the glass upon my skin, the tug at my belly and the regret, with all my heart, that I had done as I had. I want to cry tears of helpless remorse, but I am frozen with disbelief.

'You will, Annie. And you'll do another thing too; when Jacob next visits, because visit he will, you'll guide him to me. It's to me he should have come – not only because of our blood tie but because it's me who knows how to communicate with the dead.'

'You're mad,' I say.

'If Jacob has returned, he's come for a reason. I must know what it is. At the next séance I'm going to tell Mrs North to leave us. We'll touch the glass together and call my mother. And when Jacob next comes to you, you lead him to me.' She reaches into her pocket and passes me a box.

'What's this?'

'Open it.'

Inside are a candle and a feather.

'Tonight you'll burn this candle and leave the feather by your door. It's an invitation to Jacob.'

I shake my head. 'I've told you already. I'm not doing any of it. If I speak to him at all, and I have no intention of doing so, it will be to ask him to leave me alone. It's wicked.'

Anger flickers across her face. 'It's quite the opposite. It's a wonder. There's no greater gift.'

'I won't do it.'

'You will.' There is no trace of doubt.

I wonder at the change in her – gone is friendship and kindness and with it my feelings of liking. I stand shakily. 'I'm going now.'

'Sit.'

I begin to walk away but she blocks my path. 'Sit. You will hear this.'

With resignation I retake the chair.

'I know your secret, Annie.'

My insides turn to ice but I keep my face expressionless.

She smiles humourlessly and her eyes glide to my midriff. 'I've known it for some time. The spirits told me.'

'I have no secret,' I lie.

'You can't hide it. Even now it's as clear as if your first child were still latched to your breast. You fool, Annie.'

I am dizzy with horror. 'What kind of a sister are you?'

She flushes and looks away. And even now the

shadows turn in the room and night begins — slipping under the eaves like a thief and opening doors from which all that is unspeakable can flow. She looks to the window where a faint moon is sketched in the sky. 'Take the candle and feather. Do as I say and I won't tell Edward what I know.'

Almost in tears I pick up the box.

She stands, straightens her skirt and her eyes skate mine. 'And tonight call Jacob and guide him to me.' Then she leaves, closing the door quietly behind her.

I cannot face another person and so find my coat and boots. Dusk has come down upon the moor, rendering it to shadow. Soon it will be night. Pacing quickly, I try to jolt the horror out of me. There is no doubt that Guardbridge is haunted, but what of Iris? I struggle to understand how she has turned so quickly from friend to enemy and that I have so thoroughly misread her character. The band of pain that cuts my midriff is as much about the loss of her as a companion as it is the thought of what she has demanded.

How will I do as she asks? But if I do not, then surely Iris will reveal my secret to Edward. Would he have me leave? I recall Evie and her desperate escape and how he brought her back. But was it only Jacob he was thinking of? If Evie had fled alone, would he have troubled to discover her? And suddenly I am pierced through with the idea that I could lose John.

And in this moment of confusion and fear I stumble across something else entirely, and it is love; the love of John that has kept itself so hidden. I pause and close my eyes and feel the swell of it like the wave that will carry me back to shore after I have been lost at sea. Love. Oh, John.

As I return, wind blows the scent of gorse across the moor and the air is filled with the calling of finches and meadow pipits preparing for roost. Approaching Guardbridge I have made up my mind that I will do as Iris asks; there are things far worse. I truly know that now.

At the house, I have Agnes bring John and I wait until she has left. I know that I could not hide the grateful joy I feel as I cradle him to my chest or the tears that come with the knowledge of each neglected moment. And in this hour all horror pauses as I drink in the wonder of him with all of my being.

Flora has left me for the night. With trembling fingers I take the box Iris gave me and set it on the bed beside me. The candle is a darker shade than the ones I am accustomed to — fat and yellowed with a dirty patina — and a wick of black thread.

Taking a match, I heat the base and watch the tallow drip, then fix it to the chamber stick. Is it my imagination or does it burn brighter than other candles?

Dust dulls the surface of the feather and I am repelled by its texture. I lay it outside my door, then I pause and listen to the sounds of the house and take in its night scents. I shiver.

When that is done, I return to bed and pour drops of laudanum into my glass. At least I can hide in oblivion. The candle burns with a pungent aroma and in it there is something familiar, but it is not a flower or herb I can name. I let the idea pass and lie under the covers and watch the ceiling and the shapes that play upon it. My mind begins to fog. I close my eyes. What will be will be.

I dream, I am walking the passageway towards the oriel window. I am not alone. Every now and then I look down to where my hand is clasped to another's.

'Mama,' he says. 'Mama.' And the word echoes back and forth, back and forth, like a song. The ringing of Iris's glass fills the corridor and I turn to him. 'You've come a long way,' I say.

'The distance is short when measured by the heart.'

I ponder. 'You must go back now.'

'But how do I leave you?'

I do not have an answer, so I look up and point. Above us, instead of ceiling, is an arcing vault of sky where feathers drift down from the stars like a snow-storm and carpet the floor with their fall.

*

I wake. The air is filled with the musky scent of the candle. Something has woken me – some *thing*. The candle burns brighter than before, fizzing and spitting on its wick. My head is fuzzy, my vision blurred. I sit up and look to the door but it is closed. There is an unnatural chill and something in the press of air that is wrong. Utter silence. I am not alone. He is here in my room. All I have to do is look and he will be standing and gazing at me with eyes that should be blind. Dead eyes.

The flame grows and now I see fully. I gasp. He is there – in the corner. It is no hallucination. His edges are smudged – a face not fully defined but there. I cannot move. I wait for something to happen – for my voice to sound or for him to step up and touch me, this dead child, and yet I am still sitting and staring as I sense him staring back. But before I call out it is he who walks to the door and is turning the handle, he who opens it and beckons to me and in spite of everything, everything, I push back the covers and stand.

Shivering with fear and cold, I slip on my gown and walk into the freezing corridor. At the stairs I hesitate. I must take him to Iris. Pausing I turn towards her quarters but Jacob ignores me and is already at the bottom, moving through the murky hall.

Through the passageway to the scullery we go, past the boot rooms and laundry, past the cold store and pantry and to the rough wood door that opens on to a scrap of yard where in the day hens peck between the cobbles for crumbs and weeds. Into the frosty air and the sky with a littering of bright stars. I look up to the moon that hangs heavy, gilding the edges of black cloud.

He stops and waits.

We pass along the edge of the courtyard where the arch opens to a view of the river. He stops and turns his head to the sound of it and I think he is going to walk into the water from where he came and take me with him. But I am not afraid. I imagine the fierce current and a desperate part of me welcomes it – how I will sink beneath the surface until my eyes see not the pebbled bottom but that other world which I know now must exist. Tears begin to chase down my face. I think of you, and I think of John, who my heart betrayed in those first months. Perhaps death is no more than I deserve. Yet he does not go through the arch. He walks on until we reach the north wing door and, opening it, he passes through. Only the faintest light of the moon from the grimed windows touches the hallway. It must be some sort of magic that does not have me stumbling.

He does not take the stairs but a stretching hallway, rivulets of water running on wet stone from some unrepaired leak. A creature bolts from a corner and across my path. I neither recoil nor react. I only follow.

But now the depth of darkness masks the walls and I can barely see him. I put a hand out to steady myself.

Ahead, a faint glimmer from a window illuminates his outline. We come to a lobby and a servant's staircase. Up to the first floor, and up again, and finally we come to the attics where a skylight lays a film of light. Here, another staircase to the garrets above. He begins to climb. At the top he turns and beckons, but the moon is lost again and now the opacity is perilous.

I place a foot upon a step that is slippy with damp and it slides across, nearly causing me to fall. There is no rail. If I died here, who would find me? Or worse — what if I were to break a leg and not be able to make my way back? So I step down and watch until he disappears beyond. Silence. As I gaze up to blackness above, I sense suddenly that he has gone and instead of relief I am strangely bereft.

I return carefully to the main house, closing the door quietly behind me. Back in my room I strip off my damp and filthy nightdress. Even in my fogged mind I know I must hide it. I open the cupboard that held the mobile and lay it there, then back in bed I close my eyes, which feel oddly weighted, and there is something in my hand. I uncurl my fist; it is the black feather that Iris gave me. I do not remember picking it up.

*

Iris cannot sleep. She wishes it were the full moon and she could use the glass, wishes the spirits would say more, but it is as if they too are waiting for Jacob to return to Guardbridge.

Her notebook lies open but no wisdom has been imparted and she imagines Jacob walking the passage-way to Annie's room, imagines him standing before her. Does Annie not realize that there is nothing to fear? And yet, and yet, why has he returned? What is it he has come to say?

She recalls the night they died, pulls her shawl tighter and shivers. There are things there that do not bear close examination.

22

It is already late when I wake from a sleep that leaves me struggling to full consciousness. I wonder now if the night was real or some laudanum hallucination. Yet there, on the pillow beside me, is the feather. I ask Flora for tea and when she has left I try to stand, though a wave of dizziness forces me back to the coverlet. When I am steady enough, I take the candle and go to the cupboard where I find my gown and nightdress. I did not dream it.

During the morning I experience that strange return to physicality after the absence achieved with laudanum. My limbs are too heavy and my mood sunken and confused. I think about the journey to the north wing attics and burn to know what is there. And what will I tell Iris? Will I admit he came?

As soon as I am able, I make my way back, tracing the route I took last night. At the attic stairs I climb carefully to the room above. My heart races, and with each placing of my foot comes the dread that he will be waiting, this ghost child who has chosen me to be his witness. I pause at the top and catch my breath.

The door to the garret stands open to its dank and

bleak interior. I cannot turn away now, and so I step as lightly as I can inside.

He is not there.

I examine the room and its sparse and neglected furnishings – a line of toy soldiers stands in regiment on an oak chest – and I recall Mrs North once mentioning Jacob leaving the house to avoid the arguments. Was this the refuge he chose from his parents' disputes? With a pinch of sadness I gaze out of the grime-streaked window as he must so often have done.

It is then that I see a piece of paper laid carefully on a table. On closer examination I discover it is torn from something else. The page is strewn with pieces of writing, all in what appear to be different hands and I recognize it instantly as having come from Iris's notebook. Am I to assume that Jacob put it here? Or is he alerting me to the fact it was left here by Iris herself? I scan it quickly but the script is illegible, so I stuff it in my pocket and leave. It is quiet when I enter the main house and I hurry up to my chamber.

Taking the paper from my dress, I try to decipher what is there but halfway down my eye is drawn to a sentence; the letters are larger in size than the others, giving them emphasis.

If Evie and Jacob do not leave Guardbridge, they will die. Edward cannot be trusted.

My heart chills — their deaths had been predicted before the event itself, but the implicit meaning also fills me with dismay and its echo to what I found written in Evie's desk a few weeks ago: *if I do not leave here soon, I fear I shall die.* I think of Edward. How easy, I reflect, to lose control — for one act of violence to lead to another, and then, and then, to take a body and dispose of it in the river and frame it as Evie's own doing. But if I am to believe that, then all is lost. And Jacob? No, I chide myself, to kill a child, his own son, is unthinkable; I will not believe Edward has it in him to do this. Evie took her own life. She must have done, and, besides, he was not here that night, or so it has been said. And then my thoughts slide to Iris and I wonder exactly what she is capable of. Mrs North had told me of Evie's plans to send Iris away from her beloved Guardbridge. Iris must have known that.

I wish I knew when the words had been written. The two statements do not necessarily relate directly to each other; it is possible Edward was not to be trusted regarding other things — discovering Evie's secret, for example. And it is true that Evie and Jacob perished here — making the statement about them dying at Guardbridge one more thing foreseen — but Iris will have read what she wrote, and later, after Evie had fled the house and the spirits revealed her hiding place, she still told her brother — and they were brought back, sealing their fates. Did Iris not consider that?

I do not believe it was Iris who tore the page out and left it there – better she destroyed it – so it must have been Jacob. Why else lead me to it unless he wanted me to know that his death was not as I have been told and to warn me?

I look out to the cold sky and wonder when Edward will come home; he has been longer than expected. What keeps him? And I recall the visit he made to my parents and imagine him returning there and demanding that they explain their dislike and discovering what drove me under his roof.

At the dressing table I tidy my hair. There are lines on my skin that speak of sleepless nights and fear.

I call for my workbox with the intention of keeping to my chamber, dreading the moment I must face Iris. I am not ready to talk of last night or what I discovered. Try as I might, I cannot focus and, as my mind races, my needle remains idle.

When the knock on the door inevitably comes, I know it is her, and I struggle for composure. Once inside, her eyes go immediately to the candle.

'Did he come?'

'I did as you said, but no,' I lie.

She walks about the room, runs a fingertip across the dresser and desk and touches the coverlet. At the panelling where the diorama was hidden, she pauses and lays a hand on the wood, and I wonder now if my assumption that the diorama was Evie's was ever correct. Perhaps Iris herself made it and hung it there. But why? To undermine me? Or did it have some supernatural effect that Iris thought she could use against me? Did it help to bring Jacob?

I push the thread through the silk, trying to ignore her.

Iris says, 'He came.'

If I look up, she will see my deception, so I keep my gaze fixed down.

When she pulls up a chair opposite and takes the needle from my fingers I have to raise my head. And now I see her close to I am appalled at the alteration in her. It is like looking in a mirror: the shadows have grown beneath her eyes and she is not happy; all animation has gone, leaving this fraught and troubled creature.

'What did he do?'

'He didn't come,' I insist.

'Did you try?'

'I lit the candle, as you said. You can see for yourself that it was done.'

'Then you will light the candle again tonight.'

I ignore her.

'Do you want me to tell Edward your secret?'

'I've already done as you ask, Iris,' I say. 'No. Please, no.'

She puts her head in her hands; the nails are bitten

to the quick. 'Please, Annie, if Jacob doesn't want to visit me, I will bear that, but since I know it may be possible to call my mother, I'll never be at peace until I speak to her. If you understood, you might have more pity for what I request.'

'Then tell me. What is it that's so important? You talk about your peace while you destroy mine.'

Her lip trembles. 'I can't.' I gaze on, unmoved, and I am glad she does not confess. I do not want to hear it spoken aloud. I think of Edward knowing my secret and then consider Evie's. Was it worse than mine?

'What was Evie's secret?'

She sighs. 'Very well. I don't think there's any sense in not revealing it and I've asked a lot of you, so I will tell you. Evie was in love with another; had been in love with him even before she married Edward. She never loved my brother. If this were not bad enough, she continued her affair with this man throughout the marriage until Edward discovered it. She lied about everything.'

I recall Edward's twisted expression when he told me she held a secret, and it is Edward who I see now destroying her beloved instrument, punishing her for her terrible betrayal.

A sly look creeps over her features. 'Now, consider yours, Annie – what will Edward think if he knows that another woman has betrayed him? That John has a brother? Perhaps I have a duty to tell him anyway. He deserves to know about your child. He suffers not just from your silence but by what this has done to you.'

'What do you mean?'

'It's been clear from the first that you're not happy – I see your preoccupation, and, not only that, how you hardly dare love the son or the husband you are lucky enough to have. You think when Edward learns what you've hidden that it will destroy your marriage, but it's destroying it already. You walk through life like a ghost, Annie. Like a ghost.'

My throat is too full of emotion to speak; her words have stunned me. Everything she has said is the truth.

She stands, her face set hard.

'Will you tell?' I call. 'Will you?'

'Come to the next séance.'

She slams the door behind her. My hands are shaking and my heart pounds. There is no question that I will do as she asks, but will she tell Edward regardless? I do not trust her. I go to the window that will hold the moon blazing in all its fullness and shudder at the part I am going to play.

How has night come again so quickly? Time has ceased to obey its strictures and, once again, slows and speeds as if it had a will of its own. I have lost hours and now I am back in my chamber, the smell of dinner fading on the air, Flora pouring water into the tub, my white skin, veined with blue, my ribs sharp as I soap them.

Flora's hands are soft on my back and I recall my mother. How old had I been, sitting in the hip bath by the stove? Her fingers were gentle; she had washed my hair, crooning as she did. How had I forgotten that? She loved me once. She loved me. Afterwards she wrapped a towel about me, lifted me in her arms and stroked my cheek, brushed out my hair. I remember the patch of blue through the window. Gulls calling on the wind. The cat watching us from the kitchen chair.

'Mrs Stonehouse?' Flora's voice is full of concern. I had not realized I was crying. I stand, dripping suds and water, grab the towel and stumble to the bed.

'What can I do? What's the matter? Should I fetch someone?'

I can barely control my voice. 'I need a moment. Let me have a moment, please, Flora.' She hesitates, wipes her wet hands on her apron, then, casting me anxious glances, makes her way to the door. The tears will not stop. I am not crying; I am sobbing as if my heart had broken. Fear and loss pummel me in a fury of grief. I remember holding you that first time, you, my first beloved son. I recall you gone, the hands that pushed me back to the cot, the bitter taste of some cure that would send me to delirium, a voice ringing in the air. My voice: *No, no, no.*

And John — the risk of losing him too and the tears keep falling, pain swelling and receding with each onslaught, on and on until my throat is sore and the pillow damp. Eventually they diminish. I am numb. I sit up and press a handkerchief to my eyes.

I think of all the mistakes I have made. You whose name I never spoke aloud, whose name is only in my heart.

I go to the desk and take out my pen.

Dear Mama,

I hope this letter finds you and the family in good health. I have to tell you that I am not well, not in my mind, and have not been for a long time. You know from what event this sickness comes. Although I understand why you gave my son away, I cannot go on without knowing where he went and that he is safe and cared for.

It is not my intention to harm or disturb his life by revealing myself to him unless there is a way to do this that would not injure him. For now I will be satisfied with the knowledge that he is loved. But until I know this I do not believe that I can ever find peace.

If not for mine, for the sake of John.

Yours,
Anne

A fox barks on the moor and I go to the window where the moon drifts in a starry sky. The moor is in darkness. I press my brow to the cold glass. My head aches. I have never been so wretched in my entire life.

23

It starts late morning, when cloud begins to move ominously across the skies, blotting out the landscape. Soon rain hurls itself upon the house like an act of retribution. The staff busy themselves, shoring up sills with rags and placing buckets that soon ring with the sound of waterdrops. Outside, the moor blurs. The rain becomes a backdrop beat to the swell of damp air that sours the rooms.

Sometime after lunch Flora falls ill, emptying her stomach violently into a pail. But it is not only Flora — soon the rest of the staff succumb too. The source is soon identified as a stew that Bessie had left out the night before and which was served to the staff. Only the family, Agnes, who had fallen asleep and missed it altogether, and Mrs North, who eats as we do, are spared.

In the absence of servants Mrs North fusses around arranging what she can and marvelling that at least the ladies of the house remain unharmed, and by three o'clock she has seen all those who are ill to their beds, pale and sweating. Apart from the rain, the house falls to unaccustomed silence; I had not realized how much those distant whispering steps and voices, the sound of doors opening and closing, had become such a reassuring refrain.

I am surprised when Mrs North comes to my room where I sit over a sultry fire. 'Mrs Stonehouse.' Her tone is hesitant.

'Please come in. I would be grateful for companionship. Where is Iris?'

'She's in and out of trance today and will probably remain so for yet more hours in my experience. It's so chilly here.' Mrs North rubs her palms over the flames. 'I actually came to invite you to take tea with me. There's bread and cake too, in our parlour. It'll be cosier there.'

'I'm not sure,' I say. 'Iris might get up.'

'In which case you can make an exit.'

I follow a little reluctantly, but in spite of Mrs North's assurances as to the cosiness of their quarters, when I sit myself down the room is sullen and chilled. Mrs North pours tea and I take a piece of bread and butter.

'You look exhausted,' she says. 'It's been a difficult time for you all round, hasn't it?' She lowers her voice. 'Miss Stonehouse tells me everything and I hope you don't mind me mentioning it, but she informed me the spirits told her you'd had a child before.'

My heart begins to pace.

She places a hand over mine. 'Shush now, no need to say anything. She explained the circumstances of his conception. You poor child. See, men are wicked creatures in my experience and not to be trusted.'

'Not all men,' I whisper.

'Too many. But I brought you here because there's something you should know.' She pauses and the lines about her eyes deepen. 'I cannot carry the knowledge of what I've learned and remain easy, though, in telling you, I'm aware that I'm betraying a secret. But this is too important for you not to be party to. Can I trust you to keep it to yourself?'

Wind storms the chimney, spitting embers to the hearth and sending the candle flames flickering wildly on their stems. I feel the heft of something unpalatable to come.

'Yes. What is it?' I say.

'I'm truly sorry to be the bearer of bad news but Miss Stonehouse has written to your husband. Your secret is out. Please forgive me for causing consternation but since I have known I have barely thought of anything else and what he might do when he learns it.'

Faint with shock, I lean back against the chair. Dread coils in my belly. How could she? No wonder her last plea was so desperate – once Edward returns and the truth is out she will have no leverage over me.

I gasp. 'But why? She led me to believe she hadn't.'

'Miss Stonehouse is many things, and I have the deepest affection and respect for her, but I would be lying if I didn't say that she is afflicted with the hottest of tempers. Your falling-out has caused her great distress, but I also think that her loyalty to her brother is too great to ignore.'

'When?' I say. 'When did she send it?'

'I'm afraid it was a few days ago.' She looks out to the downpour. 'He's already overdue. The letter will certainly hurry him back. Do you think he'll come today?'

The bread sticks in my throat and I imagine him inside the coach, the sound of hooves splashing through puddles on the uneven road.

'He may know already,' I say, and faced now with the terrible reality of it I have to reassure myself that my secret is not as wicked as Evie's and surely, surely, when he learns that you were born out of an act in which I was not a willing participant he will not punish me. But I shudder and think of the words from Iris's notebook. *If Evie and Jacob do not leave Guardbridge, they will die. Edward cannot be trusted.*

'He wouldn't hurt me,' I say, but even as I utter it I hear the sound of my father's boot on my mother's flesh.

Mrs North stokes the fire.

'Would he?' I press.

She takes a long time to answer, then from her pocket she hands me a letter.

'What's this?'

Her eyes glide to Iris's closed door and in a voice so

248

quiet I have to lean towards her, she says, 'I think you should read it.'

I take it and unfold it on my lap.

Dear Mrs North,

I have decided that there is no other recourse than to leave here with Jacob. I think you are the only one who will understand. It was wrong of me to marry Edward when my heart belonged to another and, believe me, I tried hard to end it before I married, but I could not.

Now that Edward has learned my secret, I grow more and more afraid. He is a man of such rages. It is not a rage that passes but one that is constantly aggravated by my presence here. I believe that if I do not leave, I will die here. I do not trust the man I married.

Yours,
Evie Stonehouse

I look up, aghast.

'I understand you had a locksmith change your locks.'

I nod dumbly.

'It didn't help her.'

'What do you mean? Evie's room was on the other side.'

'No,' Mrs North says. 'I thought you knew. Before you the room belonged to her.'

'But I was told her things were elsewhere.'

'When you married, Mr Stonehouse requested that you should have new furniture and decoration. It was only her furniture and possessions that were transported to a different location.'

I think back and realize that I had never been told specifically that the room was not Evie's. It was I who made the assumption. It is then that I recall something else: when Evie died, all the staff had gone – there were no witnesses to her death. When I had asked, Iris had quickly recounted that scarlet fever would clear a house of its maids, but it had been a lie – they had never died of fever.

'When Evie died, the house was empty but for you and Iris – why was that?'

Her eyes darken. 'Do you want to know?'

'Yes,' I whisper.

'He told them all to go. Two nights before Evie and Jacob died. It was he who rid the house of all but us.'

'Edward?' Why will she not say his name?

'Mr Stonehouse,' she hisses.

I have been a fool. How have I been such a fool?

In the shock that follows comes the sound of rain on glass and the rising gale. Mrs North's face is unreadable, then she places her cup upon the table and looks at me intently. 'Didn't you ever feel the emptiness inside him?' she says gently.

I shiver. Edward? I realize I have assumed that, like

me, he has come adrift of his emotions following tragedy, which explains his aloofness. But what if that is a misconception? What if I have misread his distance from the start? What if he is empty because he contains no heart?

I must know. 'The night Evie died, he told me he was away. Was he?'

'I can't lie to you, Mrs Stonehouse. He was here.'

The lamps quiver in their globes and the room darkens. Ice slips into my blood.

I get up and pace the floor with agitation. Can I have been so mistaken? Then I think of Jacob – no, I will not believe him capable of that. It is too much. Relief comes and softens those parts of me that are pulled as tight as violin strings. But why lie about where he had been?

'But Jacob,' I say, 'even if he took his rage out on Evie, he couldn't have hurt a child? His own son. It's unconscionable.'

She looks up at me then; shadows of the rain that streams on the windows run down her face like tears. 'Didn't you know? Didn't Miss Stonehouse tell you?'

'Tell me what?'

She pauses, her eyes round with dread, then in hushed tones she says, 'That day, that day before she died, Mr Stonehouse discovered that Jacob was not his. He was the son of the lover she never gave up.'

Oh God. Now terror does not come walking but

galloping. I hear his horses on the track, Edward urging the carriage on. 'Make haste. Can't you go faster?' And he is thinking of me – of the child I have already borne, of my lies – of how, once again, he has married a woman he cannot trust.

'Mrs Stonehouse? You look very ill.'

Shock. It is shock I feel. The frames shudder as wind battles the house. The downpour hammers on the roof tiles. I have to ask; I must, although I feel myself shirking from something that is so abominable that even to think it must be the end.

'Do you believe she took her own life?'

The question is out there now. I cannot take it back.

She puts her face in her hands and, when she looks up, her eyes are grazed by tears. She shakes her head. 'No,' she whispers, 'I do not.'

I cannot stay here. I know that now. I must surely go.

Mrs North comes and puts an arm round me. 'I'm so sorry but you had to be told. What will you do?'

I cannot think for panic – my thoughts scatter like early blossom – but even as I clasp my hands in turmoil I know that staying is an impossibility.

'I have to leave,' I say, but I look at the torrent outside the window with trepidation.

Her expression crumples. 'Oh, Mrs Stonehouse.'

'How can I go safely in such weather? It will soon be night.'

She thinks. 'I haven't walked it for years, but there's

a path over the moor from the milepost on the main road. If you follow it you'll come to a hill and just beyond is a farmhouse. It's a good family that live there. They would give you shelter tonight and help you on your way.'

'But the moor will be treacherous. I must go by the road.'

'What will you do if he is returning on the same track?'

I had not thought of that.

'The path is reliable – it's a little way in but should lead you safely and it won't take long to get there.'

Bewilderment and anger billow through me. Iris must have known how Evie and Jacob died; she must have known what danger I was in. She has misguided me in every way. Yet, knowing all that, she still wrote to her brother. She never cared for me at all.

'Iris talked about having written a letter for you.'

'There's nothing she can say that I want to hear.'

'I think it must be important. Wait here.' Mrs North gets up and goes to her bedroom.

While she is gone, I ponder what Iris might have written and eventually curiosity has me go to her chamber. I scour the surfaces, open drawers and peruse her desk but there is no evidence of Mrs North's claim. I go and stand beside the bed.

'Iris,' I snap.

She does not wake but stirs, her brow furrowing as

she moans, turning under the covers as if in pain. Her skin is deathly pale. I regard her with loathing.

Mrs North joins me and puts something into my hands. It is a leather pouch. 'Take this money. It'll see you clear for a week or so.'

I can barely utter thanks. 'There's no letter.'

She too searches, then shrugs. 'Perhaps she changed her mind. It was most probably not important. It's not worth trying to wake her, Mrs Stonehouse. You won't, not when she's like this.'

But I am no longer studying her face because I am looking at the notebook lying open beside her. I do not want to see more horror but already my eyes have found those last lines and they bore into my brain.

Edward is on his way. Run, Annie. Run.

I need no more prompting. I run.

24

The clock chimes five. My mind races with practicalities but I must force myself to be calm. *John*, I think. He is the one I must think of. I will cross the moor to the farmhouse and later pay for transport to Mrs Breach. From there I must ask if Mrs Breach has friends or acquaintances who might offer me refuge while I consider the future.

As I am packing, I think of Evie. How pitiful her life became, how, like me, she tried to escape. And escape she did, but Edward discovered her. I stop still. He discovered her because the spirits told Iris her location. That must not happen again. And suddenly I become conscious of Guardbridge as if it had interrupted its course to turn its eye on me. I think of the glass and its terrible influence. *A bad place.*

The decision is made in an instant, and before I can challenge it I take scissors from my workbox and hurry downstairs. Through the hall I move until I reach the corridors of the blue room. I step quickly but even in my haste there is a shift about me. Guardbridge seems to hum and the air swarms with the gathering of a strange energy that crackles on my skin.

Outside, the storm rises and icy draughts collect in the passageway as if all doors and windows had been flung open. And I know, with some dreadful instinct, that Guardbridge knows my intention and strives to repel me. Leaves that have gathered through long neglect begin to stir and rasp across the stone tiles and the corridor becomes filled with their whispering motion across the floor. I walk on as the house garners all its abilities to repulse me – the wind becomes a howl, and hail throws itself to the windows and roofs – dust swirls in the air, agitated to fury.

At the blue room I have to use all my weight against the door to force it, and as soon as I have, silence comes down like a guillotine and Guardbridge pauses. I take a breath and walk to the glass and with each step the house awaits my next move. I reach the pedestal and look down. And now the howling gale is threaded with other sounds, soft at first – a chorus of beguiling voices. Voices of the dead. I consider all the wickedness that has come from the touch of this object – all the truths flushed from their hiding places – and how it pulled Jacob's soul from the afterlife, where surely he was at rest.

Wicked, I think, and as if hearing my thoughts the tongues grow more insistent. *Never again*. And I jam the scissor point into the lock. Shadows rush to the room and mask the light. The air shivers with the spirits, who, over the years, have been unlocked by the glass. I twist the scissors, and the crack of the broken mechanism splits the air.

Opening the lid, I stare down. Now the sky blackens and darkness creeps more stealthily into the atmosphere. Even as I watch, it coils along ceiling and floor, curling in the corners, and in it is the gaze of Guardbridge's spectral souls.

Grabbing the glass, I run from the room, slamming the door behind me. Wind chases me down the passageway, agitating the leaves into further flurries, but I do not stop until I reach the main hall. Here I gather courage. Then, without a coat, I race from the house.

It is dark now and the growing gale bends the trees and sends my skirts and hair lashing; rain and hail pummel my hands and cheeks. I pass into the courtyard and through the archway to the back of the house, going with as much speed as I can summon until I reach the river.

As I near, other sounds weave beyond the tearing of wind and rain — voices, but not of those who are alive; these are wrought by the tongues of the dead and of those spirits who continue to walk Guardbridge even after flesh has rotted from bone.

I want to cover my ears for the horror of it but, more than ever, I sense that what I am about to do is right and, lifting the glass high, I plunge it into the river.

Time stops. All noise retreats. I no longer feel the

sting of wetness on my skin or the tug of wind but have half slipped into that other world where the laws of physics do not conform to the rules of this one. No longer am I entirely an earthly creature. Around me the shadows of those souls who wait on the other side begin to emerge. Fear and care leave me as if death were a strong draught of laudanum that might last forever. As I begin to fall into its embrace there comes a pull somewhere deep inside that drags me back to the riverbank. And once more I stand, my hair running with icy rain.

The deed is done and now I hurry back to my chamber, my thoughts fixed on the task ahead. Once in my room I strip and dress in clothes more suited for hard walking. In a bag I pack all the money I can find and only what is essential for a day or so. I am nearly ready and tremble with the enormity of what I am about to do: the terrible finality of it. At the window I gaze out but I cannot see beyond. My ears are assaulted by the smashing of rain upon the moor — nothing else can be heard. I think, with fear, of crossing to the farmhouse in such weather, but go I must. My pulse quickens.

Downstairs, I take things for John from the laundry room and some biscuits and a bottle of milk. As I prepare, I estimate how long it will take to cross the moor. I am a good walker — but in weather like this and with so little moon it could be as much as two or three hours. And now the moment is upon me, my stomach churns.

In the nursery John is on Agnes's lap, finishing the last of his meal.

'Mrs Stonehouse. What a monumental storm. How are you?' She gives a weary yawn.

'I am well. And you, Agnes – how are you?' I ask, hoping she cannot read my state of agitation.

'John kept me up most of last night and to be honest I've hardly been able to keep my eyes open. I slept through lunch, which is why I missed the meal.'

'Here,' I say, reaching for John, 'let me take him for an hour or two.'

She opens her mouth to protest but then gives a grateful sigh and passes me his teething ring, and a rattle. 'I won't refuse. I don't suppose he will want to do much else but sleep either now he's fed. I can hardly keep him awake, but call me if you need anything.'

'I will,' I say. I gaze at her sadly. 'Thank you for everything, Agnes.'

She looks up, a little surprised, and gives me a gentle smile. 'It's always a pleasure,' she says.

In the bedroom I add more layers to John's clothes and then I pause and sit him on my lap. I stroke his cheek and let him take a curl of my hair in his chubby fist, and all the time he smiles and gurgles and my love for him burns through me so fiercely that I almost buckle under it.

Recalling how a woman in the village had wrapped her baby up to her body as she worked, I take a sheet from the bed. I twist and cross it over one shoulder, back round my waist and over the other then tie and pin it firmly in front. Then I tuck John in. Even through the thickness of our layers the weight of him is a comfort.

I take one of Edward's mackintoshes and button it around us. Then I sling the bag over my arm and light a lantern. I am ready. But I do not leave immediately. In the hall I look around to the place that once offered such hope. It was not to be. I gaze a final time on Evie's portrait and regard her sadly. What would she say, I wonder, were she standing here before me instead of captured in oil? She might wish me a better fate than hers.

Run, Annie, I hear her say. *Run.*

25

The instant the main door closes behind me, my courage falters. The rain comes down in sheets and the lamp rocks unsteadily, throwing a distorted beam into the night. It is bitterly cold – too cold. A moment of doubt, but I cannot afford to think what might have been. There is only now. Bag slung over one shoulder, I hold my spare hand across John's back, and I am out of the gates and on to the road that runs with streams. Within seconds my cheeks and coat are slick with rain.

As I battle into the night, my very courage is a comfort that keeps realities at bay. The noise of the storm is deafening but behind that there is silence: no owl call or that of a creature, and I imagine them burrowed in the hollows of trunks or beneath the earth – beyond the reach of the elements. The moor swells and blooms through the darkness, my lantern only brushing a faint gleam where I step. Icy wind whips at my cheeks, and my hands in the gloves grow quickly numb. The sky above is black, chased by raindrops. Then, through the sounds of the storm, there are those of wheels, and I search the gorse in panic for a place to hide – only possible, surely, if I lie flat and put out the lantern. But I do not have another match, and even if I did, I do not trust that I could use it in such weather.

I listen and the sound of wheels becomes that again of the endless spit and rush of water on stone and plant. There is no coach but the very thought of Edward gives my feet urgency, and in my haste I nearly miss the milepost green with moss.

Now I stop and open the top of my coat to look down upon John. The rhythm and heat of our bodies has sent him to sleep. I button the coat up again and turn to the moors.

The wind is against my direction now – pushing me back – as if to say 'go no further', but I step out anyway. I test the ground and shine the lamp for the path, but do not find it. I hesitate. But the words Iris had written flash again in my mind – *Edward is on his way* – and I feel him urging the carriage on. Bending into the gale, I continue.

I do not know for how long I walk, but the going is slow. I do not find the path and with each step I have to try my boot against the ground for firmness but as the deluge continues all beneath my feet begins to give. My limbs tire and I pause to take breath and gaze around. John's weight pulls at my aching back and shoulders. How far did Mrs North say? Three miles? It is impossible to see. There are no landmarks to map my course and I have a moment of chilling fear; it would be too easy to take false direction and with the weather like this I am as good as blind.

I turn back into the wind and hope that it blows true. I should have brought a stick. Stupid. I will imagine instead a warm fire and a cup of strong tea and the kind face that will greet us at the farmhouse.

The walking grows gradually more difficult and the necessity of changing direction to avoid bogs means that it is impossible to keep my bearings and, worse, the lamp is beginning to fail and cold has found its way through the layers to my skin and I shiver uncontrollably.

My foot slips and the lantern picks up the wet surface of a mire. When my heart stops thumping, I pause. Looking around, there is nothing but the inky night and the sound as wind hurls water to the earth. I would not find my way back to Guardbridge now even if I so wished it. Surely, I tell myself, the rain must soon stop and the clouds lift enough to show a moon and just over the other side of the hill I will find refuge. I think of Edward. Did he really kill his wife and child? How did he hide his character so well? Because now the extent of the danger we are in comes to me and slices my heart with terror.

Oh God. What have I done?

26

When Iris finally comes to it is from a dream that is sunk in the sound of rain – a dream full of wickedness and a coming horror that, in its very texture, is premonition-like. She wakes to the sense of something profoundly amiss.

The room is uncommonly dark, the little fireplace cold. Outside, a storm is whipping up a frenzy. She wants to call out but feels that her very voice will disturb the surface of what she has seen in her sleep and dispel it. She knows, in the way that she does, that she must hold on to what the dream was telling her.

Evie had been there. Yes, Evie, reaching out and falling. There was something in the water – a head, an open mouth. It was the place of Evie's death, and yet that was not all – for in the dream they had not been alone; someone else had stood in the shadows. *Impossible*, she thinks, but her belly turns with the trepidation of having brushed so close to that dreadful night once more. Now the sound of rain recalls the events clearly: the house all but empty and the raging storm and later the ringing absence of two souls. She gets up and goes to the window, completely opaque but for the running of drops on the glass. She rings the bell and makes her way to the door.

Mrs North is asleep, her head nodding, an empty glass on the table and a piece of knitting half on, half off her lap. Iris walks quietly to her to take it with absent familiarity from her hands, hands that over the years have bestowed such gentleness, now swollen and gnarled, an ink stain on the middle finger and nails cut straight over the small tips.

As she kneels to retrieve the knitting from the floor, she sees a roughly folded letter under the table and picks it up. It is addressed to Southy in handwriting that is badly formed and erratic, but it is the writer who sparks her interest, because there – at the bottom – is Evie's name. A letter from Evie? Southy tells her everything but has never spoken of this. She should not look – it is not hers to read – but her eyes have already captured a line. *I believe that if I do not leave, I will die here.* What? And so she takes it and reads.

When she has finished, Iris shakes her head, as if, in doing so, the letters will rearrange and form meanings that make more sense. She reads it again and thinks: *How can it be?* Because she knows her brother is not capable of causing such fear and distress – or death? Yet it is clear from what is here that Evie believed that he was.

Her dream shivers to the surface again and she feels the vibration of some further wrong-footedness beyond the implication. A shovel of rain pummels the sashes and anxiety begins to wind deep down in her belly. What is she missing? Beside her, Mrs North gives a snore and she puts the letter back where she found it.

Still no maid has come, and the room is too frigid. Opening the main door, she walks into the passage-way and calls out to the silence; the silence answers back. She rings the servants' bell again. Iris's scalp feels tight as if it had been pulled just a little out of shape with her skull.

'Southy —' she tugs at her shoulder — 'Southy, wake up.'

Mrs North stirs and jerks, knocking her cap askew, a thread of spittle at her mouth's edge and wafting the smell of brandy fumes. 'Miss Stonehouse?' She is sleep-rubbed and bleary.

'Where are the staff?'

'The staff?' She blinks and looks at the clock. 'They all went down with something after luncheon.'

Iris considers the strangeness of this. 'Not you or I, though?'

'It was a dish only the staff took and you did not eat luncheon at all.'

'And you?'

'I only wanted a little bread and butter.'

Iris thinks of the letter but it is best that she does not admit she has read it.

'Have you seen Annie and John? I had such bad dreams.'

'There now, Miss Stonehouse. Try not to worry yourself. You often dream ill.'

Mrs North rises carefully in the chair and pulls the shawl closer round her. But Iris paces anxiously, pausing at windows to witness the ferocity of the storm.

'I must find out if they are well,' she says.

Mrs North sits up higher, sways a little, then slumps back.

'I'm quite sure they're fine, Miss Stonehouse. Best stay here.'

'You're drunk again, Southy,' Iris says.

'I'm only tired and brandy helps the ache in my joints.' Her eyes glide to the bottle and she licks her dry lips. 'There's nothing wrong with Mrs Stonehouse. She visited when you were in trance.'

'Why did she come? Why didn't you wake me?'

'It's never possible to draw you back when you're like that. You're best left.' Mrs North gets unsteadily to her feet and gives an uncomfortable groan. 'I suppose I shall have to make our tea myself,' she says. 'I'll bring up some bread and cold meat, cake if I can find it – and I think that might be the only fare we get this evening.'

'Did Annie come to speak to me?'

'She came to your bed, but, as I said, you weren't awake.'

'How was she?'

'She was well other than this whole to-do with the séance, and of course she's petrified of your brother's return.'

Iris flushes. 'I shouldn't have written it.'

Mrs North shrugs. 'You said your brother should know.'

'And I believe he should, but, even so, I regret that I acted so hastily. It was wrong. It's for Annie to tell him, not I.' Remorse and guilt prick at her and she wonders now how she could have been so cruel.

'Ah well. We all do things that we later wish we had considered more.' Mrs North gazes at the sashes and gives the slightest of shudders. 'I'll be back in a jiffy.' She rises and, taking a chamber stick, leaves the room.

Iris feeds wood to the fire and returns to the bedroom for a shawl. As she is about to leave, she sees her notebook, lying open on the bed. She picks it up curiously and her eyes go to the last words written there: *Edward is on his way. Run, Annie. Run.*

Run, Annie? Why should Annie run? But it is not only the words themselves that cause disquiet; something else is tapping at her anxiety. Back in the parlour she retrieves Evie's letter from beneath the table and takes it to her room, laying both letter and book side by side. Her heart gives a twist. It cannot be. She closes her eyes and opens them, hoping that she has imagined it, but there, once again, is the strange reality that both the letter and the words urging Annie to run are written by the same hand. How can that be possible? For a moment she considers that it is Evie herself who has come to her in trance to relay this message, but as she studies it she realizes that that is not the answer, because she knows Evie's hand, and this one with its spidery crawl of letters has been forced from the nib – it is not Evie's. And now, as she studies it again, there is a familiarity to the loop of the Y and the uncertain lettering.

The shock is so great that she sits down hard. Her head swims. Checking to see that Mrs North has not returned, she makes haste to Mrs North's bedchamber and to the desk where her writing materials are kept. In the top drawer she finds a list for the next trip to town and brings it back. Once returned to her own room, Iris scrutinizes the writing again beside that of Mrs North's. There is in both the letter purporting to be from Evie and the words in her book an attempt to conceal the real author by a backward lean of the letters but in all other aspects it is the same. The looping of the Y is exact in each and there is no doubt all three have been written by none other than Southy. Her own nurse. Southy?

Sweat breaks out on Iris's palms and her mouth dries. Taking a breath, she closes her eyes and places her finger over the ink, tracing it, and in the dark behind her lids the image comes as if lit by burning torches and she sees quite clearly Mrs North curved over her own notebook with a pen. She feels the sting of outrage that Mrs North has used her notebook in this way, but then she ponders further.

Edward is on his way. Run, Annie. Run. She thinks now of how it must have been left open so that when Annie came she would surely see it. Why? Why would Mrs North put such a statement in her book and suggest in the letter that Evie was frightened of Edward? Did she show the letter to Annie? She must have done – in fact, Mrs North surely wrote the letter for no other purpose. And Annie was frightened enough already by the coming of Jacob and the forthcoming séance. But why does Mrs North seek to disturb her?

She imagines Mrs North handing over the letter to Annie. What might she have said? 'I wasn't meant to show you, my dear, but I think you should know.' Why had Southy done this? It cannot be because Edward is a true threat, because Iris knows he is not.

What must Annie be feeling? Iris knows Annie had been afraid that Edward might learn of her secret. Has Mrs North also told Annie that she has already written to him? She puts her hands to her face and to the flush of shame. Of course she has. And how had she lured Annie to her bedroom and to where her notebook lay open? She does not understand why Southy has acted in this manner, but Iris believes it explains much; Iris has felt Annie's acceleration of fear of Edward and realizes that it goes far beyond what is rational. Her feeling of foreboding gathers momentum. She is jerked out of her reverie by noises from beyond – the bang of the door, the nearing rattle of a tea tray, the tinkle as it lands on the table.

'I'm back,' Mrs North calls.

Iris looks up darkly to the panes, where a fresh flurry of wind-blown rain batters the frames. Her consciousness travels to the next room, imagines Southy easing herself into the chair and hunching over the teapot, back rounded, both hands on the handle, pouring unsteadily into the cup, how she puts the pot down to saw off a piece of bread, her mouth pursed in concentration and discomfort.

What has Southy done, and why? As Iris sits in the dimness of the room there are no stars, there is no orchestral accompaniment, just a terrible, terrible truth – a quiet, sly betrayal so profound that her world spins from its axis and she is left gasping for a sense of reality.

27

I stop to rub the rain from my eyes, but still it streams on, blinding me to what is only feet ahead. My stockings and boots are sodden, and it has grown icier; only John appears unaffected as he lies sleeping against me. The wetness has seeped through the neck of my coat and now my clothing clings to my skin, leaching out heat. I think of Edward and terror plunges me on. But the wind does not keep direction, and I have begun to lose faith in its compass. Soon I will be too frozen and weary to continue; already my legs have begun to ache and my feet cannot feel the ground below. John grows heavier and the running earth becomes more perilous. Part of me knows now of how foolish a venture this is, and another that no other choice remains.

Suddenly the gradient climbs and my spirits lift. Finally I have reached that incline of which Mrs North spoke, and even if it is not the right hill it will offer a better view once the storm has passed. I imagine arms helping us across a threshold to warmth and sanctuary.

On I go until I reach the top. Surely now I will see

the lights of the farmhouse. Lowering the lantern I gaze optimistically around but there is only blackness – no farm, no road, no Guardbridge. Then a miracle – lightning tears the sky apart, and for an instant throws its radiance across the moor. In the brief illumination I scan for the shape of a house or barn, but with dismay I realize that no building breaks the miles of gorse and heather. Nothing. I wait for another flash and look behind but with slow sinking horror it is clear that whichever way I stand the view is the same. How long have I been walking? One hour or three? Many before morning lights a path, and all the time it grows wilder, and even when the sun rises perhaps it will show only an echoing emptiness.

John begins to moan and the lamp glowers low, too low. My fingers are so numb that it nearly drops. I put it down, just for a minute or two, as I rub my palms together furiously. My whole body is shaking now with cold and my teeth chatter. With the next lightning flash I make my way back down the hill but it is slick and hazardous, and it is necessary to sit and shuffle until I reach flat ground. My heart is beating faster now – not only with exertion but with the growing alarm that I am not only lost but that I will never find the farmhouse. And if I do not? I will not think of that, not now.

At the bottom of the hill comes another streak of

lightning that reveals something a little way off – a tree twisted to the shape of wind and it is horribly familiar. I recall the split in the trunk that ends in a deadened stump. How long ago had we passed it? Hours surely. I wipe moisture from my face and try to wriggle my frozen fingers and now I am so tired all I can think of is to sit and close my eyes, only for a few minutes or so, and then, then I will be restored enough to go onward.

I huddle under a rocky overhang and tell myself that I will give my muscles ease before continuing. As I lay down the lantern it gives one final gasp before going out. I begin to whimper with cold or terror while around me the storm gathers and tears at the world as if it were its sole purpose.

28

Iris stands at the window. It is clear now that Southy wanted Annie to flee Guardbridge, but the whys are not so obvious, and it is not only that but the manner in which she achieved it. *Southy*. Southy, her friend and protector, confidante and companion. Southy, who has betrayed her by using her own notebook as a weapon. Iris is assailed with a torrent of emotion that has nowhere to go – because in this moment of truth she realizes she loves her nurse as well as she might anyone in her life, even the mother who rejected her.

She closes her eyes. *Not now*, she thinks. Now it is Annie and her affairs that are more pressing. She will deal with Southy later. Standing, she takes the evidence and locks it in her cabinet, then straightens her dress and hair and steels herself to enter the sitting room.

Mrs North looks up with a smile that Iris shrinks from.

'There you are, my dear. It was quite an adventure in the kitchen; I felt like a little mouse on the lookout for scraps.' She takes a piece of ham and cuts it neatly. 'Come and sit down.'

But Iris moves past her to the main door.

'Where are you going?'

'I have a craving for something sweet – chocolate.'

Mrs North makes an attempt to rise. 'Let me get it for you.'

'No, stay. I need to move around after so long idle.'

Mrs North does not protest, but wiggles deeper into the seat and adjusts her shawl, takes a sip of tea, a bite of bread. 'Hurry back before the pot grows cold.'

At the door Iris takes one look back then steps out. The lamps are unlit. Iris reaches the oriel window where the first streak of purpling light breaks the darkness. Petals of memory emerge from the surface of her dream – the river racing fast and furious on a stormy night, someone running towards the bridge caught in a flash of lightning, desperation and fear humming in the air. She pulls breath tightly into her lungs. *Annie*, she thinks. It is Annie who is in need now – strange, buttoned-up Annie, who came as a friend and who she betrayed. She must put it right.

A sense of doom swells through the house, its very silence a call to arms. She walks quickly to Annie's chamber and knocks hard.

Annie, run. No response.

A crack of thunder and, when she opens the door,

lightning strikes the room, and it is not so much empty as abandoned.

Now Iris checks the house and all the places Annie could be, her agitation gathering urgency. She leaves the nursery for last – because, because what if Annie is not there or, worse, John? Then what should she do? She thinks of the moors and is assailed by a wave of vertiginous dread and leans briefly against the wall. When she has gathered her wits, she knocks at the nursery and walks in. Agnes is lying back against the chair, eyes closed, head back, and knees apart. As Iris studies her she turns her head and gives a small snore – the cot is empty. Another lash of rain, another flare in the black sky.

Annie is gone and not only Annie but John too. Iris knows it as certainly as she can. Oh God, on a night like this – and who set the fuse alight that caused her to flee? Was it Mrs North's words or was it the letter Iris sent to Edward? She can only imagine how Annie felt when she left Mrs North earlier, and if Mrs North is capable of such treachery, what else might she have done to fuel Annie's anxiety?

But it is not Mrs North's actions that she is consumed with but her own guilt – she had tried to hurt Annie by making her afraid of Edward too, hadn't she? Poor Annie, who, through experience, sees danger in men already. Iris should have reassured her, not used her fear to manipulate her to her own will. If she could take it back and rescript those conversations and actions, she would. She knows why she had acted as she did. Because deep down, beyond the desire for her mother, there had also been envy and worry – worry that Annie, as Evie had done, might take against her, and envy because Annie has it all if only she knew it: a husband and home and, most of all, a baby.

How wrong Iris has played it. She should have shown Annie not that Edward was a danger but Edward as Iris knows him – in the way only a sister can. She should have told Annie how well he hides his true self – how tenderness makes him fierce, how love makes him sad, how grief makes him silent. Poor Edward. Poor Annie. They are better matched than they know.

And now Annie is out there in this cacophony of noise and rain. How long since she left? Iris returns to Annie's chamber where the fire has been long dead and goes to the window. Outside lies the world that is so familiar and so terrifying, the one that makes her panic even in its green smile of summer. But it does not smile now – now there is nothing but monstrous fury.

She swallows hard. If she leaves, the spirits have told her it will be the end, but is this not already the end? Her mother gone and Southy a traitor. For an instant an entire unlived lifetime washes through her – the possibility of friends, of parties and balls, the touch of a man who is neither father nor brother. Too painful now to ponder. And what remains here without Southy, without Annie and John? Only a brother and sister locked in tragedy and loneliness. There is no other life; this is it, and the years ahead fall like steps along an ever-narrowing spiral on and on – an endless repetition of loss.

Wind shivers in from the sashes. The sky is lit again, and she thinks of Annie, nothing more than skin and bone, out on the moor road with a babe in arms.

Already trembling with the knowledge of what she plans, Iris goes to the boot room for a coat and walking shoes. Is Southy wondering where she is? Is she on her way down to the scullery, already guessing that Iris had a different reason to leave the quarters? She does not care. *Later*, she thinks, *later. If I return at all.*

Her fingers shake as she attempts to light a lantern. Once, twice, she reaches out with the match until her hand falls upon the wick steadily enough to draw flame. Her teeth chatter even before cold has made them so. She will not think about what she is doing.

She opens the front door, sending in a sheet of blinding rain, a kick of cold and then that empty, full world that has been the thing of all her nightmares stands ahead.

She takes a shuddering breath and looks up to the moonless sky. And, holding up the lamp, she steps out and beyond.

29

The world, even in its rage, seems to welcome Iris with arms wide, as if to say, 'I have been waiting for you.' But at the bottom of the steps her legs give way and a tide of dizziness threatens to fell her on the spot. Her feet are too heavy for the weakness of her ankles, her mind paralysed, and then through the panic come the scents – a faint waft of woodsmoke from one of Guardbridge's chimneys, the dripping moors and sour mires of wet earth, and the night that is sharp and cold. It comes to her then that this sensory symphony is the memory of love, and she recalls, long ago, running across the moors to look for eggs or butterflies, the way the sun burned orange and gold on gorse, and the bleak beauty of frosted winters.

If she is to die, there are worse ways, and so, garnering courage, she walks away from the house. With each uncertain step it is as if a hand she had been clinging to slips further from her grasp, and now she is at the gates and with one more placing of her boot she will be out of Guardbridge's grounds altogether.

Iris turns and looks behind her to where it rises, dark and impermeable. Then, with another footfall, Guardbridge is adrift and a tethering is loosed, making Iris both free and trapped — one fate behind, one before. There is a moment of doubt, an instant when her pulse races too fast and her lungs are constricted in the tightness of her chest, then the sky is lit like fireworks and the moor lies before her in all its fierce glory and her soul takes courage from it.

When lightning touches a wick to the sky once more the road ahead is laid out like a silver ribbon. She scours frantically for her sister but the track is empty for as far as she can see. She walks faster into the wet expanse, trying to imagine she is held by Guardbridge but there comes a time when she realizes how far from the house she is, how far from containment, and terror immobilizes her. She waits for the world to strike her down, for the sky itself to crush her to the ground, but nothing happens, except above a cloud shifts in the dense sky and reveals the tip of a moon, and in its light Iris is once again moored to her own self.

The further Iris goes from Guardbridge, the stranger she feels, as if she has journeyed not just through space but beyond years. She has travelled past fear and to a place of fate. Thunder clamours farther off and when the lightning next comes the road ahead remains empty. Where is Annie?

Suddenly she stops, and something makes her turn to the moor and there, a mile or so off, comes a flicker of light. A lantern? She cannot think what else would be moving in the darkness. When the sky is next illuminated, she gazes at the patch with hope and there is a figure – standing straight, not a tree – and distance makes it small but when blackness falls again, the light moves as it would were it held by a walker. Annie. It must be Annie, but what is she doing there?

She looks down to the milepost. It is the part of the moor that is most treacherous; even as children they were warned never to stray this way. Iris takes a shaky inhalation but does not hesitate and, keeping her eyes fixed on that signal, moves towards it.

As time passes, the light grows closer. How long it takes, Iris is not sure, but the lantern has finally come to rest a little way off. Iris blinks and just before the flame is extinguished she sees who stands beside it and catches her breath. Not Annie. Her eyes widen in shock and wonder, then the boy is gone. But Iris is now close enough to touch the figure huddled into the rocks. Annie's eyes are closed, her skin very white, and for a terrible moment she wonders if Annie is dead.

'Annie,' she says urgently, touching her shoulder. 'Annie.'

Annie opens her lids in surprise and alarm.

If Iris had come adrift of her love for her sister before, the rush of relief to her heart brings it back now.

'Thank God,' Iris says.

'What are you doing here?' Annie's lips are so numbed that the words come out garbled and she closes her eyes again.

'Wake up, Annie, wake. If you don't keep moving, you'll die of cold.'

'I can't go back. Don't take me back.'

'How is John?'

Annie's fingers fumble with the coat but do not work and so Iris opens it to peer down and touch the warm crown and feel him stir.

'What are you doing here? Is Edward back?' Annie, coming awake, looks up with terror.

'No, I came to find you.'

'Why? Haven't you done enough harm?'

'I'm not here to hurt you. I'm here to take you home. I'm sorry for what I requested. I'm sorry for all of it.'

'I can't go back. Edward killed Evie. He'll do the same to me.'

'He won't, I promise you. Mrs North has misled you, but, either way, you can't remain here. You won't survive the night.' Iris reaches out a hand and pulls Annie to her feet and takes her bag. 'We must get back as soon as possible. Walking will warm you up a bit. Follow me.' Annie does not protest and as they move, stumblingly at first, Iris tells her, as fully as she can, how they have been deceived.

At one point, Annie grabs Iris's coat and pulls her to a stop. 'Edward didn't kill Evie? Or Jacob? Can you be sure?' Her eyes study Iris for treachery.

'Most certainly not,' Iris says. 'I'll explain later, but, come now, let me take you home. You must have wandered and come round full circle – we're not far from Guardbridge. Not far at all.'

The rain stops as suddenly as it began and clouds pass leaving the moon, bone white in the windblown night. They reach the road and Iris puts down the bag to ease her muscles.

'Iris, there's something you should know.'

Iris turns to her.

'I got rid of the glass.'

The knowledge stills her.

'Without it, I knew that Jacob couldn't return, but it was not the only reason; the spirits were the ones who told you where Evie had fled. I couldn't risk that.'

Iris's eyes sting with the pain of it. She looks up to the sky and then down to her hands. 'Is it gone for good? Can it be returned?'

'I threw it in the river. It's gone forever.'

It is too much to take in. 'We'll discuss it later; it's not the end of the night yet. I have Mrs North still to talk to. In a matter of hours my world has been turned upside down.'

'And you left Guardbridge,' Annie says. 'Do you still believe that catastrophe will follow?'

But Iris is thinking back to Mrs North and the notebook, and wondering what in it is truth and what is lies.

Finally they reach the gates of Guardbridge and Iris thinks of her Southy and dread builds again inside her. As they turn in to the drive the door is open and both Agnes and Mrs North are on the steps and hurrying down, Mrs North placing an arm protectively around Iris and Agnes helping Annie, a deluge of words and exclamations. Then they are in the warm kitchen and John is bawling in Agnes's arms as she tries to change him, and Agnes is instructing Annie to sit by the stove and take a hot drink from the kettle. Annie's eyes are anxious, and Iris knows that she is still to be convinced that Edward is no danger. Mrs North urges Iris up to the chamber so that she can get her out of the wet things.

'How did you do it?' Mrs North asks. 'To leave the house. My brave, brave girl. Look at you. What foolhardiness to go out like that – but how like yourself to take courage for Mrs Stonehouse. How did you know she was gone? What did she tell you? I knew that she was keen to leave but on a night such as this. What recklessness. Has she said anything?' And on she goes, measuring out the compliments and the chidings for her charge's brave audacity, but in all her words there are threads of uncertainty.

Iris's wet gown sweeps the floor and she shivers; it is not only her cold flesh that is the cause but the great sense that, henceforth, nothing will remain as it has been. At the door to their quarters Mrs North stands to let her pass and they regard each other with care, a dance of apprehension and concealment, but when their eyes briefly meet it is clear to both of them that everything has changed.

30

Inside her chamber, the deceit begins to steal into all those places where there had once been trust. Iris stumbles again and again on the knowledge of those faithless hands and the familiar voice that has comforted and consoled her, her entire life.

'Where did you find her?' Mrs North continues. 'Did you have to walk far? How could you dare?' She gasps as if still trying to take in the enormity of Iris's actions.

Iris does not answer, because once she opens her mouth it will be the beginning of the end. From the window wind rushes across the sodden moor; the taste of rain is still in her mouth and her scalp aches from the pull of the gale.

With each answering silence Mrs North's actions become more fervent – the endearments and recommendations. Her fingers now tremble at Iris's back and when Iris finally turns Mrs North's face is sunk in fear.

'Come to the fire,' she says, although her voice cracks. 'You must take some brandy to heat you through. Come now – what a night.'

Iris stands tall, although inside she could fold in

half. Mrs North takes her chair, but Iris remains on her feet.

'I know what you did,' Iris says finally, and with the words comes the reality of it.

There is a frantic scurrying of thought across Mrs North's face – a mouse too close to the trap that will break its spine.

'I know what you've done, Southy,' she says again. Mrs North's hands fidget anxiously. 'You wrote a letter purporting to be from Evie and you've been writing in my book.' Her eyes dart to those misshapen fingers now scrubbed of ink – did Mrs North notice them and wonder if Iris had surmised? Mrs North's hand flies to her pocket and comes up empty.

'You dropped it.'

She blanches and opens her lips but is unable to utter a sound.

'Southy.' Iris could as easily cry as scream or tear at her hair. 'Southy, don't lie to me now. Do not. If you care for me, and I believe you do, tell me the truth.'

There is a terrible silence.

Iris goes on. 'Do you want proof?' She goes to her room and collects letter, notebook and list from the cabinet. 'I know your hand. I knew, as soon as I saw the letter that is supposedly written by Evie that something was amiss, but first I could only react with shock to what was said there. I knew that Evie didn't have to fear Edward in that way so why would she write it?

And then I realized that it wasn't her handwriting at all, and I saw my notebook and knew that both came from the same pen and that pen is yours.'

'It's not true –' Mrs North begins.

'It is true – I saw the ink upon your fingers, but not only that. Your hands – I know how it pains you to move them. I've seen how, over the past years, your writing has deteriorated – you cannot properly form your letters. I took a list from your desk and compared them. They are almost the same in every respect.'

'The spirits have as different handwriting as they do voices. That's why the pen is changed and Evie Stonehouse – she was so troubled towards the end . . .'

Iris's anger rises. 'I know, in the way I often know things, that it's you. Don't pretend it's not. Annie told me you showed it to her.'

Mrs North's eyes glaze and she opens her mouth to refute it but the recognition that the deception is over leaves her in a terrible sigh. The candle flames flicker on their wicks and the last vestiges of the storm blow through the trees.

'Why did you do it? Why?'

The shine in Mrs North's eyes dies and is replaced by something else. 'I won't deny any longer, but it must be obvious why. It was for you. Everything I've ever done is for you. Annie Stonehouse would have sent you away eventually. Have you forgotten what happened with her predecessor? Evie Stonehouse tried to banish you from the home you love – forced you to face your greatest terror by stepping out of Guardbridge. Guardbridge, which is your haven and birthright. I had to make her leave before that happened again.'

'Evie wanted me gone, yes, but Annie hadn't suggested it, not even after we fell out.'

'You're too trusting. Sooner or later she would have made you go. And now you've brought her back, and she and Edward will have further children, and she, like Evie Stonehouse, will grow to detest and fear your ability more and more.'

'You don't know that.' Iris turns to the window. 'But you didn't only send her away – you sent her to a possible death. You told her that there was a house across the moor.'

'Did she tell you that?'

'Yes, and if I had not found her, by a miracle, both she and John may well have perished.'

'I don't think I said exactly that, about the house. But why would you care so much?'

'Annie was very clear that you said there was a farm a little way across the moor, and I do care. You know I do. I can't believe the wickedness of this.' She shakes her head, anger building. 'You also told Annie that Edward had been here at Guardbridge the night Evie and Jacob died. You didn't explain that you had been the one who told Edward to claim he was elsewhere.

Do you remember? You said afterwards that people would be suspicious. I remember Edward's reaction, how dismissive he was – but you, you were the one who insisted he say he was away and returned after they perished.'

'It was good advice,' Mrs North says.

'That might be so, except you used that information to contort the truth. How guilty you made him sound. Poor Annie – no wonder she was petrified – and you profess this was all to protect me? You vastly underestimate my love for Edward. Don't you think I would have rather left Guardbridge if it meant my brother's happiness?'

Mrs North has the grace to look down.

'And again you said that it was Edward who sent the staff away, knowing full well it was not. It was Evie who had begun to believe they were all against her. God, I can't believe how you have moulded things to suit your purpose. And the locks on her room – as if Edward would have broken them to get to Evie.'

'Would you have had me tell the truth? That it was you who destroyed them when it belonged to your mother?'

'Yes,' Iris says. 'I carry guilt about my mother, always, but I did that a long time ago on a night when she refused to see me.'

Mrs North makes a disparaging noise.

'I understand from the little Annie conveyed on the

way back to Guardbridge that you've used many wiles to lead her to believe that Edward was a danger,' Iris takes a breath – 'but it's not only Edward that Annie has been afraid of – it's Guardbridge too. Do you recall the diorama in the cupboard she spoke of? We thought it such a mystery, but I realize now that it could only have been you. There are still those pieces made by Evie. Was it one of them? Do you deny it?'

Mrs North raises a trembling glass to her lips.

'Southy, admit what you've done.' Iris blinks away tears. 'I feel as if I can't know you.'

'You do know me.' Mrs North's face is haggard. 'You do. I'm still your old Southy and our life is here, together. I can see you think I've done wrong, but, believe me, it was for your own good. I've protected you your entire life – from your father and mother, from Evie Stonehouse and now from Annie Stonehouse.'

'How could what you've done ever be justified? Your aim was not to force her away; your aim in sending her across that perilous part of the moor in such weather was to kill her, and not only her, John too.' She gazes at her nurse aghast, still trying to understand that Mrs North could be capable of such evil-doing.

Mrs North pales. Iris is shaking now with fury and disgust but also a growing agitation. 'Did you –' Iris's voice is hushed as if delivery might soften the truth – 'did you use the same schemes to terrorize Evie? I remember something now – Evie's piano, so beloved of her when she was unhappy. Do you recall when the strings were cut? She blamed Edward and then she blamed me, and you said it must have been Evie herself, but it was none of us – it was you, wasn't it?'

Mrs North's eyes are unreadable; she moves her lips but remains silent.

Iris holds up her book. Part of her resists knowing the depth of deception, yet she must. 'Shall I open it? Now I know your hand I'll be able to trace it back. I'll be able to see every false step you led me on – and especially when it came to Evie. Because there are pronouncements here about Evie, pronouncements that terrified her.'

'Don't.' Mrs North reaches out to snatch it, but Iris is too quick. Mrs North covers her face with her hands.

Iris flicks back through the pages. 'You see, tonight I recalled another message written not long before Evie ran away – so similar to tonight's: *If Evie and Jacob do not leave Guardbridge, they will die. Edward cannot be trusted.* Do you remember that?

'At the time I struggled with it. I struggled with it because I didn't believe that Edward could possibly have harmed Evie and yet, because my trust in the spirits is so great, I reconsidered. Had I made a mistake?

Was Edward as violent and dangerous as it suggested? I didn't tell Evie what was written because I felt, even then, that there had been some error, but I think now that you made sure she read it. I think, as you did tonight, you led her on some pretext to my bedchamber when I was in trance and left it open, because Evie believed herself in great danger, didn't she?'

'Stop,' Mrs North says. 'Please don't look any further. The spirits do tell you the truth – it's only those statements about Mr Stonehouse and the threat he presents that are lies. *My* lies. I see now I've greatly misconceived in every way.'

Iris stops. 'Wait. It's ripped out. That page about Evie.' She looks up. 'Was that you?'

'No, I swear.' There is a look of genuine bafflement on her face.

'It doesn't matter. I recall it well.' Iris continues to examine the book. 'But this, this confuses me. It is your hand without doubt, but it's not a lie.' She pauses and frowns. 'You've written here that Evie was having an affair – this is how we all learned it. I believed it, of course, but when I confronted Evie she didn't deny it; it was the truth. How did you come to know it? Surely Evie didn't confess to you?'

'We had gone to town and when we returned, she fell asleep in the coach. Her purse was open on the seat beside us and inside there were at least three letters that I was certain she had not had with her earlier. I shouldn't have read them, but I knew that there must be something in them that she wished to hide, for why else hadn't she had them sent to Guardbridge?' Mrs North looks at Iris as if expecting praise for her cleverness. 'My first thought, as always, was you – perhaps it was arrangements to have you leave.'

'So you read them?'

'I don't deny it, and I don't regret it.' A righteous flush colours her cheeks. 'It's true that they didn't contain what I was concerned about, but I learned something else, something of great importance – I learned what kind of woman she really was and how she had deceived us all. It made it even more ridiculous that she might try to have you set up home away from Guardbridge.'

Iris's heart is pained at the memory of this revelation, because when Iris had confronted Evie, Evie had not only confessed but had been relieved to share her secret with someone. She had wept and begged of Iris, 'What am I to do? Tell me, what should I do?'

Tears of regret ache in her throat. 'You used me. Why didn't you tell Edward or myself how you came to learn this? Why do it this way – so that I had the responsibility of it?'

'I'm only the lowly nurse, Miss Stonehouse, a mere servant. Who would believe me if she denied it? And if I had been found out in snooping, I don't think Mr Stonehouse would have looked kindly on such behaviour, do you? He would have sent me away. But Mr Stonehouse always listened to you. Evie Stonehouse was a wicked creature. Her lie poisoned their marriage and hurt poor Jacob.' Mrs North's eyes narrow. 'But even then I wouldn't have interfered until I learned that she planned to send you from Guardbridge. How I went about it was wrong, I see that, and of course I never wished her dead, but do you think I would have done such had your life here not been under threat?' Mrs North reaches across, love suffusing her face, and tries to take Iris's hand. 'It was all for you, always; always, for you my dear.'

Iris shrinks away with revulsion. 'I blame you for her death. I blame you that she became so wretched she took her life. You betrayed us in the worst possible way.'

'If I had known she would go so far . . .' Mrs North does not finish. 'I thought she would run away again and that it was for the best. I felt sorry for poor Evie Stonehouse – I helped her escape, you know. I gave her money and organized the coach. I didn't seek to harm *her* even though she wished to harm *you*. You see, we all would have been happier if she went to her lover. Mr Stonehouse need no longer have been tortured by her betrayal and you could remain happy here. Better if the spirits had never revealed where she'd gone.'

'Happy?' Iris says. 'You think we would've been happy without them? Edward loved his son, even if he didn't know then that the father was another. It broke his heart when she ran away.' She gasps at his remembered pain and then she stops, as a thought of something so heinous comes to mind. Not that surely. It would be too much. But she is filled with dread and shakes her head. 'Southy, no, you wouldn't be so cruel and do something so abominable.' But she thinks now that she could – and Iris's fingers work over the notebook. 'Tell me it wasn't you.'

Mrs North's expression fills with fear.

Iris traces back, back until she reaches the statement. Now she hardly dare look, not wanting confirmation, but her eyes have already found the words inked across the page – the same back slant and the letters irregular and ill formed. *Jacob is not Edward's child.*

She looks up winded. She can barely articulate for disgust. 'You lied about Jacob – he was always Edward's child – all the time. Oh God, Southy. What have you done?'

Mrs North shakes her head but her eyes dart with guilt in her stricken face.

'How could you? How could you?'

Mrs North does not answer but picks helplessly at the antimacassar and then smooths it on the arm of the chair, repeating the action again and again. Iris's heart will surely break for Edward, who still does not know, who believed what Iris said. For it was her own lips that spilled that monstrous falsehood. Now tears run fiercely over her cheeks. 'I can hardly believe you would have done such a thing. How could you have ever cared for me if you told your lies through my tongue, if you gave me the burden of destroying my brother's life? Because that's what happened, isn't it?'

Mrs North shrinks further into her seat and rubs her palms. 'You always thought too much of your brother.'

'How dare you? You know as well as I that Edward's a good man,' Iris says.

'You make too much of his virtues. He's just a man, like his father, like all men. Edward is not a good man. He's a faithless excuse for humanity like them all.'

'I said, "How dare you?" How can you speak of him in such a way?'

Mrs North's lips thin. 'You know nothing of men. They're not like us – they weather these sorts of emotional furrows without coming to harm. Men pick up or put down a woman as they please – the heart doesn't come into it. Your brother married again within months of his wife's death, which goes to show how little she mattered to him.'

Iris paces as if doing so will ameliorate some of the poison that leaks forth from Mrs North's mouth. How can she describe her brother's nature in such a way?

'He did marry again, yes, but he's not whole – how can he be after what he went through? Do you think that just because he believed Jacob was not his that he could just shut his love off as he might put something away in a drawer? It's nearly destroyed him – how could he open himself to Annie after that – or even to John? He carries with him the guilt of their deaths. And now he has to learn again that Jacob was his own all that time he believed otherwise.'

Iris's dream shimmers to the surface then and nudges itself out of hiding. She recalls, once more, that other presence in the driving rain, a witness to Evie and Jacob's deaths, a witness or worse, and she knows now what the dream was telling her.

She turns horrified eyes to Mrs North. The words will not come loose – to speak them would be to unleash an evil beyond imagining. She can only stare as the dream rips open. 'You,' she says finally. 'She didn't take her own life. It was you.'

'Oh no. No.' Mrs North attempts to get up from the chair but defeated sinks back to the cushions.

'Look at me so that I may see the truth.'

Every line is visible in Mrs North's face now. 'I swear not that. It was an accident, a terrible, terrible accident.'

'I don't believe you. How can their drowning have been an accident?'

'You must. You must believe me. I haven't denied the other things but I'm not the murderer of Mrs Stonehouse and Jacob.'

'But you were there, weren't you?'

The room falls to a foreboding silence. Mrs North trembles as she reaches for the glass and when she finally speaks her voice is veined with regret. 'I was there, yes, but I didn't kill them. It started earlier that night. You had been in a trance, and I went to your desk and I . . .' She lifts guilty eyes. 'I came to write in your book. I came to write those very words that you quoted tonight. I didn't know it but Jacob was in the room with you, and when I entered he must have hidden. You remember what he was like? He was always snooping. Well, he was far from stupid and he'd been told enough that nobody was to write in that book but you.'

'He saw you and you blame him – when you were the one who did wrong?' Iris's rage swells.

'He watched what I was doing and when I had finished he stood up from behind the bed and ran to where I was, and before I could cover it properly he had read what I'd put there. He was clever enough to understand at once and he told me he'd tell his mother. I had to stop him. He pelted down to the ground floor, calling for her, but I went by way of the servants' stairs and managed to corner him in the hall; the only escape left was the front door, so he went out.

'Mrs Stonehouse had heard him by then and come to find out what it was all about. We both followed him out into that terrible storm. Dear God, it was hard to see, but we kept on. The wind was so strong I could barely stand, and then there was lightning, and Jacob was running alongside the river. Mrs Stonehouse called out to him again and again and eventually he heard and turned suddenly.' She stops, her cheeks drained of colour. 'He slipped.' Tears now. 'He slipped and Mrs Stonehouse was there, screaming and wailing for him. I will never forget her expression and, God forgive me, she tried to save him by plunging in after.'

Iris thinks she will be sick. She cannot observe Mrs North for a second more.

'I hate you,' she hisses. 'You're despicable. I can't be in the same room as you any longer,' and she goes to her door, banging it behind her. Once inside, she sits on the bed, filled with grief and dismay. She folds her arms to still the tremors and tries not to imagine that night as Evie watched her son fall into the water. And Edward – what will she tell him, what will she tell him now?

Pain leaves her gasping. She wonders how they will all go forth from this point? What will the future hold when so much of the past has been disassembled? Her notebook is still in her hands. What is true and what is not? With the glass gone, will she ever write through the spirits again? And who will be there to comfort her when it is too much to endure? And the part that has leaned on Southy all her life leans that way still with a longing that takes her breath away.

She thinks of Guardbridge, her beloved home, and how Mrs North's influence has coiled about it like a snake.

The door opens, framing Mrs North.

'Get out,' Iris shouts. 'Just get out.'

'Please.' Mrs North's face is fearful. 'Please. Haven't I been everything to you?'

'I said, get out.'

'Iris.' Mrs North wrings her hands. 'Please don't be so hard. My intention was always to protect you. I would lay my life down if it meant saving yours.'

'If that's your way of protecting me, I'd rather you didn't interfere.'

'I wonder if you can ever understand that I meant only good. Perhaps in the future you might forgive me.'

'How can you talk of forgiveness? It's not me who has been most harmed – it's my brother. What will you say to him? I don't think you ever did what you did to protect me, but only to injure my poor brother who you clearly hate.'

'We don't need to tell him.'

'Are you mad?' Her voice has risen. 'Not tell him that Evie's and Jacob's deaths were an accident? He is cowed by the guilt that he drove her to it. I won't let him carry that burden any longer than it's in my power to remove it. And even now I wonder if I believe it was an accident. I can't listen to any more lies. You have to leave.'

'*Leave?*'

'You can't stay at Guardbridge. How can you imagine that's possible?'

A change comes over Mrs North's demeanour. Gone is the apologetic stoop, gone the beseeching look and now there is something steely. When she speaks, it is unflinching.

'If you knew the truth, you wouldn't speak to me so.'

'What do you mean?'

Mrs North is beside her now, her black eyes gazing into Iris's with strange intensity. 'You ask me not to protect you. Do you want to know why I do? I've not understood why you never guessed. Why the spirits didn't tell you when every single day the evidence has been there. I waited and waited and still you didn't see or know it.'

The cold that had begun in Iris's midriff now spreads icily through her. Mrs North snatches a hand mirror from the dressing table and holds it up to Iris's face.

'Look, Iris. Look in the mirror.'

Iris does not want to.

'Look.' She presses it closer and Iris traces her features and her heart shrivels.

'Your father promised to make me his wife when your *mother*, precious Annabelle, died. He promised I would claim my rightful relationship to you and my place here as mistress. I thought your father was a gentleman and honourable. How stupid could I have been? He was just like all men, and your mother was no sooner stiff in her grave than he was off to town and coming back smelling of those cheap women men seek. He never intended to wed me – why should he? It was never love that he felt; it was always that thing men want. I was a fool.'

Hatred spills from her lips in a stream of long-felt rage. 'And when Annabelle died, how could I prove my claim? Who would have believed me? Once I threatened to tell you, but he said he would send me away and deny it.' She tries to take Iris, who sits in stunned rigidity, in her arms, but Iris shakes her off.

'Yes,' Mrs North says, with a sigh that has been waiting for twenty-two years. 'I was the one who bore you.'

'Get out!' Iris shouts. 'For God's sake, get out.'

Gathering her skirts, Mrs North returns to the parlour.

Annabelle was never her mother. Is it true? Can she trust what Mrs North has said? But as she had followed the lines of her face, the reality was there in all her features. Not my nurse, my mother. No wonder Annabelle disliked her. The pain and bewilderment are devastating. Then Iris is back to the night of the fire: she had stayed up late to finish an embroidered purse and, impatient that her mother receive it, had waited until the servants were in their beds before taking her candle and making her way through the house to the north wing.

Her mother was already asleep, and Iris lay the gift upon the covers, but she had been so still she might have been dead and Iris had bent her head so that her ear was close to her mother's lips and waited until she felt the soft warmth of her exhalation. A sound from somewhere close made her jump and she had knocked her mother's chamber stick to the coverlet.

Righting it, she checked that it had not caught, then fled, hurrying back towards the main house. As she did, there had been the nearing of light footsteps as one of the maids came along the passageway, and keen not to be seen out so late Iris moved back into the obscurity of an alcove. The steps came closer and Iris had blown out the candle and held her breath as someone whipped past.

Iris had barely fallen asleep when the shouting came. She had gone to her window and gazed out to where orange flames pressed against the glass in her mother's chamber and the night air was filled with the smell of charred timber. She had run to Mrs North.

'*Fire!*' she had gasped. 'There's a fire in the north wing. My mother.'

Mrs North had risen slowly from her chair – a look of alarm in her eyes. But not just alarm – Iris had felt the quiver of her excitement and known somehow that she was pleased, but of course she could not be and so Iris had dismissed it.

Until now, that is. Iris has spent the years since her mother's death believing that she was responsible; that the candle had in fact caught the linen of the bed and that she had missed it, but now she gazes back into the memory with doubt and astonishment. What if it had not been her at all? Who other than Mrs North had a greater motive?

Iris returns to the sitting room and focuses wide unbelieving eyes on Mrs North, who shrivels under the scrutiny.

'You set the fire that killed Annabelle,' she says. 'It was you, wasn't it?'

Mrs North's pupils glitter in the candlelight and Iris sees her clearly for the first time, sees beyond the face shaped by Iris's love – to the selfish, misdirected heart that sits inside.

'She didn't deserve you.' Mrs North's tone is relentless.

'So much so that the only recourse was murder?'

'Every day that woman was alive, her rejection of you caused you more wounds. She didn't merit the right to live, even for another hour.'

'So you killed her.'

'Don't look at me like that; she was ill by then, ill and in pain. She was on so much medicine she didn't feel a thing. In truth, it was more like an act of mercy.'

'Of mercy? If she'd wanted to die she could easily have managed it herself – her room was an apothecary's dream.'

'I did it to save you.'

'Save me? You didn't save me. Her death has left me destroyed by guilt.'

'Why would you blame yourself? You weren't even in the same wing.'

But Iris will not tell her. 'I believe you did it, not for me, but because you thought it would put a ring on your finger.' Mrs North gasps in outrage, but it is clear that she has hit upon the truth. 'I don't think now that you did any of this to save me but only to save yourself. You have made Guardbridge your home; you have professed to me often enough how leaving here would be such a sadness for you. But it is more than that, you feel it's owed to you. If I left, there would be no place for you here. You'd have to go.'

'You're my daughter.'

Iris shakes her head. 'You trapped me, didn't you? For how many years have you misdirected me? I wonder now if it was you and not the spirits who told me that to leave Guardbridge would end in tragedy? If I had married, what would have happened to you then? Did you write that in my book?

Condemning me to years confined within these walls like a prisoner. Did you?'

Mrs North begins to cry.

'Oh God, what misfortune gave me two mothers who cared so little? I can't see you again, not ever.'

Mrs North lifts her head. 'But where do I go?'

'Go? You're responsible for murder. When Edward comes it is to the police you will go.'

Mrs North begins to beg but Iris is beyond reasoning. She will not hear another word.

Annie, she thinks. *I need Annie.*

31

The last of the storm has blown the sky as clear as glass and lit it with stars, and when I finally climb into bed, still trembling with cold, I ponder the many strange turns of events the evening has brought. After changing, I had brought up hot water, lit the fire and unhooked my gown, and in all those small domestic necessities the world once again made sense. Now, although I ache with exhaustion, I am wakeful and alert.

As I returned across the moor, and in all the moments since, the idea that Edward is not the man I had come to believe grows easier to trust. In everything that Iris told me I felt the truth and then, reflecting over our time together, realized that at no point had he ever behaved in a way that hinted at violence. How quickly I had taken up the suggestions, but I had grown up with a man who ruled the house with anger. Why would Edward be otherwise?

When I close my eyes, I see Iris standing over me, hair bedraggled, grey eyes both relieved and shocked as she helped me from where I lay. Her courage leaves me awed. I wonder what will happen to us all now. If

Iris can be brave, I must too. Tonight has changed us both.

Edward must soon return and what a great deal he will have to learn. Edward. I give a shiver of anticipation or fear; I do not know which.

An image comes to me again of the winter day we first met, and how I had been afraid of the strange certainty that had come to me and foretold that our fates were entwined. I remember how we sat in the parlour, taking tea, my parents courting him as much as he courted them, and a moment when, across the conversation, our eyes had met. All about me had faded to silence until there was only the two of us, and I felt so many things – his sadness meeting mine, the tacit recognition of it, and upon his face a look of such tenderness that those heavy features were transformed and I had thought, *I could happily look upon him for the rest of my life.*

That night my heart raced with liberation and I wondered what it might be like to live at Guardbridge and to have money, and before the night was over I had already bought a wardrobe of pretty gowns, sat over a hundred sumptuous meals and borne a family of well-behaved children. Then later, just as sleep was beginning to claim me, I thought of Edward himself and that look he had passed me, and in some deep part of me that I kept closed a spark came, and I thought perhaps other things would be possible for us too. Now I recall that flame and hope it is not too late.

There is a knock at the door. When I unlock it, it is to find Iris, pale and distressed.

'What happened?' I say, taking her arm. 'What happened with Mrs North?'

'Help me, Annie. I don't know what to do.'

I guide her shaking frame to the bed and help her in, then climb in beside her and wrap us both in a blanket. For some while she is mute from shock and grief and all I can do is comfort her. But eventually she takes a deep breath and relays all that took place, the wickednesses unfurling one after the other.

I do not interrupt until she has finished, reeling and stunned to silence.

Taking her cold fingers, I say, 'I can't believe what she's done.'

'It's too much to take in. What am I to think?'

'I don't know,' I say. 'Things will make more sense in time. I'm pleased you no longer have to believe that you were responsible for your mother's death.'

'Yes,' she says. 'Yes. You have no idea how much it has tortured me.'

'What will you do with Mrs North, knowing what she's done?'

'It doesn't seem real. I can only think how she's treated us all. She claims it was for love of me, but it was she who wrote in my book that disaster would

315

fall if I left the house. How could she trap me so if she loved me?' Her voice breaks.

'We will bear it with you,' I say. 'Do you believe that Evie's death was as she said?'

'I felt she spoke the truth, but how will I ever know? Once you learn that someone has built a life on lies, it's impossible to pick out the truths. But for all her cruelty I don't think that she could have harmed Jacob in that way. It's clear now what motivated her to act as she did. I think she felt Guardbridge belonged to her – that she deserved it for all she suffered at the hands of my father. My poor brother, Annie – I don't know how I'll tell him what I know. However things are between you, will you promise me that when he returns you'll try to help him bear it.'

'I will if he lets me.'

I place my arms round her. 'We must think of the future now. There's so much waiting for you beyond Guardbridge,' I say.

'Although she has unlocked the cage, I still feel safer within the bars, and I have too much to think about before I make decisions. I can't face Mrs North again, not tonight.'

'Stay here,' I say. 'You can borrow a nightgown.'

She nods. 'You know, I was thinking earlier how serendipitous for Mrs North it was that the staff fell ill when they did. It was perfect to get you away. I recall now the stomach complaint that followed the time I left Guardbridge as a child. What if she was the one who put something in my food to prove that leaving Guardbridge would bring misfortune? If so then she's used that ploy before. Do you think she did that?'

'I hadn't considered it, but now you mention it, it's likely – every one of them out of the way while she played her final cards into my hand. She couldn't afford for me to use the coach and horses or for one of the maids to stop me.'

Iris goes behind the screen to change, and I walk to the window to draw the curtains, but the beauty of the night sky captivates me.

When she is dressed, Iris joins me. 'It will soon be dawn. I've behaved so badly to you, haven't I? Will you ever be able to forgive me, Annie?'

'I forgive you, Iris, and will you forgive me for what I did to the glass?'

'Those insights I gained were not always comfortable, sometimes I learned things I would rather not have known, and for all its magic it failed me in that which was most important: the deception wrought by Mrs North. I wonder now the value. Southy was right inasmuch that I was growing worse after each sitting. Perhaps it was the best thing. Time will tell.'

'And Jacob,' I say, 'will he be at rest now?'

'I believe that those spirits when returned to the

afterlife find peace, but, Annie, I wasn't sure whether or not I was going to tell you, but . . .'

'What is it?'

'Jacob was with you again tonight.'

'What do you mean?'

'I didn't find you by accident. I was guided across the moor by a light. I thought at first it was you, but just before I reached you I caught a glimpse of the one who held it; it was a child, Annie, Jacob. And when I found you half dead by the rocks your lantern was cold.' The moon reflects white on her skin. 'If it were not for him, you and John may well have perished.'

I shiver. 'He saved us?' I recall the spectral appearances of before and my conviction that he had come only to harm. 'But all those other times, what was his reason then?'

'It makes no sense that he ever intended to be the source of so much fear in you – I think he always came to help you.'

'But I felt so much malice.'

'Was that him or was that your own agitation conjuring it?'

I recall the time he led me to the north wing and to the piece of paper ripped from Iris's book. 'Wait here.' I go to my desk and take the page, passing it to her. 'That night you gave me the candle, he took me to the north wing attics. This was on one of the chests.'

Iris looks down. *If Evie and Jacob do not leave Guard-bridge, they will die. Edward cannot be trusted.*

Her face tightens in anger. 'This is Mrs North's writing. I remembered this comment tonight and went to look for it, but the page had gone.'

'But surely it was left there to frighten me. To make me think Edward would harm us.'

She grabs my arm. 'No. Don't you see? He wanted you to believe the opposite. Perhaps he thought you would recognize that the hand was really Mrs North's or perhaps that you would bring it to me. I think if you had, I would have looked at it in a different way and considered the treachery.'

I reframe my memory of the hand that clasped the corner of the wall, not with stealth but timidity or shyness. The words on the glass: *See me.* He wanted acknowledgement, and I only fled in terror.

'What will he think of me? I felt only horror at his presence.'

'The spirit world is different from ours. Time is meaningless – a baby can grow to a man much sooner than he could here, and spirit children have insight and intelligence far beyond their years. I'm sure he understood; after all, he came back to help you again.'

'What will happen to him now?'

'I think because the truth is known, he will return and grow in the spirit realm – to become the man he was destined to be in life.'

And then I realize that by the time Jacob had stepped on to the moor, the glass had already gone. 'Iris, the glass was in the river by then. How did he come?'

Iris stills. 'It means that magic exists beyond the glass, that the universe can arrange for strange and wonderful events to occur.' She blinks hard to clear the moisture that springs to her eyes.

'But if he has gone, how can I show him my gratitude? If he were here now, I would thank him from the bottom of my heart.'

She puts a steadying hand on my shoulder. 'Perhaps he knows already.'

We climb into bed and I lean over and blow out the candle so that she will not see the tears that suddenly burn so fiercely.

32

My dreams are filled with the moor – with the night-time creatures and a storm that rips the heavens apart, but there is also a boy, who stands, wet hair clinging to his cheeks and boots sinking to the sodden earth, who holds a light that flickers on his unearthly countenance.

We are woken by knocking.

I get out of bed, wincing at the soreness in my limbs, and unlock the door. Flora wears a distraught expression. Beyond me she sees Iris. 'Oh, thank goodness Miss Stonehouse is here. We couldn't find her and feared the worse, but you must come straight away.'

'What's the matter?'

'It's Mrs North.'

'What about Mrs North? What has she done?' Iris asks.

'I'm sorry, miss.' Flora's eyes fill with tears. 'Mrs North died in the night.'

Iris sits up and pales. 'Are you sure? She's dead?'

'Yes, miss.'

Iris looks ill. 'Are you certain? Dead? How?'

'There were empty bottles lined up on her table.'

Iris slumps back against the headboard. 'Oh God,' she whispers when Flora has gone.

'Her future didn't look good, Iris. She'd admitted to murder. Once the police were involved, if she were found guilty, she would hang.'

Iris shakes her head in disbelief. 'She was my mother. I can barely believe any of it today, but it's true. It's all true. And now she's dead.'

We wash and dress in shocked silence and then make our way to Iris's quarters where the staff hover, silent and subdued, Bessie mopping her eyes with a handkerchief. They part to let Iris through to where Mrs Ford stands at Mrs North's bedside.

Mrs North is beneath the covers, still dressed, death having taken the colour from her skin.

Iris does not say anything but sits heavily on the chair, her face bathed in disbelief.

'George has gone for the doctor,' Mrs Ford says. 'But it'll be an hour or two. Did she say anything to you last night?'

'A great deal,' Iris says weakly, 'but I'm too exhausted to recount the details now.'

Mrs Ford nods and is about to ask more when I say, 'Perhaps you could leave us, please.'

When we are alone, Iris turns to me. 'Oh, Annie, even knowing what she was, my heart is breaking. Tell me it isn't my fault?'

'She committed the worst sin possible. You have no responsibility for that. She could not have remained here. It was over. You know that.'

'She was my mother.' Iris gazes at Mrs North's immobile features, mask-like in the cold dawn. 'My mother. For all she did, for all the harm, why is it that I'm so unbearably sad?'

Getting slowly to her feet, she moves to the bed where she kneels and takes one of Mrs North's hands, pressing it to her lips. 'I need to be alone a while, Annie,' she says.

Over the next days, the house falls under silence, the muted whispers of staff, our own sombre exchanges, and we all move from room to room, treading more softly as if we do not wish to disturb fate further. Iris spends much time in unhappy reflection, her loss as devastating as any she has suffered. Only John is oblivious, howling if he needs something or shrieking with pleasure when happy. Still Edward does not return, and with each day my anxiety builds.

When Iris is not mourning alone, we spend time in each other's company. Often we go to the nursery or have John brought down to the drawing room where both Iris and I enjoy his moments of levity. When I am with him now, gone is my fear, gone is my doubt, leaving gratitude and joy in its place. The storm has passed, fully leaving the scent of spring, and the maids open windows to chase out the winter air and beat rugs in the weak sunshine. A few days after Mrs North's death I say, 'Iris, it's a beautiful morning. Come for a walk with me.'

She looks up anxiously from her work. 'Not today,' she says. 'I'd like to finish this.'

'The longer you leave it, the harder it'll be.'

She gives a great exhalation and puts her scissors down. 'You've found me out. How can I remain so afraid when only two nights ago I left here in the midst of a raging storm? Although I can still hardly believe it.'

'Why don't you accompany me? You must long to be outside and there are not many days as pretty as this.'

Sunlight touches the ends of her lashes as she turns to the window, then she gets up from her chair and gives me a faltering smile. 'If I don't, I never will.'

Flora helps us with coats and boots, and then we are standing at the open door. A cool wind ruffles our hats and brushes our cheeks; there are the chirrups of birds and the sound of the river. We step down and into the garden. We do not speak, walking past the north wing and then beyond to where the path takes a turn. A flock of geese pass above us and Iris tips her head to watch them.

It is only as we take a course past the lake and to the drive and gates that she hesitates.

'Shall we leave the grounds?' I ask.

'Don't give me a choice.' So I take her arm and we walk on, on to the road and to the moor itself.

'Edward has been long returning,' I say.

'Edward? Yes, he doesn't usually tarry so much. You must be thinking that it's my letter that detains him?'

'I am,' I say. 'I imagine he's not looking forward to seeing me again now that he's learned the truth.'

'I shouldn't have written it,' she says.

'It was something he should have known from the first. If you hadn't, I don't know that I would ever have found the courage.'

'Are you afraid that he's planning not to come back?'

'I've wondered that.'

'He'll return, Annie, and is your secret such a bad one? I'm sure he'll understand why you couldn't tell.'

'I hope so. Do you think your correspondence regarding Mrs North and all that she did has reached him?'

'I think so. If he had moved on from the inn, he would have left an address.'

'It's such a terrible thing for him to know. I'd expect him to come back immediately.'

'You don't know Edward as I do yet. At a time like this he'll want to be alone, to consider the news and to grieve again. Do you want him to come home?' she asks.

I give a shiver. 'I don't know.'

'That's only because you're afraid.'

The twist in my belly confirms her supposition.

'Have you told Edward that Mrs North was your mother?'

She nods. 'He knows, and you know, but there's no advantage in spreading the word further, particularly as we've learned what else she did. Can you imagine the gossip?'

'I think that's wise. There's no benefit to anyone discovering the facts. I also think I shall never tell Edward that Jacob came. At least that is something he can be spared. And the glass, Iris. What do you feel now?'

'With so many weightier things to consider, I barely think of it. In some way it's a relief to say goodbye to the spirits.'

'They haven't visited?'

'Not once.' She pauses. 'The house is changed, you know, and I'm changed. Perhaps it's that I'm still too shocked and grieved by what Mrs North confessed, but I have not gone into trance or felt the presence of the spirit realm since the night of the storm. Maybe life is telling me that I must look to other things now.'

I smile and raise my brows. 'And there are many, many other things when you're ready.'

There are wheels on the road as we turn back and the sight of a coach. I think instantly of Edward, but Iris tells me it is the undertaker. We accompany the men to where Mrs North lies in a little parlour away from the main house.

Iris stands tall, her expression fierce in its determination not to show emotion. When the men return with Mrs North's body, we follow the coffin to the hall and Mrs Ford opens the door, bringing in the spring sunshine and birdsong. We watch it carried to the coach. The servants gather on the steps beside us. Iris takes my arm and we stand in silence until it is out of sight.

In the following hours I distract myself in the nursery, where I help sort clothes for John and make lists of what he will soon need. Agnes talks of her past charges and the life she had growing up on a dairy farm in Northumberland. We are so engrossed in our task that I jump when I find Iris behind me. Her eyes are red from crying but her manner is urgent. 'Annie, you'd better come now. I've something to show you.'

Agnes and I exchange curious glances and I follow Iris to her quarters. It is strange to enter their main room – I expect the familiar sight of Mrs North in her chair. Her workbox remains on the floor where she last left it. Beside it, on a table, are a bottle of almond oil and the tonics she used to soothe her joints.

Iris leads me to Mrs North's bedroom where she has emptied drawers and cupboards, laying things on the bed for removal.

'I could have left the servants to this, but I was

interested, and quite right too.' She passes me a box to view the contents.

I gaze, aghast. 'My necklace.'

'Not just yours. See that brooch? That was Evie's, as was this silver bracelet.'

'Why would she do such a thing? I agonized over the loss of it.'

'I believe she wanted to make you feel incompetent. These are quite valuable. I don't think that Edward would've been pleased.'

'He wasn't. But, Iris, you don't need to do this alone. I'll help you.'

Together we sort out Mrs North's things as the sun turns in the sky. Dusk is falling when wheels on the drive send us to the window.

'Annie, it's Edward,' Iris says.

My heart bangs painfully and I stand, suddenly afraid.

Iris takes my hands. 'Trust him,' she says. 'Just trust him.'

33

As I take the passageways to meet him, I am conscious of the house in a new way: every smell, every sight, reaches me and is felt in the same moment. And I feel that, at some point in the past, I must have lost pace with myself and have since been walking a little ahead, outrunning what I wanted to escape. But finally the misalignment is corrected.

As I reach the top of the stairs, Edward's voice sounds from below. I pause and lay a hand on the banister. At the sound of my shoe he looks up and we see each other, as if for the first time, and I am no longer afraid.

We stand, transfixed, then Bessie and George are bringing in the trunks and Bessie drops Edward's umbrella to the stand and the noise is the starting gun for us to take motion – Edward being helped from his coat and for me to descend to the hall. I reach the bottom where he is waiting and I search his face for anger but there is only sadness and trepidation.

'Annie.' His tone is sombre and together we go to the drawing room where he takes his customary place and in all his movements I feel his desire to delay the moment we must begin. I had imagined myself gushing apologies and explanations, but instead I feel only the overwhelming sorrows that have beset us, and in this instant of truth I recognize that I am not yet ready to talk of you.

'You received Iris's letter about Mrs North?' I ask.

'I did.'

'I'm sorry, Edward. About Evie and Jacob.'

'What I now know about Evie and my son doesn't alter what I felt for them. I loved Jacob even when I believed he wasn't mine.' Pain breaks across his features and he cannot speak.

'I'm glad that he was.'

He inhales, and it takes him a while to gather his emotions. 'I've done a lot of contemplating while I've been away. I realize I've not been able to think clearly since the day they died. In retrospect, I believe perhaps it was unfair to marry you. I thought doing so would distract me. It was selfish.'

'Do you regret it?' I ask.

'Only if it has hurt you,' he says.

I think about this, and about John. 'No, it's not hurt me. I too wasn't ready for marriage – only the escape it offered.'

We gaze at each other for a long time. Then he says, 'Iris explained everything. You could have told me about your son.' His expression is tender, and I wonder how I could have ever thought him otherwise.

And now the time has come my mouth is dry. 'I believed that if I did you wouldn't marry me.'

'I suppose many women would have reason to feel that way, but I'm not one of those men.'

'I didn't know that.'

'We hardly know each other, do we? And I've not been forthcoming, leaving you to imagine things rather than tell you the truth.'

'Would you have felt the same about me had you known?'

His face colours. 'I think I would have been more careful with you, more considerate, and it would have explained how you sometimes behaved when I was there.'

'You were never unkind, and if I was afraid of you, it was only that I embellished your silences and Mrs North's suggestions.'

Anger flushes him. 'We will talk of that another time, not now.'

He comes and sits next to me and takes my hand. 'Annie –' his voice is grave – 'there's something I must tell you.'

Suddenly I am afraid.

'Look at me, Annie.'

I cannot. Something has struck me so deeply and with such fear that I fix my eyes on the floor.

He tips my head towards him. 'I visited your parents after I received Iris's letter about you.'

I do not want to hear this. I do not.

'Your son.'

I will not hear it. I will not. But his voice goes on, tearing at the past.

'Your son didn't live.'

I rip my hands from his and cover my ears. I am falling fast now, through time and space like a comet to that sticky summer morning you were born. *No, I think, it is not the truth.* You are in my arms again and I am looking down to see the monster that I imagined I had carried, but what I hold is not a monster. It is a baby – you – and my heart has opened like a flower.

'Annie,' my mother murmurs.

'It's a baby,' I say.

Your warmth against mine, your perfect mouth, the curve of your skull and tiny ears. My mother hands me a blanket and I wrap you tight, rock you to me and there is such silence, and still I cling to you.

My mother tries to take you, a gentleness in her tone that fills me with terror.

'No,' I say.

She tries again. 'Annie.'

But as I clutch you I become aware that you do not cry or move – that those perfect fingers do not crawl across my chest in first exploration, that your mouth does not reach for my breast. And something, something that had been hanging only by a fine thread finally snaps and I have been falling ever since – until this moment – caught in a net of grief that has been impossible to bear.

'Annie,' Edward says and takes my hands again.

The sound that comes from my throat has been waiting to come since that very day. I begin to weep and Edward pulls me to him, to the sensations of another human skin, another beating heart and finally, finally I acknowledge the loss of you.

34

Evening drifts to night, and the corridors to darkness. The wet moor seeps into the rooms – with the smell of gorse and candle wax. As I make my way to bed, the passageway is full of whispers, as if, even without the glass, Guardbridge is still under a spell.

My heart aches with loss. It seems impossible now that I wove a web about you in which I kept you alive when, all this time, you never opened your eyes. I recall how they took you away, you, who I named without ever speaking it aloud: Nathaniel.

Did I truly believe you were elsewhere? Because now I am not sure that I ever did, only that I found comfort imagining you growing older with the years. And I did take comfort. I saw you at every age. At two, with dimpled knees and curly hair. Then at three and four with your limbs grown long. If I close my eyes now I can still see you – not a bundle cooling in my arms, but the child you have been to me. Who you will always be for me – a child who, even never having taken breath, was ever less loved.

Later, when Flora has left, Edward comes to me and we lie in the near dark with moths that flutter about the wicks and the fire that spits softly and the sound of owls from the woods. He wraps an arm about me, not only for my comfort but also for his.

I do not know what wakes me. I listen. I hear only silence but something is changed and I am filled with a strange certainty. Sitting up, I move quietly so as not to wake Edward and, with care, push away the covers and stand.

Out in the darkened passageway I hardly dare breathe. I need no lamp to guide me, only the inner one that tells me that this is what I must do. It takes me to the landing where I wait, my palm cool on the banister. Then I make my way down to the empty hall. Moonlight spills from one of the windows and brushes the tiles silver, but it is up that I look – up to the top of the stairs where I sense you crouch in the shadows.

Air stills. Time lengthens and hesitates. And you are there. As I knew you would be.

'I see you,' I whisper. 'I see you now.'

Your hands clasp the spindles and I recall that night your fingers came round the wall. It was always you – it was never Jacob. Only you.

Shyly you stand and show me the face my heart did not recognize, and love squeezes and strains inside my chest.

'Will you forgive me? I hope you know that I've always cherished you, Nathaniel.'

You look down, and there can never be minutes

enough to drink in your face. Slowly you descend, closer and closer as I marvel, and then you are near enough that if you were flesh and blood I could take you in my arms. I reach out, but instead you take one further step and move through me, leaving something within changed forever.

And then you are truly gone and I know you will not return but I gaze until my eyes burn and my skin chills.

There is only quiet now – and something enchanted upon my heart. Then, wonderingly, I climb the stairs – where Edward and John are waiting.

Acknowledgements

I want to thank my wonderful editor, Clio Cornish, who has been such an inspiration to me on this journey and who continues to add so much value to anything I deliver with her insight and skill.

With gratitude to the very fabulous team at Michael Joseph, once again, for all the hard work that goes on behind the scenes in bringing a book to the shelves. Thank you to: Emma Plater, Emma Henderson, Kallie Townsend, Jessie Beswick, Helen Eka. Apologies if I have missed anyone.

To my lovely agent, Hayley Steed, for all her support and commitment.

I thank my writing friends, who are always there to encourage and help and who I don't know what I'd do without, and not forgetting my non-writing friends for letting me bore-on about writing and hiding the yawns.

Lastly, heartfelt thanks to my family: Hugh, Tom and James, who are accommodating of my long hours and who are ever supportive. To Anita Frank for her wisdom and for always being there when I need help. And to my sister, Julia, with whom I share endless silent Zoom calls while we work on our books – not quite a coffee shop but as close as we can get. I wouldn't want to do it without you.